T0301052

The CHRISTMAS EVE MURDERS

The CHRISTMAS EVE MURDERS

NOELLE ALBRIGHT

QUERCUS

First published in Great Britain in 2024 by

Quercus Editions Limited
Carmelite House
50 Victoria Embankment
London EC4Y 0DZ

An Hachette UK company

The authorized representative in the EEA is Hachette Ireland,
8 Castlecourt Centre, Dublin 15, D15 XTP3, Ireland (email: info@hbgi.ie)

A CIP catalogue record for this book is available from the British Library

HB ISBN 978 1 52943 985 4
EBOOK ISBN 978 1 52943 987 8

2

Typeset by CC Book Production
Printed and bound in Great Britain by Clays Ltd, Elcograf S.p.A.

Papers used by Quercus are from well-managed forests and other responsible sources.

The CHRISTMAS EVE MURDERS

CHAPTER ONE

'No, no, no, oh God, please no . . .' Maddie Marlowe moaned at her blue Nissan as it ground to a halt halfway up a snow-laden hill, somewhere in the Yorkshire Dales. A faint, but utterly offensive, burning smell filled Maddie's nose as she pulled on the handbrake to prevent the vehicle from rolling backwards. In a bid to convince herself she couldn't smell anything sinister, certainly nothing that might indicate her car was completely kaput, she pressed the Engine Start button. 'Come on, come on, you know you want to . . . just for me, come on,' she pleaded in her soft Edinburgh accent. 'There's a full wax and polish in it for you if you start now . . . OK, OK, you drive a hard bargain, but I'll throw in a complete interior valet service too. Please. Just. Start.' However, as Maddie pushed the button over and over again and made increasingly expensive promises to her transport, nothing at all happened.

Maddie's journey north from the newspaper office she worked at in Manchester had already been plagued with enough obstacles that, had she been anyone else, she might have whimpered her words, rather than tried to sweet-talk the car engine. But given that her parents were of Scottish stock, she'd never be able to look them in the eye again if she whimpered out loud. Far better to act like you're completely doolally by talking to your car directly and offering it services you couldn't afford if you saved every penny for a year than be caught in a whimper. Even if there was nobody around to hear it. Even if she was stranded in the dark, icy reaches of . . . where exactly was she again? A narrow road on the outskirts of some lonely settlement with far fewer street lamps than a person might prefer, and not one soul out walking their dog or delivering last-minute Christmas cards. But on December 24th in rural England that description didn't exactly narrow it down.

She'd definitely seen signs for Skipton and Settle not long ago . . . Quernby . . . hadn't that been the name on the sign as she'd entered the village? Not that it mattered much what the place her car had broken down in was called. What was important was that the village in question was too small to be connected to anywhere else by bus or rail. That it was already six o'clock on Christmas Eve, so even if there were mechanics who worked here who might have had a bash at fixing her car, they'd have long since shut up shop for the day. At this rate, she was not going to make it back to her parents' house on the outskirts of Auld Reekie for Christmas.

Something about that hard, cold fact stirred the part of Maddie's brain that dealt with creative thinking in a crisis.

The British Automobile Club.

She had full breakdown cover. It was another monthly instalment she couldn't really afford, but her dad had insisted on it when she'd bought the car.

'Why is it that when there's something sensible needs doin' you've got a list of excuses as long as the Tay not to do it? Cancel yer Disney Plus if you're that hard up,' Maddie remembered her dad barking down the phone at her in his sharp Perth accent when she'd quibbled over the cost of the fee. Maddie wagered any other thirty-one-year-old would be outraged at being spoken to this way by their father but she had learnt the hard way over the years – as had her mother – that there was no changing her dad. And, though he invariably bungled the delivery of such sentiments, she knew everything he said did come from a place of love. Consequently, she'd learnt to deal with such outbursts by finding the funny side and had had to put a hand over her mouth to keep from laughing at yet another example of how irate he got at the smallest things. The thought of his no-nonsense straight-talk made

Maddie smile again even now. Considering her current predicament, she was glad he'd been so dogged about it.

Twenty-four seven, three hundred and sixty-five days a year, that's the support the British Automobile Club policy had promised. Times like this were what membership fees were paid for.

Reaching into her coat pocket for her phone, Maddie swiped the screen with fresh hope that she might yet get a bowl of her mum's cock-a-leekie soup before bedtime. Within seconds, however, all such hopes were dashed as she noted there was not so much as one bar of mobile signal.

Maddie stared out of the windscreen, trying to keep her breathing steady, and failing. It was starting to snow again and it was eerily quiet. Faint yellow lights gleamed from a few houses in the distance but that was the only sign of life. Glancing in the rear-view mirror, she saw nothing but a dark, empty expanse there too. Returning her gaze to the front window, she took pains not to catch the green eyes she'd inherited from her mother in the mirror. The last thing she needed was to see fear swelling in them right now. A long time ago, she had seen first-hand what could happen to young women who found themselves alone in remote places. She shook her head. Trying, at the same time, to shake away that image, that memory, that always found her without fail in stark, quiet moments.

She had to do something.

Knock on somebody's door and ask to use a landline?

It wasn't really the done thing in the modern era, to bang on a stranger's door for help, but needs must. All she needed was to make a quick call. She needn't wait in the house if whoever she found in at home was severely put out by her presence. It would be far from cosy without the heating on, but she could just make her way back to the car and wait there. The only seeming alternative to imposing on strangers was sitting here in the car all night, alone with no help on its way and no means of contacting her parents. That was surely a recipe for getting hacked to pieces by an axe murderer.

Maddie unhooked her seatbelt and braced herself for the cold. Just as she did so, however, a loud knock came to the driver's side window that made her cry out in shock.

By the dim glow of a street light a wee bit further up the road, Maddie could make out an older gentleman standing outside her car. She frowned. How had he crept up without her noticing? Perhaps he had turned some corner behind the car that she could not see in the dark. However he had manifested, Maddie could have done without a shock like that just then.

With her heart still in her mouth, she surveyed the figure outside the car window. A neatly trimmed white beard, which was bushier around the moustache, framed his face. Presumably he had the hair to match but that was impossible to verify as it was covered by the ear flaps on his winter hat. His watery grey eyes stared at Maddie in such a manner that she almost wondered if he were cross with her for some reason. Had she 'parked' on the hallowed grounds of a permit holders only street? If there was one thing she'd learnt in her time as a Scot who'd moved to England for work purposes, it was that, in these parts, parking was a big deal.

The man was leaning on a walking stick, and only on registering that detail did Maddie notice that he also had a black Scottish terrier by his side. The dog had a bushy moustache to match his master's and was wearing a rather festive crimson coat with a white fluffy trim. It must have been a particularly obedient hound, as it wasn't on a leash. The sight of the animal made Maddie relax a bit, though she had no idea why. The family canines they'd had over the years were far more interested in where the next sausage was coming from than the moral integrity of their masters.

All in all, Maddie had to concede that the man looked harmless enough but she had seen every last episode of *Happy Valley*, so wasn't about to take any chances just yet.

Unable to open the window due to the engine failure, she simply looked expectantly at him, hoping he'd get the hint and say whatever he wanted to through the glass.

'Terribly sorry, didn't mean to startle you, it just looked like you were having a spot of trouble,' was his opener, just loud enough for Maddie to hear through the barrier between them. His articulation was much posher than she would have expected to find in rural Yorkshire.

So, this man was only concerned about her welfare and not cross at her for some unspecified parking violation. The hard intensity she'd previously read in his eyes must simply have been part and parcel of his natural resting face.

'Is everything quite alright?' he added.

Maddie found herself nodding, even though that was a wholly inappropriate gesture under the circumstances. 'My car's broken down, that's all.'

That's all? That's enough, isn't it? she thought, before relaying the real issue at hand: 'And I've got no mobile signal to call for help. I've got breakdown cover but no way of reaching them.'

The man pressed his lips together. 'That *is* rotten luck, on Christmas Eve too. I thought I heard a car engine failing when I was walking along Aysgarth Road, there. With the weather, it seemed only right that I come along and see if I could be of assistance.'

Ordinarily, Maddie would have been impressed by a person, perhaps particularly an older person who might have difficulty with hearing, being able to pick out the sound of a car breaking down a couple of streets away. But it was so quiet here, and as it rolled to a stop her vehicle had made the most horrific grating noise that, at a best guess, indicated every piece of the engine was disintegrating all at once. It would be difficult to miss a racket like that in the stillness of a Yorkshire village as small as this one.

'Listen,' the man said enunciating as he spoke through the glass. 'I'm walking to the village pub, The Merry Monarch. It's closer to this spot than my house, just shy of half a mile. There's a phone there you could use and if you can't get anyone out to you tonight, they've got rooms upstairs. I can show you the way if you'd like.'

Maddie thought for a moment. She received nigh on constant reminders via her job as a reporter for the local newspaper, *The Trafford Times*, that this wasn't the kind of world where a woman travelling alone could trust offers of help from a seemingly well-meaning stranger. If she wandered off into the dark with this man, would she ever be seen alive and well again? As a reporter, she knew just how the headline to an article about her own death would read. And how foolish the living would think her for leaving the relative safety of her vehicle to go for a walk with a person she didn't know from Adam.

'I know it's a bit of a walk, but, even in a place as safe and as small as Quernby, I really don't think it's a good idea for a young woman like yourself to be stuck in a car out here all night,' the man added when it was clear Maddie was hesitating.

Maddie nodded to herself in resignation. The few houses she could see didn't have any lights on, the residents were probably out somewhere visiting family or having Christmas Eve drinks at the very pub this man had suggested walking to. She didn't know her own way to the pub, had no way of summoning Google Maps without any signal and, when it came down to it, didn't really have other options. She had to trust this man who had, so far, done nothing but show concern for her wellbeing.

She offered him a vague smile as she tentatively opened the car door, pulled the small case that had been sitting in the passenger footwell with her, and made sure the vehicle was all locked up before leaving it.

'My name is Curtis, by the way,' the man said before gesturing to the dog. 'And this is Barkley.'

At this the terrier let out a surprisingly deep, but singularly controlled bark.

Curtis chuckled, 'He knows his name.'

'He certainly does,' Maddie replied. 'I'm Madeline, but everyone calls me Maddie.'

At this, Curtis scrunched up his face. 'Why on earth must people shorten names? I'm sure people would call me Curt if I gave them half a chance.'

Given how stern his face looked in repose, Maddie couldn't help but think this might not be such an ill-fitting nickname for the man.

'Still, in your case Maddie is better than them shortening your name to Mad, I suppose,' Curtis added.

'I've been told we have to be thankful for small mercies,' said Maddie, doing what she could to force a smile but Curtis's reaction told her she wasn't fooling anybody.

'Try not to worry, my dear,' Curtis said. 'A car breaking down is just a little mishap in the grand scheme of things. I've lived in Quernby since I was a young man. This is a very safe village, and if any ne'er-do-wells, or raving lefties, do cross our path, I'm lethal with this.'

At this comment, the man raised his walking stick and performed a kind of strange karate chop through the air with it.

'I believe you,' Maddie said. In spite of herself, she was unable to suppress a little smirk at Curtis's antics. His comment about 'raving lefties' offered her a litmus test of the politics in the village. Maddie made a note not to make her feelings about any political policies clear until *after* she'd accessed a phone or secured a warm bed for the night. His comment also made her reflect again on her earlier musings about the indiscriminate affections of dogs. *Oh, Barkley*, she thought. *In the time-honoured tradition of hungry wee hounds, it sounds as though you might have sold out for sausages here.*

As they walked together towards the promised warmth of the village pub, their shoes crunching through snow so thick that poor Barkley was half-buried in the stuff, Curtis pointed out The Merry Monarch standing in the near distance. Between the darkness and the weather it was impossible to make out any intricate details, but Maddie did notice that it was more brightly lit than the other few scattered houses that surrounded it. Like many travellers to the Yorkshire Dales likely had before her, she did her best to focus on the welcoming yellow of those lights. While she was on, she tried to think more positively about her situation.

This was a safe village, Curtis had assured her of that. And The Merry Monarch had both a phone and rooms to stay in if it came to it. She might not get the Christmas she had hoped for but so long as she could reach her parents on the phone and let them know where she was, everything would be alright. That's what Maddie told herself as the snow fell heavier and yet heavier still.

But the logic wouldn't quite stick.

Perhaps it was the eerie silence of the dale or the fact that there was not another soul to be seen, not even so much as the headlights of a car driving in the distance. Whatever spurred the strange feeling that overcame

Maddie as she looked over the wintry landscape, there was no denying that something about Quernby village put her on edge. It gave the distinct impression of being the kind of place where if anything untoward did befall you, nobody would hear you scream.

CHAPTER TWO

On the way to The Merry Monarch, Curtis had mentioned, in passing, that the pub had an open fire. This tiny nugget of information had steeled Maddie to trudge forward through the growing blizzard. On pushing open the heavy oak door of the establishment, she was vaguely aware of Curtis and Barkley heading over to the bar and greeting whoever was behind it, but *her* top priority was to find said fireplace at once.

Her walking companions were seemingly used to nights as Baltic as this one had been so far, and thus had no interest in warming themselves up after a stint in the snow. In Barkley's case, he had both his own fur coat and a festive jacket to protect him, putting the pooch at a decided advantage over Maddie. Yes, growing up on the outskirts of Edinburgh, she had seen her fair share of snow. But that stuff so rarely settled and melted almost as quickly as it fell. Maddie made a personal pact with herself right then to never live in a place where weather as glacial as this happened frequently enough for people to get used to it. She missed the luxury of having feeling in her hands too much. And the end of her nose. It might seem like a trivial thing to some, but Maddie had become quite accustomed to being able to sense the end of her own hooter.

Given the size of the village, there were more people gathered than Maddie might have expected in the small bar area but she was too cold to be polite and acknowledge a single one of them, even in passing. On spotting the fire over on the right-hand wall from the entrance, she strode straight to it, pulling her luggage behind her, and stood as close as she could without catching alight herself. Peeling off her sodden woollen gloves and stuffing them in the pocket of her navy duffel coat, Maddie held up her reddened hands to the flames until the feeling started to return to them. Only when the warmth had reached her frozen core, did she take a few moments to properly assess her surroundings.

It was quite an odd little pub in some respects. There were small snugs in the corners of the room, complete with frosted glass tinted red and green, sheltering parts of the space from prying eyes. Maddie couldn't remember the last time she'd seen a layout quite like it, perhaps in one of the old coaching houses she'd visited in Pitlochry while on a weekend away with her ex-boyfriend, Lance. To Maddie's mind, these secluded little areas added a certain antiquated charm to the place.

There was certainly no mistaking that it was Christmas in here. The owners had really gone to town with the decorations. While warming her hands, Maddie had noticed that a long, green garland hung around the fireplace, decorated with ornaments in the shape of robins and partridges. A large Christmas tree stood at the opposite end of the room and Maddie was struggling to think of the last time she'd seen so much tinsel. It snaked around the branches in streaks of blue, silver and red to the point that it was almost difficult to spot the greenery. An angel, whiter than the snow now falling outside, sat atop the tree, overlooking the various baubles, bells and other trinkets that adorned the boughs below.

It seemed that Christmas cards had been strung up in every spare bit of coving and Maddie also noticed that thick bunches of mistletoe hung here and there in one or two of the smaller snugs.

Unlike the bars she frequented in Manchester, The Merry Monarch didn't smell of stale lager and sweat. Instead, the scent of pastry browning in an oven somewhere filled the room. Quite possibly, it was the smell of a very good steak pie cooking. At the mere thought of hot puff pastry and tender steak, Maddie's mouth began to water. Her depressing lunch of a brought-from-home cheese roll felt like a very long time ago just now. Unlike a lot of companies, the paper didn't pay its employees before Christmas so Maddie had brought cheese rolls into work for lunch for the whole of December in order to afford some nice gifts for her family.

Glancing around the tables, she noticed a couple of guys seated near the bar. Sure enough they had a steak pie apiece and were tucking in with great enthusiasm. It was difficult to remember a time when she'd been this jealous of another person. After being so disciplined during a month when everyone else tended to loosen the purse strings, and after the truly horrendous journey she'd had, didn't she deserve a wee treat? Perhaps, if she had a wait on her hands for the car to be fixed, she could enjoy a quick bar meal and drive the remaining distance to Edinburgh full and satisfied. The food here probably wasn't too expensive. At this rate, it would be well after midnight by the time she reached her parents' house so she'd definitely need the extra energy.

Beneath all of the festive accoutrement, it was possible to get a sense of what the pub was like at any other time of year. Maddie noted that the pub's decor was just as traditional as the dishes on the menu. The interior walls were built of the quaintest stonework, each block its own irregular shape, but the stones had been arranged in such a manner that every piece appeared to be in just the right space. The walls were adorned with a miscellany of vintage paraphernalia, including an oval mirror with an intricate brass frame, a set of bronze pans and several wooden plaques into which local landscapes had been etched. There were also numerous shelves lined with books and old pottery, but one object in particular made Maddie start to look at it. Tacked up next to one of the shelves was an old, hand-painted mask. Probably made of enamel or some other similar material. The face was divided diagonally in two: one half painted black, the other white. On the black half, a teardrop had been marked out in white, right next to the eye. Maddie couldn't quite put her finger on what was so creepy about it, but a shiver ran through her and she decided to divert her gaze somewhere else.

Unfortunately, this strategy didn't much help matters.

Turning around to face the corner of the room that had thus far been behind her, Maddie came face-to-face with a snarling leopard standing on its hind legs. Since this was the last thing in the world she had expected to see in a snug in the corner of a quaint pub in the middle of the Yorkshire Dales, she let out a sudden, and very high-pitched, yelp. Blinking hard, she stumbled backwards and put a hand to her chest in a bid to recover herself as she realised that the creature poised to attack was, in fact, stuffed.

'Eeee, I 'ope Cindy Clawford dint scare yer, lass,' a man standing behind the bar called over. He laughed then and the buttons on his checkered shirt, which already looked like they were under considerable strain, pulled each time his stomach inflated. It wasn't that the man had a particularly large tummy, though he was quite stout in frame. It just looked as though perhaps the shirt he'd picked out was a little small for him. 'She is a bit of a sight to be'old if you're not expectin' it,' he added.

That's the understatement of the night, Maddie thought as she raised an eyebrow and looked the creature up and down. 'Cindy Clawford's a good name though.'

'Aye, sadly I can't take credit for that. Mind you, I like to think I would have come up with somethin' just as clever. That was the name the seller gave 'er. We got 'er on Etsy,' the man said.

'Barkley's not a fan of Cindy,' Curtis added, standing at the bar with a glass of whisky. As if to confirm this fact Barkley, who had been lying out on the maroon weave carpet that seemed to have been laid in every part of the pub, raised his head and let out a short growl at the mention of Cindy's name.

'Without wishing to offend you in any way, I think I might be with Barkley on this one,' Maddie said, making her way over to the bar.

Again, the man laughed at Maddie's reaction to the beast.

'This is Mickey, the landlord,' Curtis explained. 'I've already relayed to him the unfortunate predicament with your car.'

'There's a public phone over there, love,' Mickey said, pointing over to the other side of the room, 'next to the grandfather clock. And if for any reason you can't get 'elp there are a few rooms left upstairs. They're not the biggest rooms, mind. The biggest one's already been booked but . . .'

Maddie held her hands up to indicate Mickey didn't have to qualify the help on offer any further. 'If for any reason I can't get the car moving tonight I'll be grateful of any available warm bed. I appreciate the help. I can't have any alcohol in case I do need to drive tonight but while I'm on the phone do you think you could make me a hot drink of some kind? I'm not fussy, I'll take anything you can make with hot water.'

'Can't believe a woman as blonde and beautiful as you

needs a drink to warm her up, you're hot enough as it is, aren't you?'

Maddie was so taken aback by this comment that it took her a moment to realise who exactly had said it. Certainly not Mickey or Curtis. And unless Curtis had been modest about his dog's talents, probably not Barkley.

Slowly, Maddie turned her head in the direction of where the comment had come from. A younger man had appeared behind the bar. He wore a black shirt unbuttoned low enough to reveal a small tuft of chest hair and his face was haloed by a thick crop of brown curls. He wasn't Maddie's type, not that she really had a type, she just knew that he wasn't it. Looking into his blue eyes, however, she could imagine quite a number of women her age finding him attractive enough to date. Perhaps on the agreement that he kept any talking to a minimum. Maddie couldn't think of anyone she knew who wanted to hear lines like that.

'James!' Mickey barked at the younger man. Maddie hadn't meant for any distaste to show on her face but even when she didn't voice her opinion on something out loud, her expression regularly gave her away. Mickey clearly didn't appreciate James making his customers feel uncomfortable and Maddie couldn't much blame him, that kind of thing was hardly good for business.

'Don't mind 'im, love. James is me son. Twenty-eight

and 'e's still got a lot to learn about communicatin' with people. You'd like to think that would be a basic life skill but, somehow, it's passed this idiot by.'

James didn't look put out one iota by his father's words, which Maddie found quite strange. She and her parents had their differences at times but there was no way they would speak like that about her to other people.

'My name's James,' he said as though he hadn't heard a word of what his father had just said about him, and maybe he hadn't. He leant over the bar to add: 'But most folk around 'ere call me Jack, as in Jack the lad. Know what I mean?' At this he winked at Maddie, which only deepened her confusion. Was it her imagination or was James proud of his nickname? He seemed to be. So proud in fact that Maddie wondered if he fully understood the negative associations with that phrase.

'She doesn't need yer life story, James,' Mickey interjected. 'She needs a hot beverage to warm 'er up and nowt else out of you, thank you.'

James gave his father a sour look which Mickey completely ignored.

Instead of engaging with his son, the landlord turned back to Maddie and asked: ''Ow about a 'ot chocolate? Eeee, my wife Sofia makes a cracking 'ot chocolate. Marshmallows. Whipped cream. The works.'

'Oh, it's a great shame that your wife is already married,

Mickey,' Maddie said in an attempt to lighten the mood after the harsh words he'd exchanged with his son. 'With those credentials I'd snap her up in a heartbeat.'

The thick crease that had settled along Mickey's brow subsided at her comment and he cackled in appreciation. 'I'll get Sofia to sort you the 'ot drink and you see what you can do about yer car.'

'I'll be here when you get off the phone in case I can be of any more assistance,' said Curtis. 'I don't know exactly how I might help but I was a solicitor before I retired so I'm quite the dab hand at conflict resolution.'

'Oh, that's kind of you, Curtis, but it's Christmas Eve,' said Maddie. 'If you've got other plans you shouldn't let my wee drama get in the way of them.'

'It's not putting me out in the least,' said Curtis. 'Barkley and I will be here quite late this evening, you see, we're taking part in the Christmas Eve scavenger hunt.'

'We do one every year,' Mickey clarified. 'Being so remote we don't do big business on a Christmas Eve so at eight o'clock we send the few who aren't takin' part 'ome to watch *Morecambe and Wise*, again, and everyone else stays for the scavenger 'unt.'

'Mickey's doing a good job of skirting around the fact that he puts it on so that those of us without anywhere else to be, or anyone to be with, can enjoy a bit of company on Christmas Eve,' said Curtis. 'Since my wife Edith passed away six years ago, I've been glad of the tradition. I know several others feel the same.'

Mickey didn't respond verbally to Curtis's words, he simply patted the old man on the shoulder and gave said shoulder a squeeze.

'I'm really sorry to hear about your wife, Curtis,' Maddie said. She never quite knew what to say to people who had lost someone they loved. Though death was a fact of life, it was still such a difficult and sensitive subject and no words, no matter how well-meant, were going to heal a wound like that for someone.

'Thank you, my dear,' Curtis replied. 'Perhaps if you end up staying here tonight, we'll be on the same scavenger hunt team?'

Maddie smiled. 'You can count on it.'

Turning from the bar, Maddie scanned the room and soon picked out the grandfather clock Mickey had mentioned, and the phone sitting next to it. On doing so, however, Maddie noticed that the men who had been tucking into their steak pies earlier were watching her with more than passing interest. How long they had been watching her, she did not know, but they weren't being particularly subtle about it.

One of the men was shorter than the other, with a round face and jet-black hair. The taller of the two was much softer in his features, or maybe Maddie just felt that way because he was dressed in a thick grey jumper that looked like the cosiest garment she'd ever seen.

But no, it wasn't just that.

The gentle waves of ash-blond hair around his face and the soft curve of his jaw lent his features an air of sensitivity his companion did not have.

When the pair realised that Maddie had caught them looking over at her, they both averted their gazes and continued whatever conversation they had been having before their curiosity about her interrupted the flow of it.

And that's how she chose to read the strange look they'd given her.

Curiosity.

This place was hardly a grand metropolis after all. They probably knew every other face in the pub except hers. They were bound to be wondering who she was and what she was doing here. Yes, Maddie told herself, she was sure it was no more sinister than that.

Walking over to the phone, she picked up the receiver and, after pulling up the number in the contacts list on her mobile, dialled the number for the BAC.

As the phone rang in her ear, Maddie noticed the two men sitting near the bar were once again looking in her direction. Before she had a chance to react to this unwanted attention, however, an operator picked up at the other end.

'Hello, British Automobile Club, Nancy speaking, can I help you?'

'Oh,' Maddie said, looking at the men, who were still looking at her, 'yes, I really do hope you can.'

CHAPTER THREE

Caught in a morose daze, Maddie slowly put down the receiver on the phone. Nancy from the British Automobile Club had not faltered once in her cheerfulness as she'd relayed the bad news: the heavy snowfall had made all roads that led to the part of the Dales Maddie had broken down in impassable. On confirming that Maddie did have somewhere she could stay for the night and would not need an emergency airlift out of the area, Nancy advised her to stay put until morning came. Maddie admitted privately that she was tempted, just for a second, to lie and pretend she did need the airlift. That's how badly she wanted to see her parents and be back home in Scotland. But, of course, she could never bring herself to do such a thing. While they were needlessly airlifting her, they might be unable to help somebody else who was in actual physical jeopardy. Nancy had assured her that if the snow stopped, they'd be able to get someone out to her the next day. Since there was nothing else to be done, that would just have to be good enough.

Maddie took a deep breath and tried to blink back the tears pricking behind her eyes. If her parents frowned on whimpering in public, they'd most definitely disapprove of her wailing over something that was well beyond her control. She could just imagine how her dad would respond to such a thing. 'You've got a bed for the night, haven't yae? And yer not going hungry? Well it can't be the end of the world then, can it, bucko?' And he'd be right of course. So why, then, did it feel like it was?

If she was honest with herself, she'd admit that the move she made to Greater Manchester the October before last had been more difficult for her than she'd expected it to be. When the position at *The Trafford Times* had popped up in an online job search just two weeks after she'd broken up with Lance, it had seemed like the perfect move at the perfect time. She needed to be somewhere she wouldn't be reminded of everything that gowk had done to her before they'd parted ways. And there was a much lower chance of running into Lance and his new, thinner, younger girlfriend in Manchester than there was in Edinburgh, which had made the idea all the more appealing.

What she hadn't counted on when she took the leap and

moved to Lancashire, was the homesickness. She missed the misty mountains of the Highlands so much it hurt. She also missed having the Scottish accent in her ears on a daily basis, something other than her own soft Edinburgh tones. She missed looking out over the Firth of Forth and meditating on what tomorrow might bring. And after just over a year's worth of perspective, Maddie cringed at the thought that she had given all that up for a good-for-nothing boy who had shacked up with someone new two minutes after he moved out of what was once *their* flat.

Maddie looked back over to the bar, unsure of what to do first. Secure a room or call her parents? One glance at the scene over by the bar, however, made the decision for her. Mickey and James were standing on the other side of a swing door that separated the serving area from the kitchen. She could see their faces in profile through a round window cut into the door. Maddie didn't know what James had done to aggravate his father now, but their discussion looked heated to say the least. Mickey was shouting right in his son's face. She could also just make out his finger pointing aggressively in his son's direction. For his part, James was looking at his father like it was nothing he hadn't heard before. As jovial as Mickey had seemed earlier, Maddie sensed this was not the moment to interrupt them and so, instead, turned her attention back to the phone.

She knew that hearing her mother's melodic Inverness intonation just then was going to make fighting the tears back even harder, but she had to let them know what was happening. Break the news that she wouldn't be home in time for Christmas morning.

Sighing, she dialled her parents' number and twirled the telephone wire around her finger as she waited for someone to pick up.

'Hello?'

'Mum? It's Maddie.'

'Och, I was just wondering where you were on the road, hen. I—'

Her mother was interrupted by her dad shouting in the background. 'Who's that on the phone on a Christmas Eve? Haven't they got anything better to do than be on the phone to yae? Tell 'em to pour themselves a whisky and settle down for the night.'

Maddie couldn't help but smirk at her dad's trademark insensitive comment. Imagine if it was somebody who did have nothing better to do? Someone widowed, like Curtis, or alone for other reasons. How would they feel hearing her dad shout something like that out in the background? Though that would be a mortifying situation if it happened for real, her dad's devil-may-care attitude to social etiquette was blackly entertaining in the abstract.

'It's our Maddie, Callum. Pipe down, will yer, so I can

talk to my own daughter,' Maddie's mother said, before adjusting her tone to address Maddie again. 'Sorry, hen, you know what he's like. Were you calling to let me know what time you'll be landing?'

'Not exactly,' Maddie said, 'I'm stuck in the Yorkshire Dales tonight, at a pub called The Merry Monarch.'

'The Yorkshire Dales? What're you doin' all the way out there?'

'There was a pile-up on the M6 after an accident so I decided to try an alternative route. Anyway, that wasn't a good move because my car broke down and the BAC can't come out because heavy snow has made the roads impassable.'

There was a pause then, much colder than the snow drifts outside.

'So you . . . you won't make it to us tonight then?'

Maddie could hear the sharp disappointment in her mother's voice and that alone was enough to break her heart. The smile she was still wearing after her dad's little sideshow faded and she was back to fighting the tears again.

'I'm really sorry, Mum. I'm just as down about that as you are but there's nothing I can do. The pub has accommodation so I'm going to hole up here for the night and pray the snow has melted enough for the BAC to get my car started tomorrow.'

'Well, I suppose the important thing is that you're safe,' said Maddie's mum. 'But och, I was really looking forward to seein' you tonight.'

'I know. I really wish this wasn't happening but there's nothing much I can do about it. Hopefully the snow will clear overnight though. And when it does, I'm going to do everything I can to be back with you for Christmas dinner. I—'

Maddie was about to tell her mother just how much she'd missed her but was interrupted by an odd clicking sound.

'Mum?' she tried, but there was absolute silence at the other end of the receiver. Panicking more with each moment that passed, Maddie put down the phone and then picked it up again in the hope of redialling, but it was no use.

The line was dead.

CHAPTER FOUR

Not one to give up lightly, Maddie frowned and tried the same process of putting down the phone, picking it up and redialling one more time for good measure, but it yielded just the same result.

No dial tone.

No life in the phone at all.

Looking back over in the direction of the bar, Maddie noticed that Mickey was serving Curtis another measure of whisky. The landlord was smiling again and there were no signs of his earlier anger. As for his son, he was nowhere to be seen.

Now seemed as good a time as any for Maddie to make sure she had somewhere to sleep tonight. At the very least, if she sorted it out now, she could secure a room without James offering to escort her up to her quarters. Even the thought of that made Maddie shudder. She would like to presume that James was all talk and that his coming on strong with the ladies routine was just a sign that he was a bit of a chancer who hoped that, one day, he'd strike it lucky. That's certainly what his nickname *Jack the Lad* would suggest. And Maddie was fairly sure Curtis would have warned her to steer clear of him if he was a real threat. But, then again, people turned a blind eye to those kinds of things all the time and with James's type one could never be sure. Consequently, she made it her mission right there to make certain she didn't find herself alone with him between now and check-out tomorrow.

'Mickey, I'm sorry to bother you,' Maddie said after striding back over to the bar.

'You're not botherin' me, love, here's yer 'ot chocolate. I'll warn you though, Sofia dint hold back with the chocolate powder. It'll be quite the sugar 'it, mind.'

At this, Mickey put the biggest hot chocolate Maddie had ever seen down on the bar. The vessel looked more like a soup bowl than a cup. And Mickey's wife Sofia had not scrimped on the whipped cream and marshmallows. The whole thing was dusted lightly with cinnamon and there was a piece of Christmas gingerbread sitting on the saucer. The warm, chocolatey smell of the beverage momentarily distracted Maddie from what she'd really come over to the bar for.

'Thank you, that looks . . . well delicious doesn't quite

cover it. I can tell you right now it won't last long. Perhaps you could add the cost to my room bill though, as it turns out I am going to need a bed for the night.'

'No luck with the BAC?' said Curtis.

Maddie shook her head. 'The breakdown service can't get to me because of the snow. If things clear up they will come out tomorrow morning but, until then, I'm stuck.'

'Not a problem, I'll get that all sorted for you,' Mickey said.

'And, sorry to ask for anything else,' Maddie said, 'but do you have another phone? I was just speaking to my mother and got cut off. The line seems to be dead.'

'Oh bloody 'ell, it must be bad weather out there. This 'appens sometimes when we get really 'eavy snow,' Mickey said, taking off his glasses for a moment and rubbing them clean with a nearby cloth. He wore the same kind Maddie's grandad used to sport when he was alive. Tortoiseshell frames and brown tinted lenses. 'I'll check the phone in the kitchen, see if that's workin', but it's safe to say if that one's out then they all are.'

Maddie smiled her gratitude as Mickey pushed through the swing door. In his absence, she took the opportunity to pick the marshmallows off the top of her hot chocolate and swipe them through the whipped cream. The mixture in her mouth felt like the height of indulgence and that warm feeling that spread through Maddie whenever she showed herself kindness kindled inside. Making a living in journalism was no easy task and, as such, she was prone to pushing herself harder than was healthy. As she gulped down the first few mouthfuls of hot chocolate, she tried to capture a strong mental impression of just how good this feeling was. To stop. To savour. To enjoy. There should be more of that in her life, she admitted to herself. There was never any time but she needed to *make* time and make more of the time she did have. It was just so difficult to do that when work was so busy.

When Mickey returned a few minutes later he was shaking his head.

'I'm sorry, lass, there's no dial tone on the one in the kitchen either. Which means the phones are down, and the WiFi with them. What's more, mobile signal up 'ere is like gold dust. I'm afraid we'll 'ave to wait for the snow to melt.'

'Not to worry,' Maddie said, as much to herself as to Mickey. 'I managed to tell my parents where I am and that I'm going to do my best to see them tomorrow so they know I'm safe.'

'The main thing,' said Curtis, who had been respectful enough not to interrupt her communing with her hot chocolate but had been listening in to Maddie and Mickey's exchange, 'is that your parents know you've got somewhere to stay and are not alone. And, I know it's not the Christmas Eve you planned, my dear, but you can now take part in the Christmas Eve scavenger hunt.'

'Oh I . . . Curtis, I'm not sure,' Maddie started, more than a little sheepishly. She had said before that he could count on her as a teammate but that was when she thought the likelihood of her having to take a room at The Merry Monarch for the evening was low. The mere idea of having to put on a show of festive cheer when she'd already endured one of the most obstacle-ridden nights of her life, and it wasn't yet seven p.m., did not appeal in the least.

'Don't give me that,' Curtis said, making it clear he wasn't going to have Maddie rowing back on her promise anytime soon. 'It's Christmas Eve. And you are alone, far from your family. You can't spend the evening locked away in your room.'

'Can't I?' Maddie said, though she was more asking permission to do just that than questioning Curtis's logic.

'From what I've 'eard, sounds like a light-hearted game might just be what you need.' This comment came from neither Curtis nor Mickey but from a woman who had joined the two men sitting near the bar. The same two men who had driven Maddie to Steak Pie Envy earlier and who had taken more than a passing interest in her since she arrived.

The woman in question was older than her companions.

If Maddie were to guess she would say she was probably in her fifties. She had shoulder-length hair which, judging by the grey at the roots, had been dyed a rich, dark shade of brown. An olive-green bucket hat with a large brim sat on the table next to her and, even though it was toasty in the pub, she still wore a scarf in the same shade of green around her neck.

'Sorry, that were quite rude of me to interrupt, weren't it?' she said, with thin lips painted in pink lipstick. 'I didn't mean to be rude.'

Maddie smiled. While part of her couldn't help but wonder what the woman had heard about her when she had been in the pub less than an hour, she reasoned that it was no different in the local ale house near where her parents lived: strangers you didn't recognise were fair game to be gossiped about and conversation was a bit of a free-for-all. If you overheard something you wanted to chip in on, nobody was going to stop you. Besides anything else, this woman clearly meant well with her comment and Maddie wasn't in the business of making any enemies here. She just wanted to get a bit of food inside her, take a hot shower and go to bed. And, it seemed, in the interim she was going to have no choice but to participate in a festive scavenger hunt, but there were worse things for a person to endure.

'Madeline, this is Jeannie,' said Curtis. 'She runs the

village convenience store. And is the village seamstress. She keeps us all in bread and milk—'

'And those little mini cans of sour cream Pringles,' said the man with the jet-black hair.

'Oh God, here we go,' Jeannie and the blond man, who was also sitting at the table, said at once while rolling their eyes in unison.

'What's the matter?' Maddie said, fighting a smile at their synchronised reaction.

'This is Donny,' Curtis said, gesturing to the dark-haired man.

'Don,' the man corrected. 'People called me Donny when I were a kid but I'm twenty-five now. No matter 'ow many times I tell people I'm not six any more, they keep callin' me Donny.'

'Sorry, Don,' Curtis said, with a slight curl to his lip. Maddie remembered Curtis's distaste for shortening names. If he had his way, he'd probably be introducing Don as Donald. 'He works as a police officer with Alex here up at the Yorkshire Dales Constabulary. And Don has a bit of a reputation for being addicted to sour cream crisps.'

Maddie considered making a crack about crisps making a change from donuts given that Don and Alex were police officers, but thought better of it. That was really more of an American stereotype and, anyway, like most of

Maddie's jokes, it wasn't particularly funny so was likely to fall flat to an embarrassing degree.

'It's not the addiction to the crisps we mind, you understand,' said Alex, the blond-haired man who up until now had remained very quiet. 'It's the fact he brings them up at every opportunity. It's become a pretty wearing conversational track, to put it politely.'

'I second that,' said Jeannie. 'I do love spending time with me nephew,' she squeezed Alex's arm as she said this, 'but 'e always brings Tweedle Dum along with 'im, which means at some point I'm bound to get quizzed on when I'm getting more sour cream Pringles in stock because 'e eats them faster than I can buy them in.'

Don crossed his arms at these comments, clearly put out at being shamed for his pious devotion to sour cream Pringles.

'Well, I think there's a lot to be said for a person who can find real joy in the smaller things in life,' said Maddie. Words that brought an immediate smile to Don's face, every inch of which was covered in faint freckles. 'I'm happy to join in the game,' Maddie continued. 'But I really must get a room sorted and freshen up after the walk here. I can only imagine what the snow has done to my hair. I did brush it before leaving the house this morning, honest.'

The group chuckled at Maddie's self-deprecating comment

while Mickey went to fetch a key for Maddie's room. With the phone lines down, Mickey said he would take payment the next day, or over the phone after Christmas, but on being told what the bill would be, she was relieved that the accommodation prices in these parts were fairly modest. At just sixty pounds for the night, however, Maddie did wonder if Mickey had taken pity on her and offered a reduced rate without saying anything. With finances being what they were at the moment, she wasn't going to question any such charity pushed her way.

'The game starts at eight,' said Curtis. 'So, make sure you're back down before then. You don't want to miss orientation.'

'No, wouldn't want that,' said Maddie, and she tried really hard not to sound tart about it because Curtis had been very helpful to her.

Mickey, Don and Alex all offered one after the other to help Maddie with her bag up the stairs but it was only one flight and, as friendly as everyone seemed, she really did need just a few minutes to herself to adjust to the new Christmas Eve plan.

If she was really honest, she wanted to go upstairs for a good cry. Of course, there was no pressing need to do so. She wasn't injured. Hadn't suffered any humiliating verbal attack. But she knew, after the blow of not making it home this evening, that she would feel better just to let it out. And as Maddie thought over the trials of her journey: her boss, Gavin, not letting her leave at the time they'd agreed because a story about a local drug ring broke, the pile-up on the M6, her car breaking down, the breakdown cover being no bloody help whatsoever and the phone lines cutting out, she felt nigh on entitled to have a ten-minute sobbing session in the privacy of her own quarters.

And then, as she made her way up to the corridor of bedrooms upstairs, another thought occurred to her. That was a lot of bad luck for anyone to endure in the space of one evening, just by chance. Maddie didn't believe in fate per se. But maybe, for some reason she did not yet understand, she hadn't been meant to make it home that night. Silly as this may sound to any scientific-thinking person, it was certainly beginning to feel that way. As if some force was keeping her here at The Merry Monarch.

As old floorboards, hidden by fraying rugs creaked beneath her feet, Maddie quickened her pace along the corridor, which had been painted bottle green and thus felt like quite a dark, dingy space. It was the kind of environment in which her imagination could quite easily run away with her and she could do without that right now.

Before turning her key in the lock of her room and bundling her case through the door, she raised her eyes to the ceiling and said: 'Gavin, M6 pile-ups, car malfunctions, snow, dead phone lines, anything else?'

As soon as the words were out of her mouth, however, she bit her lip and wished with all her might she could take them back. After the evening she'd had thus far, tempting fate seemed like a bad move. One she would surely come to regret.

CHAPTER FIVE

After all of the unwanted drama she had suffered through earlier in the evening, Maddie could barely believe it, but within thirty minutes of making her way back downstairs to the pub area, she was laughing harder than she had in a very long time.

'Stop it, stop it, please!' she begged of Alex and Don. Curtis was also sitting at the table with them, a sly grin on his face. Though Jeannie had obviously heard this schtick before, she too was chuckling along at the antics of her nephew and his work colleague, who were ridiculing Curtis for being able to appear as if from nowhere and disappear just as quickly even though he had a walking stick and the bad hip to accompany it.

'Nobody knows 'ow 'e does it,' Don said. 'There's been a bloody BBC *Panorama* about it and even they couldn't get to the truth. It's the biggest mystery since Wagatha Christie.

Mind you, in recent years, there 'ave been rumours that 'e's a distant relative of 'arry Houdini and that maybe the trick 'as been passed down the family.'

'Houdini has got nothing on me,' Curtis said, raising what must now have been his third glass of whisky and taking a sip.

Maddie giggled at just how much pride he was taking in his reputation and creased up all the more when she remembered how startled she'd been by his sudden appearance by her car. In her defence, when he performed his act on her, she had only just broken down in an eerily quiet village in the Yorkshire Dales. Now that she'd got to know him a bit, however, she felt somewhat foolish for being so jumpy about the way he'd manifested out of thin air. Little had she known then that he was renowned village-wide, and possibly even further afield than that, for such trickery.

'So long as you don't try to replicate Houdini's naked escape act,' said Alex, 'I do not fancy arresting *you* for indecent exposure.'

'You finished with your plate, love?' Sofia asked as she passed by their table. After Maddie had described how jealous she had been watching Don and Alex tuck into their steak pies, Sofia had insisted that the last one in the oven went to their unexpected Christmas Eve guest.

'Aye, thanks for that, Sofia,' said Maddie. 'I'm beyond

thankful not to have missed out on that pie, it was just as delicious as I imagined it to be. And are those chips homemade?'

'Oh aye,' Sofia said, there was a shine to her deep blue eyes as she placed her hands on her wide hips and took an unmistakably dignified stance. 'My family moved to England from Belgium when I was just a bairn, and, as you might be aware, fries are quite a big deal where I come from so I pride myself on those.'

Maddie looked closer at Sofia. She hadn't realised when she originally spoke to her that she was from the other side of the English Channel. It was her accent that had made her seem like a local, born and bred. It wasn't quite as broad as Mickey's but the vowels were round and flat enough that she didn't notice much difference in the way the two spoke. Of course, if Sofia had lived here a long time, it was only to be expected that she'd adopt the local way of speaking.

'Mmmmm! When me and the girls were on a hen do in Bruges we lived off Belgian fries pretty much exclusively,' Maddie said in response to Sofia's brag about the chips. 'But there was something different about yours. Somehow, they taste even more . . . golden. If that's even a word you can apply to taste. I can't quite put my finger on what it is.'

'And you never will,' Sofia said, wagging a finger at

Maddie, 'it's a family secret and if you ever guessed it, well, I'd have to kill you.' With that Sofia let out a sharp little cackle, picked up Maddie's plate and took it back into the kitchen.

Maddie, as certain as she could be that the death threat was made in jest, chuckled at Sofia's comment and sighed the sigh of a woman whose stomach was stuffed full of good food.

Don took this pause in the conversation to shoot a funny look in Maddie's direction that she had no hope of reading.

'What's that look for?' Maddie asked.

'Nothing,' said Don, shrugging in an attempt to shrug off Maddie's question.

'No, seriously,' said Maddie, her smile fading. She hadn't completely forgotten the strange looks Alex and Don had given her earlier when she went to call her mother. If something was up, she wanted to know what it was.

'It's nowt really,' said Don. ''Cept, I were just wondering if everything . . . er, if everythin' were alright with yer room?'

'Don,' Alex said, his voice carrying a sharp note of warning. 'Don't start with that.'

'Don't start with what?' Maddie said, looking between the two of them. She couldn't work out what they were getting at. The rooms at The Merry Monarch were very welcoming. Hardwood floors covered in thick rugs. Crisp white bedclothes accented with, presumably seasonal, red and green checkered cushions. Botanical wallpaper that looked as though it had been rehung in recent years. It was a damn sight more presentable than some of the other places she'd stayed over the years. 'Everything with the room was fine . . . why?'

'Trust me,' said Curtis, 'if it's what I think it is, you're better off not knowing.'

Don cast a glance over at Alex, clearly considering his prior warning but choosing to disregard it. 'It's just me and Sita – she manages the local charity shop – we've got this theory. We think this place is haunted.'

'Oh God,' Alex said, covering his face with his hand. 'You are an absolute embarrassment sometimes. Do you know that?'

'Haunted?' Maddie said. She didn't believe in ghosts, at least not on the whole. But she had to spend the night in this place and the last thing she needed was someone telling her stuff that was likely to send her imagination running wild.

'There's nowt to it, love,' said Jeannie, perhaps sensing that Maddie was more than a little uncomfortable with this line of conversation. 'And frankly I've 'eard Donny go on about this subject more times than I can count so I'm going to make another trip to the ladies. The cold outside is doing nothing for my bladder.'

'Aww, Jeannie,' Don grimaced. 'TMI.'

Jeannie scrunched her face up at Don. 'I don't know what that means. And my bladder isn't going to let me 'ang around to find out. But while I'm up, I might as well take some of these empty glasses through to the kitchen.'

'Watch yourself, Jeannie. Keep helping out like that all the time and Sofia will have you on the bar rota before you know it,' said Alex, as Jeannie collected up the empty glasses and scurried over to the swing door. Since most patrons would simply take the glasses to the bar rather than all the way to the kitchen, it seemed to Maddie that Jeannie must be constantly in peril of being offered a job by Mickey if she was allowed into staff-only territory without permission.

The smile returned to Maddie's face at the warm interplay between them all. They clearly had a lot of affection for each other even though Don obviously rubbed Jeannie up the wrong way at times.

'So, about this ghost?' Maddie said once Jeannie was out of earshot. She said this in part to bait Alex. She'd seen how fed up he'd looked when Don had brought it up. She also admitted privately, however, that she wanted to satisfy her own curiosity. It had been a long time since anyone had told her an actual ghost story. She was probably about eight and at a sleepover last time it happened.

'Must you encourage him?' said Alex. 'There is no ghost.'

'I have to agree with Alex on this one,' said Curtis. 'The whole thing is utter nonsense. An overblown fairy story cooked up by tourists not used to the sounds that carry across the Dales at night.'

'Not all of it can be put down to that. Some guests 'ave reported really strange 'appenin's,' said Don. 'Things movin' around, not bein' where you left them.'

'The people who reported that were in their nineties,' said Alex. 'They probably just forgot where they put their reading book, or whatever it was they lost.'

'Well, what about the strange noises in the middle of the night? Not outside, before you put it down to the Dales, but inside the property,' said Don.

'Probably Mickey's snoring,' said Curtis. 'I've been around when he's dropped off sitting in one of the armchairs over there, and I can tell you strange noises are in abundance when Mickey's enjoying some shut-eye.'

'Oh, you're just a bunch of unbelievers, it's no good talking to you about it. But I've been collecting these stories from different people I've met over the years and, let me tell you, there are a lot of patterns runnin' through the different accounts I've heard. Besides, Sita has tuned into the energies in this place and she says there's a ghost 'ere and I believe 'er,' said Don.

'And Sita manages the village charity shop and is also some kind of . . . expert in the paranormal?' said Maddie.

'You've hit the nail on its proverbial head there,' said Curtis.

'Yes, by day she'll sell you a dog-eared copy of a John le Carré mystery and by night she'll read tarot cards, or your tea leaves or your aura, all for a reasonable fee,' said Alex, his voice laced with disdain.

'You are so sarcastic,' said Don. 'She runs the charity shop because she cares about the environment so much. Whether she's sellin' old books or old tennis rackets, it doesn't matter if it's helpin' the planet, does it?'

'Alright, no, I didn't mean to be dismissive . . . at least of that particular life choice,' said Alex.

'Thank you,' Don said, before continuing on his spooky conversational track. 'Anyway, she says she's not surprised by all the stories I've 'eard about this place because there's definitely a spirit living 'ere that she can't identify. She can always identify spirits. But not in 'ere. Like, this is the only place she's never been able to reach out to them. 'Ow creepy is that? Eh? Eh?'

'Pretty creepy,' Maddie said with a nod while shooting Alex a knowing smirk.

Alex offered no more than an eye roll in response.

'Aye,' Don continued, off in a world of his own by this point. 'And you just know it's going to end up being one of those freaky little girl ghosts that show up in ’orror films runnin’ about in their nightie. Ooh, it sends a shiver right through me, it does.’

‘You’ve watched too many of those bloody ghost movies,’ said Alex. ‘Sita can’t identify the spirit, because there is no spirit here. There never has been. It’s a load of rubbish.’

‘That’s what you think,’ Don said. ‘Some of us are more open to the unknown wonders of the world.’

‘You’re an unknown wonder of the world,’ came Alex’s response.

At this juncture, Jeannie returned to the table and sat herself down. ‘Please tell me ’e’s not still talking about ghosts.’

‘No, he’s not,’ said Alex. ‘We’re done talking about that, aren’t we Donny?’

‘Well, I ’adn’t fully finished making my case—’ Don began, but he was quickly interrupted and Maddie noticed relief flood Alex’s features at this fortuitous interjection.

‘Right, you lot,’ Mickey said, approaching their table. ‘Things are about to get serious in ’ere. We’re ushering out anyone who isn’t takin’ part in the scavenger ’unt now, so you’d better start pickin’ yer teams. In a few minutes, Sofia will come around and put all the mobile phones in the safe box so, if the WiFi comes back online, there’s no chance of anyone cheating. Once that’s sorted, I’ll do a full orientation in five minutes when everyone is sittin’ with their group. There should be a total of three teams so bear that in mind when you're dividin' yourselves up.'

'We . . . have to hand over our mobiles?' Maddie said to Alex. She wasn't one of those people who constantly scrolled on their phones but the device did have personal data on it and she didn't much like the idea of handing it over to someone she barely knew.

Alex smiled at the alarm that was no doubt written across her face. 'It's only for a few hours and Sofia locks them in the safe so nothing can happen to them. They have to do it that way now because of a long-running feud between Curtis here and Mrs Fazakerley. Three years ago there was an argument between the pair that lasted over an hour. Even with training as a police inspector I couldn't defuse the situation any quicker than that. She claimed she saw him using his mobile for help with one of the clues and all hell broke loose. Trust me when I say, we'll all just have a lot more fun if phones are taken out of the equation.'

'Alright,' Maddie said, though she still felt far from alright about the prospect of handing over the most expensive thing she owned. 'Well, it goes without saying that I'm on your team, Curtis.' There hadn't been any follow-up to his earlier comment about *raving lefties* so she was hopeful that the topic of politics would be off the table for the duration of the evening. That should make it safe enough to muddle through a couple of hours of riddle-solving with him.

'No offence to you two,' said Jeannie, directing her gaze first at Alex, then at Don, 'but I'd like to go one night without sour cream Pringles being mentioned so I'm going to go over there and join the Kapoor family on their team.'

'I'm not surprised you've chosen that team, I found it a peaceful change last year,' said Alex. 'I'm sure it's only a matter of time before Curtis starts complaining about how the scavenger hunt is rigged.'

'Well, in my defence it is, you know,' said Curtis.

'Yeah, well, no offence, Curtis,' said Jeannie, 'but I am familiar with yer feelings on the subject so I am going to 'ave a change of scenery. I'm not joinin' your rival, either mind. I don't want to 'ear Mrs Fazakerley 'arp on all night about 'ow she's undefeated in the game, any more than I want to 'ear Don talk about Pringles. In short, I'm choosin' the quiet life for the evening.'

Maddie looked over to where Jeannie had gestured and saw a mum, dad and daughter at a table nearby. James had reappeared for the first time since his argument with Mickey and was sitting with them. From what Maddie had overheard when she was in her room earlier, however, Jeannie was definitely not choosing the quiet life by sitting at that particular table.

About an hour ago now, Maddie had just enjoyed a hot, steamy shower and was lazing about on the bed wrapped up in a white fluffy towel when the people in the room next door had started a screaming match. She'd tried to ignore it at first but it was just so loud. As far as she could tell, there was only her and one other party booked in upstairs, and for some reason Mickey had seen fit to board her next door to them. It had been a very long time since she'd heard people bellowing that way. The sound was quite distorted through the wall and it took her a while to get the gist of what the argument was about. Ultimately, however, she realised that it was a father shouting at his daughter about a boy – and the boy in question was James.

It seemed the landlord's son was really hedging his bets when it came to the ladies that night as, from what Maddie had heard, the father was livid about the fact that James had been flirting heavily with his daughter in the bar earlier. 'You're nineteen and still living under my roof so you'll do as you're told,' the father had shouted over and over at his child. A fact that had only heightened Maddie's dislike of James.

What was a twenty-eight-year-old thinking of, going after a nineteen-year-old? Of course, Maddie had a fair idea why a girl in that age bracket might appeal to James and it turned her stomach. She recognised that later in life people often formed relationships in which there was a bigger age gap and it was not an issue. By that point, the parties concerned had grown up and learnt a little something about the world, and themselves. But she wasn't convinced that at nineteen a person had really had enough life experience to assert their views and make themselves heard in their chosen relationship. Particularly if the other person was a lot more experienced than they were. Did James just see this girl as an easy target? Someone he could manipulate as he chose? Maddie didn't know for sure and wasn't in a position to judge, but she could understand the father's concerns. Even if she wasn't thrilled about the volume at which he was expressing them.

When it became obvious that Maddie wasn't going to get any peace in her room, she had quickly dressed. When she left to go down to the pub, the Kapoors happened to be vacating their room at the same time. Before bustling on ahead of them, she had smiled as politely as she could in the hope that they wouldn't guess she had overheard their screaming match. Of course, she hadn't known their name then. Or that they would be joining in the scavenger hunt. Just because they were staying the night at The Merry Monarch didn't oblige them to join in the activities. But there they were, across the room, the three of them and James in a potentially explosive seating arrangement. With Jeannie on the brink of joining them without a clue of what she might be getting herself into.

CHAPTER SIX

As Jeannie got up from the table, just for a moment, Maddie wondered if she should warn her that sparks might fly on the Kapoors' team, but who was she to do that? She didn't know Jeannie, or anyone else that well, so how would it look if she started gossiping behind people's backs? She shouldn't have even been listening to the argument taking place on the other side of the wall from her. Not that it had been possible to really avoid doing so. After listening to said argument, Maddie was surprised Mr Kapoor was willing to sit on the same team as James at all. Was he tired of arguing with his daughter about it? Or had he and James reached some kind of understanding? Regardless, for better or for worse, Maddie decided to stay quiet about what she had witnessed, leaving Jeannie to pick up her hat and saunter over to take part in what would surely be the most awkward team dynamics in the room.

Meanwhile, Don looked around in an overtly casual manner as though he had yet to decide the best team for him. 'Think I'll go and join Mrs Fazakerley's team.'

'Oh, will you now,' said Alex, 'there's a big surprise.'

'What?' Don said, blinking rapidly in such a way that suggested he knew just what Alex was getting at.

'Well, it just so happens that's the team Sita's on. What a coincidence,' Alex said.

'Oh, is Sita over there with 'er? I 'adn't noticed,' Don said with a quick shake of his head. 'But I did want to ask about 'er plans for the upcyclin' event she's holdin' after Christmas. So that works out quite well.'

Don wasn't convincing anyone with his innocent act and, from Alex's tone, Maddie gleaned that Don had something of a wee crush on Sita. Presumably this was part of the reason he'd been so quick to argue for the existence of ghosts in The Merry Monarch. Maddie hoped this was a factor as, based on the meagre evidence presented, blindly believing there was a ghost here did make him seem a bit naive to say the least. And this guy was a police officer. Wasn't he supposed to be just a little bit streetwise, like Alex seemed to be?

'Nothing wrong with taking a shine to someone, Don,' said Curtis. 'I think I spotted some mistletoe in the corner there . . . though I would do a bit of recon before you commit. Based on the conversations I've had with her when she's served me in the charity shop, I can't be sure, but I think she might be a Labour voter.'

Maddie bit her lip. Looks like it was somewhat optimistic to assume that politics would be off the conversational agenda.

Alex, however, wasn't going to be drawn into such serious territory. Not when the opportunity to thoroughly roast Don about something still hung in the air.

'A kiss under the mistletoe at Christmas and a summer wedding, how does that sound, Donny?' Alex teased, his blue eyes sparkling as he did so. 'Although she'll probably want some kind of weird, New Age, hippie-dippie wedding come to think about it, knowing what she does in her spare time and all that. Mind you, with your love of the supernatural, I'm sure that will be right up your street, won't it?'

'New Age wedding?' Don stammered. 'I mean . . . I've got no idea what you lot are on about.' The slight blush in his cheeks suggested otherwise. 'I'm just going over there to even out the teams. If any of you could do simple mathematics, you'd see it makes sense. Mrs Fazakerley and Sita can't just do the game as a twosome. The Kapoors 'ave got five on their team now with yer Auntie Jeannie. If I go over there to Mrs Fazakerley's team, we'll be a trio and you'll be a trio. A foursome including Barkley.'

'Yes, he's quite smart for a dog, but I'm not really sure riddle-solving is his forte,' Curtis said.

Barkley let out a sharp yap at this, as though he somehow gleaned his intelligence was being questioned.

'Whatever,' said Don. 'Me being on Mrs Fazakerley's team just makes it more even. And I shouldn't have to point out such simple sums to two people who are allegedly so educated and so much smarter than I am.'

'Alright, stop it, you're embarrassing yourself. Just be off with you over to the other table, Captain Wentworth,' said Alex.

'Was . . . that a Jane Austen reference?' Maddie said, trying to hide the surprise in her voice and failing. Perhaps it was unfair of her to assume that a police inspector from the Yorkshire Dales wouldn't be caught dead with a copy of *Persuasion* in his hand; people were individuals after all. Quirky. Idiosyncratic. Still, Maddie couldn't help but be a bit taken aback.

'No, it's a Dakota Johnson reference,' said Don, without missing a beat. After the hard time Alex had given him about Sita, he clearly wasn't going to pass up a chance to repay the favour.

'What's a Dakota Johnson?' asked Curtis.

'She's an actress in the latest film version of *Persuasion*,' Don said. 'Alex is mad about 'is darling Dakota. 'E goes and sees all 'er films. Even if 'e doesn't understand 'em. 'E dragged me to the pictures to see that one. It were *so* boring. But of course 'e didn't think so because 'is darling Dakota were on the screen.'

'I'm not mad about her, thank you,' Alex said, 'but even if I was, I've probably got more chance with Dakota than you have with Sita.'

This wiped the grin off Don's face. He opened his mouth to say something else but thought better of it and went over to join his chosen team.

Once Don was out of earshot, Alex turned to Maddie. 'Please, pay no attention to Donny's talk about ghosts. He only believes in all that because he's a bit green and wants to get into Sita's . . .' there was a pause then as though Alex remembered who he was talking to, 'good books,' he finished at last.

Maddie offered Alex a smile and a nod in return for the reassurance. So, Don was a bit wet behind the ears then, and his principles were easily swayed by the women he found attractive. Maddie wasn't sure these were particularly winning qualities in a police officer but she had to concede that Don seemed harmless enough and his heart was in the right place. That counted for more than most people realised.

'Right, my friends,' said Curtis. 'Now that the most distracting member of the table has gone elsewhere, it's time to engage in the serious business of sizing up the competition.'

Slowly, Curtis gazed around the room and, after a few moments, both Alex and Maddie followed his stare.

'The Kapoors are at an advantage with five on their team,' said Alex, looking over at their table and frowning. Maddie looked more closely at the team in question. James was talking almost exclusively to their daughter whose name, Maddie had gleaned through the wall, was Zainab. With her long flowing brown hair and the luscious red lipstick that matched her dress, Maddie couldn't blame James for having his head turned by this particular young woman. It seemed his charms weren't lost on her either as whenever she looked at him, a dreamy expression crossed over her face. This was made more noticeable by the scowl she threw at her father whenever she looked in his direction. It seemed Zainab did not appreciate his opinions on her new potential suitor.

Zainab's mother sat sighing on the other side of her husband. She looked like one of those bored and glamorous types. Her thick eyeliner had been applied with an expert precision Maddie could only dream of. The vibrant turquoise trouser suit she was wearing fit so snugly, and was so elegantly cut, Maddie wondered if it had been especially tailored. However the garment itself had been put together, it contrasted beautifully with a delicate gold pendant hanging around her neck. Regardless of what was going on behind the scenes in this little family unit, this woman's demeanour definitely didn't match her vibrant couture. Perhaps she felt caught in the middle of the feud between her spouse and her daughter. Given how despondent she looked though, Maddie wagered such spats were quite a regular occurrence in this household.

Periodically, Jeannie was trying to engage Mrs Kapoor in conversation but was getting short, flat responses. No doubt Jeannie was already regretting her choice of teams. She'd probably rather listen to Don talk about sour cream Pringles all night than be sat with a bickering family on Christmas Eve.

'It's true that the Kapoors have five teammates,' said Curtis, disturbing Maddie's line of thought, 'but one of them *is* your stepbrother.'

'You're right. That . . . does even the playing field somewhat,' Alex conceded.

Maddie scanned the table the Kapoors were sitting at. Other than Mr Kapoor, the only male on the table was James. So that meant . . .

'James is your stepbrother?' Maddie tried not to let the distaste ring out in her voice but it was no good, even she could hear the judgement in her tone.

Alex nodded. 'Mickey's my dad. He left my mum for Sofia when I was twelve and they started a new life at The Merry Monarch.'

Quickly, Maddie did the maths in her head. Mickey

left twenty years ago and James was twenty-eight. Which means he was having an affair with Sofia for almost a decade. That was a very long time to deceive a spouse, and the likelihood was that Alex's mum knew nothing about the other child until Mickey left her.

'I—I'm sorry, I didn't know the connection,' said Maddie. She made a note to be more careful about what she said for the rest of the evening. There was something about the ambience of The Merry Monarch, it lulled you into a sleepy haze and made you almost feel as though you were sitting in your own living room. Despite how warm and cosy it felt, lolling about in here with the open fire blazing, she mustn't forget these people were relative strangers and, as such, it would be easier than she'd like to put her foot in it.

'Why would you guess the connection?' said Alex with a shake of his head. 'It's not like we look alike and there's nothing to be sorry about. I've had twenty years to get used to the situation. Same for Jeannie. You see how she gets on with Mickey and Sophia now. It's all water under the bridge.'

Alex's clarifications answered a question in Maddie's mind: was Jeannie's Mickey's sister? But no, it would seem from Alex's phrasing that it was more likely she was a sister to Alex's mother. As he said, Jeannie seemed very at ease with them. When it came to how Alex felt about this situation however, Maddie wasn't quite so convinced everything was settled. His words were amiable enough but there was something about his tone that made Maddie wonder if he really had come to terms with the fact that his dad had left him to start a new family. That would be a bitter pill for any twelve-year-old to swallow and, as Maddie knew all too well, the difficult stuff that happened to you when you were a kid tended to stick and stick hard.

'I'm sorry if I spoke out of turn, Alex,' said Curtis, clearly embarrassed at having accidentally revealed a good chunk of Alex's family history to a total stranger.

'You didn't,' Alex said. 'And besides, you're right about James putting the Kapoors at a disadvantage. Mr Kapoor's really quite good at solving the clues though so maybe that will even things out. I was on his team last year and he was the one who solved the hardest of all the riddles.' Alex turned to Maddie at this point. 'Mr and Mrs Kapoor are teachers in the local school, you see, to say they're smart the understatement of the century. And he, in particular, loves the figuring out, you can see it in his face while he's thinking. He just loves it. His wife and daughter aren't as into it as he is, mind.'

'I can understand this might not be the most thrilling Christmas Eve outing for someone Zainab's age,' said Maddie. 'And maybe that's why Mrs Kapoor doesn't exactly seem ecstatic to be here. She looks like she might be much happier drinking cocktails in the city than sitting in a country pub competing in a scavenger hunt.'

Alex nodded. 'You're not far off. The Kapoors got married against the odds. She was from a highly regarded, and very well-off, Pakistani family. Mr Kapoor . . . Well, let's just say he was from the other side of the tracks. The way he tells the story, they married for love but I'm not too sure how well it's working out for them. They moved to the village five years ago and I don't know if I've ever seen her look happy here.'

'Why are they staying at the pub if they live in the village?' said Maddie, wondering if the Kapoors had money to burn. On her salary, she certainly couldn't justify a hotel in the same village or town she lived in, even for one night.

'They live way out in the dale,' said Curtis. 'It's a good two-mile walk from here on foot. They like to have a drink or two, it being Christmas and all. And frankly by the time the scavenger hunt is over everyone is exhausted so a two-mile walk in cold weather isn't an appealing prospect. From what I understand, Mickey gives them a reduced rate on the biggest room in the place, since they're local, you know.'

'That's good of him,' Maddie said, looking over at Mrs Kapoor again. This time, however, her expression was no longer listless. Her charcoal eyes were full of a fiery intensity, and it took a moment for Maddie to realise what, or rather who, Mrs Kapoor was looking at.

It was James.

And, while Zainab was busy looking in her handbag for something, James was looking right back at Mrs Kapoor. His stare just as intense as hers. Even from across the room, Maddie could sense how thick the air was between them. And it wasn't until Mr Kapoor, who had been having a quick word with Mickey, turned back around to the table that the spell was broken. Both Mrs Kapoor and James flinched when Mr Kapoor caught them studying each other and quickly averted their eyes. From the subsequent scowl on Mr Kapoor's face, it was obvious something else was going on here. But Maddie could not fathom what.

CHAPTER SEVEN

'I know I've got a reputation for getting overcompetitive about the scavenger hunt, having failed to win it in all previous years,' said Curtis, forcing Maddie to return her attention to her own team. 'But let's be honest, nobody will be taking this more seriously than Mrs Fazakerley.'

'Why's that?' Maddie asked, looking over at the table Don had joined. There were two women seated with him. She guessed that the younger woman of the pair with a short, black pixie cut and slender frame was Sita, who Don was apparently pining over. The other lady was much older. Her grey hair was firmly set in curls that didn't seem to so much as ripple when she moved her head and she wore very thick tights that were clearly supposed to be natural in shade but looked burnt orange in hue.

'Mrs Fazakerley always wins the scavenger hunt,' said Curtis. 'It doesn't matter what team she's on, what setbacks she has, somehow she always wins. Nobody knows exactly what's behind her streak of exceptionally good luck, but I suspect she'll be working quite hard this year to hold onto her title.'

'Yeah, OK, Curtis, I know it's tough for you that Mrs Fazakerley always wins but let's not get onto your conspiracy theories about her having an inside track on the scavenger hunt,' said Alex, barely able to contain his amusement as he did so.

'You shouldn't be so dismissive of my theories,' said Curtis, his tone far more serious than the look on Alex's face. 'Rumour has it she knows her way around all the secret passageways in the pub.'

'There are . . . secret passageways in this place?' Maddie said, trying not to let out an audible gulp as she did so. Rumours of ghosts. Secret passageways. Unsettling masks hanging on the wall. In her mind, Maddie was beginning to recategorise The Merry Monarch, moving it from its previous position under the *cosy* heading into the *creepy* column. 'The passageways are not involved in the scavenger hunt, are they? It's just that I'm a bit claustrophobic,' she added.

'Occasionally there's a clue that leads you down one of them,' said Alex. 'But don't worry, I'll go in solo if necessary. And anyway, I used to play in the secret passageways when I was a teenager so if that's Mrs Fazakerley's only advantage then I can match it.'

'No, no, no,' said Curtis. 'The gossip is that there are more secret passageways in this place than most people are aware of and only Mickey, Sofia and Mrs Fazakerley know about them. Secret secret passageways.'

Alex shook his head. 'If anything like that existed, I'd have found them when I was a kid.'

'I don't know so much,' said Curtis. 'Mickey told me even he's not sure he knows about all the secret passageways in this place. Says he's happened across one or two of them he hadn't a clue about in recent years.'

'But how would secret passageways help Mrs Fazakerley win the scavenger hunt?' said Maddie.

'The clues are scattered all over the building,' Curtis explained. 'If she knows some secret ways of getting about the building more efficiently, she'd likely be at a time advantage if nothing else.'

'Oh, Curtis,' Alex said, beginning to chuckle. 'Please don't start again on this topic. My ribs can only take so much.'

'I don't know why you find it so funny,' Curtis said, scrunching up his face.

'Well it's the way you go on and on about Mrs Fazakerley like she's some kind of criminal mastermind.'

'Not criminal,' said Curtis. 'Just a morally bereft mastermind. We can't trust her to play fair, I'm telling you.'

Alex shook his head and muttered to Maddie: 'Last year, when Mrs Fazakerley won, he started a fifteen-minute rant on how she'd cheated and manipulated the game. I wish I'd had him down the nick so I could have got it all on record. It was the kind of stuff that would give you a laugh on even the worst day in the office.'

'Do you often have bad days at the office?' Maddie said. 'I mean, it seems fairly quiet around here but looks can be deceiving.'

'Nah, you get the odd, unexpected tragedy and some low-level drugs stuff but most days at the Yorkshire Dales Constabulary make old episodes of *Heartbeat* look exciting. And I'm OK with that. Started out in the cities during my training when I was eighteen. I did my time in that world. I'm not saying I'll stay local forever, but I think I've earned a bit of peace and quiet . . . and er, that's my life story. Apparently.' Alex pressed his lips together and widened his eyes and Maddie laughed at his expression.

Being off-duty, he'd had a couple of beers, which might have loosened his tongue a little, but this wasn't the first time someone had told Maddie more than they meant to in conversation.

She wasn't sure what it was about her that set people at ease. That spurred them to share details they wouldn't share with anyone else. Perhaps, somehow, the people in question knew she was really listening to them. Over the years of doing her job, Maddie had come to understand the unique power of really listening to another person. Of taking in each word they said and considering all possible meanings. Consequently, over time, she had become much more accustomed to listening in a conversation than she had talking. Possibly, this was, in part, because she already had her outlet, her opportunity to make broadcasts of a sort, with her newspaper articles. Whatever it was about Maddie that enticed people to speak openly with her, she considered it a gift, and it had certainly come in handy during her time as a journalist.

Maddie was about to say something to set Alex at ease about how much of his autobiography he'd just offered up with almost no prompting, but she was interrupted by Sofia clanging a spoon against a glass to get everyone's attention.

'Right, folks,' she said, raising her voice a wee bit louder than necessary considering how few people were now left in the room. 'It looks as though you've all made your choices when it comes to your allegiances for the evening.'

Looking over again at the team with Jeannie, the Kapoors and James on the table, Maddie couldn't help but note that Sofia had chosen an interesting turn of phrase with *allegiances*. Between the argument the Kapoors had back in their room and the strange look that had passed between Mrs Kapoor and James, it was difficult to say where any of the allegiances lay on that particular table.

'I am now going to come round and collect up the mobile phones before handing you over to my glamorous assistant, and husband, Mickey,' Sofia said, regaining Maddie's attention. 'The time has come for the games to begin!'

CHAPTER EIGHT

'Right,' Mickey said in a bid to get everyone in the room looking in his direction. He was still jovial enough but Maddie noticed a certain sharpness to his tone that hadn't been there earlier. 'Sofia's just told me that everyone's 'anded in their phones and she's on her way now to take them to the safe. You'll all get 'em back once the game is over in a few hours, or sooner if one of the teams is up for breakin' some records. I know 'ow seriously you lot take what is supposed to be a jolly Christmas scavenger 'unt so let's go over the rules now so there're no arguments later. We don't want a repeat of last year where we were up until one a.m. on Christmas mornin' arguing the toss. Sofia is 'anding each team an envelope. The colour of that envelope determines the colour of yer team. We've got a red team, a blue team and a yellow team. Do not open that envelope until I say so.'

A strange excitement fizzed up in Maddie as Sofia dropped a yellow envelope onto their table before distributing the red envelope to the team Jeannie had joined and the blue envelope to the team Don had joined. Scavenger hunts weren't really Maddie's thing. In fact, she wasn't much of a joiner in general but the others were so it seemed bad form to let her dislike for organised activities show. With a bit of luck, she would just get swept along in the merriment of it all. Which, besides anything else, would make the fact that she couldn't spend the night with her family more bearable.

'This first envelope,' Mickey explained, 'contains yer first clue. Each clue will lead you to the next and there are twelve in total. The first team to solve all twelve clues, one for each day of Christmas, and come back with a certain item we've 'idden at the end of the trail, will win a Christmas food 'amper and a fifty-pound bar tab.'

At this remark, the room erupted into a high-pitched *woooooooo*, not dissimilar to the kind of sound you'd hear on a game show when an exciting prize was announced. Maddie laughed at the sound, which was clearly slightly mocking in tone. She hadn't been prepared for pantomime responses to Mickey's orientation speech but she reasoned that it was Christmas so pantomime was sort of the done thing.

'Yes, thank you, thank you, I know, *Who Wants to Be a*

Millionaire? has got nowt on us,' Mickey said in response to the unsolicited *woooooooos.* 'The second team to solve all twelve clues will win a thirty-pound bar tab. And the last team . . . well, you win a kiss with Cindy Clawford under the mistletoe which will be duly caught on camera for our social media page. And before anyone comments, any of you 'orrible lot would be lucky to 'ave 'er. She's a creature of unrivalled beauty. Mind you, you might 'ave a bit of competition. She's still talkin' about the smacker Alex gave 'er last year.'

At this the whole room burst into laughter and Alex, to his credit, joined in. 'She was quite a good kisser,' he confided in his teammates. 'The best I had last year, anyway.' Maddie and Curtis chuckled at his words. The image of Alex, a respected police officer, smooching a stuffed leopard under the mistletoe was a mental picture that wasn't going to leave Maddie alone for some time to come.

'Now, because we know 'ow 'igh tensions can run in this game,' Mickey continued, 'we 'ave made sure that the first clue sends each team to a different part of the buildin' so you'll 'ave a bit of space to talk through the riddles and, more to the point, won't get into any immediate confrontations. Mrs Fazakerley, I'm looking at you.'

Mrs Fazakerley glared back at Mickey through thick-rimmed glasses. 'It's not my fault everyone's bitter about my winning every scavenger hunt to date. If people are that put out about it, they should try exercising their brain on a more regular basis. The lot of you are scrolling on your phones from breakfast till supper and wondering why the old grey matter is failing you. If you took a leaf out of my book and spent your time reading instead, you might solve the clues a bit quicker that way. No point crying to me if you don't use your brains.'

Maddie glanced over at Curtis to see him gritting his teeth at Mrs Fazakerley's comments. Just behind him, there was a soft, cuddly Santa sitting on a shelf, doing its bit to lend a bit of Christmas cheer to the pub. The rosy-cheeked smile of the toy made such a stark contrast to Curtis's expression that it was almost comical. From Maddie's perspective, it almost looked as though Santa was sitting on his shoulder, taking great amusement in how irate he was getting over a bit of festive fun. Alex had made it more than clear that Curtis and Mrs Fazakerley were competitive but Maddie just couldn't understand how anyone could take something as frivolous as a scavenger hunt this seriously.

'Yes, thanks for that TED Talk, Mrs Fazakerley, I'm sure everyone's taken that advice on board,' Mickey said with a knowing grin. 'Now, if you 'appen across an envelope in yer travels that is not yer team colour, it must not be tampered with in any way. If I find out from anyone that their envelopes 'ave been tampered with the whole game will be called off and there'll be no winners and no prizes and no scavenger 'unt next year. Me and Sofia are a bit sick of sorting out disputes like that. It is supposed to be fun, somethin' I think you lot forget sometimes. And it is Christmas, let's remember that. A time of generosity and kindness and I'm addin' good sportsmanship to that list.'

A grumble went around the room at this, but the bulk of the volume seemed to come from Mrs Fazakerley's table. Or, to be more accurate, from Mrs Fazakerley herself.

'If it gets to eleven o'clock and no team 'as decoded all twelve of our clues,' Mickey said, 'then the winnin' team will be the team who 'ave solved the most clues out of the twelve. With this in mind, you'll want to 'old onto all the clue cards you find so that they can be counted up at the end in case an outright winner isn't declared.'

'Wait a minute. What if there's a tie between two teams?' Sita called out. She had the most dazzling white teeth Maddie had ever seen on a person outside a television set. 'What if two teams solve the same number of clues before eleven? What then?'

'We've got a tie-breaker question organised for that eventuality,' said Mickey, 'or at least, we will 'ave by eleven o'clock. Me and Sofia will remain completely impartial throughout. But, so none of you are tempted to try and bribe the answers out of us,' at this Mickey shot yet another look in Mrs Fazakerley's direction, 'we'll spend most of the evenin' in our livin' quarters up in the attic. We'll come down now and again, like, to make sure there 'aven't been any fisticuffs, or worse.' Mickey laughed at this, but Maddie was starting to see a bit of a pattern in all of the rules he was dishing out. Were all scavenger hunts like this? Did people always play so rough? This was the first one Maddie had ever been to so it was difficult to know for sure but there seemed to be a lot of ground rules being laid down. Leaving her wondering exactly how high tensions had soared in previous years.

Alex must have read Maddie's expression as he shook his head and rolled his eyes as if to suggest Mickey's performance was all very over the top. She hoped very much that he was right about that. Maddie supposed that the residual fear of being stuck in a broken-down car in an isolated village could still be playing tricks on her. Despite Mickey's numerous digs about their capacity for foul play, everyone she'd met so far had been friendly. Arguably, in the case of James, a wee bit too friendly. The odds were that there was nothing to worry about. If anyone could assess how much jeopardy she was in with clear eyes, it was someone like Alex. A trained police officer. Mickey was probably just poking fun at how seriously the villagers took what was supposed to be a bit of light entertainment on a Christmas Eve.

'Right, without further ado,' Mickey continued, 'the time 'as come, on my mark, for each team to open their first envelope. Everyone at the ready? And three, two, one. Off you go and may the best team win!'

The sound of paper crumpling and tearing momentarily muffled the Christmas music that had been playing at a low volume in the background. This was quickly followed by frantic murmurs as each team read their first clue and started conferring in hushed tones.

Curtis opened their yellow envelope and turned the yellow rectangle of card so that Maddie and Alex could read it along with him.

In the kitchen is where you'll find me.
Small, as small, as small as can be,
with a gesture fit for royalty.

Alex, Curtis and Maddie all frowned in unison as they contemplated the words before them.

On reading this first clue, Maddie at once regretted agreeing to partake in the game. Though she loved words as a means of creative communication, she had always been rubbish with cryptic riddles and generally avoided any activity in which they were likely to feature. She wasn't all that bothered about being no good at such things in general, but in a team setting this kind of shortcoming could be pretty stressful. She always felt like she *was* the weakest link and, as such, any team would suffer for having her on it.

'Hmmm, nothing is immediately springing to mind,' said Curtis. 'Perhaps if we go to the kitchen itself and look around, something will come to us.'

'In my experience of these games it's definitely better to be in whatever room is mentioned in the clue,' said Alex. 'Look, all the other teams have already had the same idea and vamoosed, we should follow suit.'

Maddie looked around the room to see that Alex was indeed correct. The other teams had scuttled off to whichever corner of the building their first clue had sent them, and Mickey and Sofia must have made a sharp exit up to their living quarters.

As she scanned the room, it looked . . . emptier than expected to her somehow. As though it was missing more than just the people who had but moments ago been muttering to each other about the contents of their envelopes. Something obvious was absent from this scene, but for the life of her, Maddie couldn't put her finger on what was causing her to feel this way.

'The fire's gone out,' she said aloud. Since this was the only thing she could obviously see that was different from before.

'Oh yeah,' said Alex, 'Mickey must have put it out when

he went upstairs. Maybe there's something about insurance, that the fire has to be watched by a staff member at all times or something.'

'Yes. That makes sense,' said Maddie, though she still couldn't shake the feeling that there was something else amiss. Something she couldn't put her finger on.

'I'll have to stand on this side of the kitchen door with Barkley while you two go in,' said Curtis, returning Maddie's attention once again to the scavenger hunt. 'I don't want to leave him tied to a chair in here on his own. And it's not hygienic to have this little ball of fur pattering around Sofia's freshly mopped floors.'

'That's fine,' said Alex. 'Me and Maddie will go into the kitchen for a look around. If you have any big brainwaves, you can shout them through the door to us.'

Alex's words, banal as they seemed, stirred something in Maddie's mind.

'Brainwave . . .' she said. 'Brainwave. Brainwave. Brainwave. Wait, let me see the clue again.'

Alex handed her the yellow card and Maddie reread the riddle.

'A gesture fit for royalty. Wave. Could it be the royal wave?' she said once she'd finished reading.

'And small, as small as can be . . .' Curtis mused for a moment. 'Micro. Microwave.'

'Can that really be it? Maddie said, feeling somewhat

deflated that the clue wasn't as complex as she'd expected. The way Mrs Fazakerley was talking, Maddie had thought she was going to be dealing with the kind of puzzles that wouldn't be out of place on *University Challenge*. 'That didn't take too much figuring out.'

'The clues tend to get harder as the game goes on,' said Alex. 'I don't think Dad and Sofia like anyone to feel stumped by the first one. It's a bit off-putting for people if that happens, you know, makes them feel like they can't take part.'

'Well, if we've already determined where the next clue is hidden, it's pointless going as far as the kitchen door while my whisky's sitting here,' said Curtis. 'I think you two are more than capable of finding a microwave between you. Me and Barkley will wait for you to retrieve the next clue.'

'Alright,' said Alex, 'hopefully we won't be long. If there's nothing in the microwave and we've misinterpreted the clue, we'll come back and regroup and . . .'

Alex broke off at this point and sniffed the air. He frowned and then he did it a second time, this time taking a bigger, longer sniff.

'Do you . . . do you two smell that?' he said.

'Smell what?' Maddie said, taking a deep breath in an attempt to detect whatever Alex already had.

'I don't smell anything in particular,' Curtis said.

Alex sniffed again. 'No, never mind, it's nothing. It . . . it doesn't matter.'

'O-kay . . .' Maddie said, sincerely hoping that Alex hadn't smelt gas in the air. With the luck she was having this evening she couldn't rule out something catastrophic like a gas explosion, and the strange expression that had crossed Alex's face when he asked if she or Curtis could smell anything had set her on edge.

'It wasn't gas you could smell, was it?' Maddie said, unable to quiet her mind on the issue.

'No, nothing like that, I'm just imagining things. For reasons I won't bore you with, Christmas Eve is a bit of a weird day for me,' said Alex, before making his way behind the bar. Not particularly reassured by his cryptic response, Maddie trailed after him and pushed through the swing door into the kitchen. The room, which largely consisted of polished wooden worktops and the expected electrical appliances, had been set seemingly in readiness for serving Christmas food the day after and perhaps Boxing Day too. Several jars of cranberry sauce were lined up on the counter. Sofia must have put a turkey in to slow-cook on her way upstairs as, by the oven light, Maddie could see a large bird stuffed in there on a low heat. A basket of cutlery wrapped in red and green napkins also stood next to a kettle. On examining the room more closely, Maddie realised something: 'There's more than one microwave,' she said.

'I count three in total,' said Alex.

'Three? Where's the third one?'

'Over there in the corner.'

'Oh yes,' said Maddie, 'I see it now. I'll go and check that one out. You look in the other two.'

Nodding, Alex walked over to the microwave nearest the door. It was positioned on one of the wooden worktops, next to a toaster. Maddie strode over to the other side of the room towards the microwave in the corner.

'There's only a blue envelope in here,' said Alex. 'So that one's not for us.'

'No tampering now,' Maddie teased. 'We wouldn't want Mickey to call the whole thing off.'

'Is my surname Fazakerley?' Alex jibed back. 'That envelope will be returned to the microwave exactly as I found it, thank you very much.'

Maddie chuckled as she approached the microwave and opened the door on it. 'Yep, I've got the next clue. The next yellow envelope's in here,' she called over.

'Nice one,' said Alex.

Maddie grabbed the envelope, closed the microwave door and was just about to turn to follow Alex out of the kitchen when something next to the wall caught her eye.

Taking a step closer, she blinked hard in case she was somehow hallucinating. As she continued to look at it, her breath became quicker.

'Alex . . .'

'What's wrong?' he said, immediately gleaning from Maddie's wavering tone that something was indeed wrong. Very wrong.

'Is this the junction box for the phone wires?'

Alex hurried over to where Maddie was standing. Crouching, he examined the small white box and then picked up a frayed wire that was lying on the floor.

'It is, and it looks like . . . I mean, I suppose I can't be completely sure but at a best guess somebody's cut the wires.'

'W-why would somebody do that?'

'I don't know,' Alex said, with a shake of his head.

'Earlier, when I was on the phone to my parents, I got cut off. I asked Mickey if he had another phone and he said he'd check the one in the kitchen. How come he didn't notice that the wire was cut then?' Maddie said, suddenly starting to wonder if Mickey was as friendly and trustworthy as he had seemed. He owned this place, which lent him a certain authority within the community, and thus she had believed him when he'd attributed the loss of landline service to the weather. But what if something else was going on here?

'The phone is much nearer the swing door than the junction box,' said Alex. 'There's no reason for him to have suspected that the wires had been cut. He probably just picked up the phone, realised he couldn't get a dial tone and then reported to you that the phones were down because of the weather.'

'Yes, you're probably right,' Maddie said, though she wasn't much convinced by that theory.

'Wait here and just guard the junction box for a minute, will you?' said Alex. 'I don't think that anyone's about to tamper with it any further but I don't want to leave it unattended just in case. I'll nip upstairs and get Mickey and see what he's got to say about this. It is strange and we should at least try to get to the bottom of it before we continue playing the scavenger hunt.'

'Agreed,' said Maddie. 'If there's a simple, silly explanation for this, I'd like to hear what it is.'

'Alright, I'll be right back,' Alex said, starting his journey back across the kitchen.

He was about half way between Maddie and the kitchen door when every appliance and light bulb in the room cut out, leaving the pair in absolute darkness.

'Oh God,' Maddie said through the blankness, tears threatening though she held them back. Her breathing had almost turned to gasping now. She couldn't believe how dark it was in here. The pub was so remote there wasn't any light outside and everything inside had gone dead all at once. Maddie tried to steady her breathing but there was simply too much about this night that had left her unsettled. The breakdown. The BAC refusing to come out to her. Getting cut off on the phone to her mother. The Kapoors' argument spilling through the guest room walls and now this. Phone wires cut. Power off. Maddie had seen this movie a million times and it never ended well.

'Alex . . . What's going on?'

No response.

'Alex?'

'I'm still here. Try not to panic,' Alex's voice said through the black tar of night that Maddie now felt was invading every orifice. 'It's probably just a power cut. It happens sometimes in bad weather. Of course it had to happen on the one night of the year that I'm separated from my smart phone and can't use the torch function.'

'What about candles?' said Maddie. 'Do you know if they keep any in the kitchen or in the bar?'

'I don't know if they do and, frankly, by the time I try and find both candles and matches in the dark, we'd be better off waiting for Mickey to turn on the emergency generator, which is probably what he's trying to do right now. There's a fire escape ladder from their bedroom that will lead them pretty much right to it. It has to be switched on manually outside, but I know Mickey keeps a torch in his room for just such an emergency and once it's on it will provide lighting and heating through till morning.'

'Do you . . . really think it's the weather causing this?' said Maddie. It wasn't a question she actually wanted the answer to but, being a journalist, she was trained to ask those kinds of questions.

'Yes,' Alex said, his tone not in the least bit convincing. 'I'm pretty sure that's going to be it.'

If Alex had seemed surer of himself, Maddie might have been able to stay calm. But as it was, the many unsettling thoughts that had been whirring around her mind for the last few minutes overtook her all at once. Regardless of what her Scottish parents would think of the outburst that was about to come, Maddie couldn't help herself. The resolve she'd done her utmost to hold onto all evening started to unravel.

'But, but, but, Mickey blamed the phone lines on the weather too,' said Maddie, her words leaving her mouth faster and faster with every syllable. 'And that wasn't true. It wasn't. Somebody tampered with them. Somebody cut them. What if they've cut the power off too? Who would do this to us? And why?'

'Maddie,' Alex's voice was surprisingly stern. Stern enough to stop her babbling. 'We don't know what's happened with the phone lines. Something could have gnawed through that power line. A mouse or something. They are quite common in the country no matter how hygienic your kitchen is. The power cut could just be a coincidence. One thing I do know is, in situations like this, panicking gets you nowhere. I need you to calm down.'

'OK,' Maddie said, letting a deep breath fill her lungs before slowly exhaling. 'OK, I'm sorry. I'll try to get a hold of myself. I'm just . . . I'm just not where I expected to be tonight, and all this weird stuff is happening.'

'There's no need to be sorry, I just don't want you worrying unnecessarily. Now, give me a minute, I know the layout of this kitchen quite well and I'm going to try and navigate my way back to you to lead you out. If at all possible, we both need to avoid injury while doing so.'

Maddie remained quiet, trying to focus on taking slow, calm breaths. In and out.

In and out.

All she had to do was wait for Alex to find her in the dark and—

But Maddie didn't get to finish that reassuring thought.

Out of the darkness, from the pub area, there came a desperate, ear-splitting howl that turned Maddie's whole body cold. She had never heard a noise quite like it, and yet she knew exactly what the noise was.

It was the gut-churning sound of a man screaming for his life.

CHAPTER NINE

'Alex?' Maddie whispered in the darkness once the screaming had finally ceased. She couldn't bring herself to call out to him any louder than that. She had no idea who had screamed on the other side of the kitchen door. Possibly, it had been Curtis as he had been the only person in the bar area when she and Alex had left it. Regardless of who had made that unforgettable sound, however, there was no doubt in Maddie's heart that something terrible had happened to them. And calling out without knowing what that something terrible was seemed like a bad idea. Her mind flitted back to what Don had said earlier about the pub being haunted. She didn't believe in ghosts. But the phone lines were dead. And the lights were out. And if she was wrong about the existence of paranormal spectres, she didn't fancy being the spirit's next victim.

When Alex didn't respond to her whisper, however, it

was clear she was going to have to raise her voice in order to get his attention.

'Alex!' she called, as loud as she dared.

'I'm still here,' he replied. 'I'm still finding my way to you.' Though his voice felt very far away. Probably the dark and the scare of that scream having their way with Maddie's powers of perception. At least that's the only explanation she could come up with.

'If a hand grabs you in the next five seconds or so, don't jump, it's just me,' Alex said, his voice noticeably closer now.

'I feel like I should keep making noise so you can – oh, there you are,' Maddie said as Alex grabbed first her shoulder and then felt his way down to her hand. Maddie didn't hesitate in holding Alex's hand in return. It was definitely a bit of a forward move to make on a man she'd known only a few hours but she wasn't going to risk getting separated from him. Maddie also privately admitted she was glad to feel the warmth of another human being at her side. Too many unsettling things had happened to her this evening.

'Who was that screaming?' Maddie asked.

'I don't know,' Alex said, tentatively taking steps forward and sideways through the kitchen, and pulling Maddie along with him. 'I think the more concerning question is why somebody screamed out like that. I'm afraid, given my line of work, I have to at least try and be the first on the scene to find out. Which means you might see some things you don't want to see.'

'You're being optimistic about the fact that we'll get the lights back on again, then,' Maddie said. 'Because neither of us are going to see anything until that happens.'

'If I had to bet,' Alex said, 'I'd say that Mickey and Sofia are already outside working on getting the generator going. Until then, we're just going to have to see if we can find something out by calling to other people.'

'I really hope Curtis is OK,' Maddie said, her words betraying her worst fears for him.

'That makes two of us,' Alex replied.

After several minutes of feeling their way around the kitchen in the dark, Maddie and Alex pushed through the swing door that led back into the pub. Maddie's breath quickened as they did so and she suddenly found herself feeling dizzy at the thought of what might lie beyond the kitchen door. Regardless of what they found on the other side, however, she guessed that there were few better people to have with you than a local police inspector.

'Curtis?' Alex called out through the dark.

While they'd been navigating their way out of the kitchen, Maddie had heard Barkley yapping. But after that unforgettable scream they'd heard, the little mutt's barking had been the only sign of life from the other side of the door.

'I'm here,' Curtis's voice returned Alex's call, but it sounded weaker than before. As though the volume had been turned down on it.

'Are you alright?' Alex asked.

'I'm not physically hurt but . . . embarrassingly enough I . . . I think I might have fainted,' said Curtis. 'I've never fainted before. First time for everything, I suppose.'

'It wasn't you who screamed out then?' said Alex.

'No . . . and I didn't see anyone else enter the room. But I think the scream is what knocked me out. I didn't fall or anything so I'm not hurt. Just slumped down in my chair. But dear me, that doesn't say much for my levels of courage, does it?' Curtis said. Though Maddie couldn't see his face in the thick blackness of the room, a sense of shame was more than evident in his tone.

'Locked in a pitch-black room with someone screaming like that, I think I'd faint too – and as a Scot I don't say that lightly,' Maddie said, hoping her words might lighten the mood and make Curtis feel less self-conscious about passing out.

'Situations like that make your blood pressure plummet,' Alex added for good measure. 'It's very common for people to be overcome. Happens to the best of us. The main thing is, you're not hurt.'

'No,' said Curtis. 'I'm not, but given the sound I heard

bellowing over from the other side of the pub I'd imagine someone else is.'

'Alex,' Maddie said. 'The fire is out.'

'Yes, we covered that point earlier,' came the dry retort.

'No, I mean, with the fire out, there is no light in here at all. You said that Mickey had probably put it out. But what if . . .'

Maddie didn't dare finish her sentence. It was too terrifying to consider why someone might want to plunge this room into total darkness. Especially after that scream that even now still rang out in her ears. If her suspicions were correct, if whoever was behind the power cut had also gone to the lengths of putting out the fire, there was only really one assumption to draw from that: that the person in question wanted to do something under the cover of darkness they didn't want anyone else to see. Between the phone lines and the lights, there was no doubt in Maddie's mind that, whatever had taken place when that man screamed out, it had been planned. Premeditated.

'Is anyone else in here? Hello?' Alex called, an urgent note sounding out in his tone after Maddie's observation about the fire. No doubt he had come to the same conclusion she had. Whoever was behind this, they hadn't just struck upon the idea tonight and, somehow, the calculated nature of these events made them all the more sinister.

Nobody returned Alex's call and a heavy silence settled in the room.

'They could be unconscious or otherwise unable to respond,' Alex muttered, seemingly to himself but Maddie still had her hand locked in his so was close enough to hear his every word.

'Hello?' another voice, a woman's, came out of the gloom.

'Who's that?' said Alex.

'It's Zainab. Is that you, DI Beaumont?'

'I think Alex will suffice in this kind of situation, don't you Zainab?'

'Alex,' Zainab repeated. 'I'm so glad I found you. I was in the laundry room when the lights went out and the only thing I could find in the dark was the stairway. I called out to the others but nobody answered. My team split up because James suggested we scoured the building first to see if we could find any red envelopes just by looking so we weren't together when it all went dark.'

'That splitting-up strategy is not really in the spirit of things, is it?' said Curtis, while Maddie marvelled at his ability to care a jot about the scavenger hunt after all that had unfolded.

'No, maybe not, but James said if we split up we'd find the clues as quickly as possible. Dad was so excited to get his hands on the puzzles that he reluctantly agreed with

James and insisted that was what we were going to do. He's like a little kid with this stuff. I— Hang on a minute, is Dad down here?' said Zainab.

'Not that we know of,' said Alex. 'Nor your mother, I'm afraid, it's just me, Curtis and Maddie.'

'Hopefully they won't be far away,' said Zainab, a note of concern in her voice. 'When it all went dark, I did my best to feel my way back down here. Pretty surprised I managed it, to be honest. Talk about achievement unlocked. What's happened to the lights? Has there been a power cut or something, like there was a few years back?'

Neither Maddie, nor Alex, nor Curtis answered Zainab immediately. Perhaps she hadn't heard the scream they had all heard. And Maddie was pretty sure there was no way she could know about the severed phone lines. There were too many disturbing factors at play here to give Alex's nibbling vermin theory any credence.

Since Zainab was blissfully ignorant of these other factors, however, and they had yet to locate her parents, it seemed cruel to put the poor girl on edge until the power was restored and they had a better chance of ascertaining what had really happened.

'We don't know exactly what's going on with the power,' Maddie heard herself say in a more comforting voice than she would have imagined she could muster under such circumstances. 'But Alex says there's a back-up generator outside. Mickey's likely already on his way out there to turn it on. So, with a bit of luck, we shouldn't be left too long in the dark.'

Just as Maddie said this, a call came out from the other side of the room.

'Alex?'

'Don?' Alex replied.

'Aye, and the rest of my team,' said Don.

'Poor Donny,' said a voice that Maddie was relatively sure belonged to Sita. 'Me and Mrs Fazakerley are the bread and he's the sandwich filling right now.'

'I can't think he'll mind that much,' Maddie heard Alex mutter under his breath, before adding, 'If you're coming down the stairs, mind how you go. We can do without emergency airlifting anyone to A and E tonight. And, to be honest, getting in touch with the emergency services under the current circumstances would be difficult to say the least, so really, really watch yourself.'

'No stairs involved,' Don confirmed, 'we were in the little office room near the toilets when the lights went out.'

'Hello? Alex?' came another voice from the blankness.

'Is that you, Jeannie?'

'Aye, I've just run into Mickey, quite literally,' said Jeannie. ''E said 'im and Sofia were on the way out the back now to try to turn on the back-up generator. Lights should be back on in a minute or so.'

'Has anyone seen . . . er, sorry, I mean, bumped into James or my parents?' said Zainab.

Everyone around the room called back in turn that they hadn't.

'Oh God, I hope they're alright,' said Zainab. 'If they're not back by the time the lights are back on, we need to go and look for them.'

'We will, Zainab,' said Alex. 'Don't worry. Some people tend to think it's better to stay put in this kind of situation, rather than fumbling around in the dark. And there's sense to it, you're more likely to get injured if you roam around. So they're probably just waiting for the lights to come back on before they rejoin the group.'

'I'm sure you're right,' Zainab said, though her tone seemed less than certain and Maddie wasn't too sure about that theory either.

A man had called out in the darkness, there was no mistake about that, and two men were as yet unaccounted for. Had there been some kind of altercation between the pair? Was one of them lying in this very room, unconscious . . . or worse? And if so where had the other crept off to? And what about Zainab's mother? Where had she been while all these unsettling events were taking place?

Maddie thought again about the look that had passed between James and Mrs Kapoor. She thought also about the look Mr Kapoor had given when he saw them have their little moment. Jeannie had run into Mickey and Sofia, so they were accounted for. Could it be coincidence that the three people caught in some kind of weird triangle of high emotions were the only ones yet to call out in the dark?

As it transpired, Maddie wouldn't have to wait too much longer to get at least some of the answers to her questions. A few moments later, the lights flickered on. The yellow glare of them was almost painful after standing in darkness so long and a murmur of relief rippled around the room from everyone present.

Uncoupling her hand from Alex's as politely as possible, Maddie blinked a few times and, over the course of a few seconds, her eyes began to adjust. Her attention landed first on Curtis, who was sitting, just as they had left him, at a table near the bar with Barkley at his feet. The dog was yapping excitedly and running around in circles on the spot in a way that suggested he hadn't enjoyed his stint in the dark any more than the rest of them.

Zainab, Don, Sita and Mrs Fazakerley had managed to manoeuvre themselves across the room, near to the door through which Maddie had originally entered the pub. They, like Maddie, were blinking and looking around the room, trying to get used to the light again.

Jeannie was the only one standing out on a limb, with her back to the now-extinguished fireplace and the snug next to it. As Maddie looked harder at those present, however, she realised that Zainab, Don, Sita and Mrs Fazakerley all had a simultaneous shift in their expressions. They began staring at Jeannie in such a manner that they seemed unable to believe what they were seeing. Maddie glanced at Alex and it was obvious from his expression that the change in that group at the other side of the room hadn't escaped his notice.

Manoeuvring around the bar, Alex strode over to where they were standing and Maddie followed after him. At once, she spotted something in the snug behind Jeannie.

'Oh, thank the Lord, the lights are back on,' Jeannie said, rubbing a hand over her face before pressing it against her chest. It took her a moment to register that everyone in the room was looking at her. Slowly, she took a few steps towards the rest of them. 'Is everyone alright? You all look so shaken. You're not alone like. I don't think I've ever been so scared in all me life as when those lights went out. I was in the guest library at the time. I never thought of it as a creepy room but, let me tell you, you don't want to be alone in there in the dark.'

'Jeannie,' Alex tried to get her attention, but she was still mid-flow.

'Especially after listenin' to Donny banging on about ghosts and this place being 'aunted. I'm going to 'ave nightmares for a month after that. I – what? What are you all lookin' at me like that for? What is it?'

In the time that Jeannie had been talking, oblivious to the scene behind her, Maddie had realised that the limp object in the snug was not an object but a person slouched in a chair by the rapidly cooling fireplace, in the lunging shadow of Cindy Clawford. A frown weighed on Maddie's brow and her breath quickened as she tried to convince herself something else was going on. That maybe some kind of practical joke was being played. Or that she had actually fallen asleep on her bed after the warm shower she took earlier, and had never left her room, and was dreaming.

But in her heart, she knew exactly what she was looking at. She had that feeling, the same feeling that had filled her up to the brim when she had been playing amongst the fir trees of Reelig Glen twenty-six years ago. The day she discovered something she would never forget. The day that would haunt her for ever. In that respect, Maddie did believe in ghosts. When they came in the form of regrets.

On recognising the truth about the dreadful sight before them, every face in the room had fully riveted on the crumpled figure behind Jeannie's back and a chorus of gasps filled the air.

'Jeannie, listen to me,' Alex said. 'Whatever you do, don't . . .'

If Alex was about to tell Jeannie not to turn around, his warning came too late. Following the startled gaze of all other eyes in the room, his aunt turned to see James slumped in a chair, pale and bloodied in the snug. His face a portrait of fear, a corkscrew sticking out of his neck.

'Oh . . . my . . . God!' Jeannie said and followed it up with a scream. 'Noooo. No this isn't real. This isn't happenin'.'

'What's not real?' Curtis asked, before standing and joining the others to see for himself the scene that had caused this reaction.

'Somebody tell me this is a joke,' Jeannie said, shaking her head. 'It can't be . . . 'e can't be . . .'

Dead.

Since nobody could seemingly bring themselves to finish Jeannie's sentence out loud, Maddie finished it for herself in her head.

James was dead.

Murdered no less.

And Mr and Mrs Kapoor were still nowhere to be seen.

CHAPTER TEN

Considering he was looking at the dead body of his own stepbrother, Maddie thought it quite impressive that Alex was able to slip into detective inspector mode in a matter of seconds. However, she had, during her time as a news reporter, come into contact with the police and, from what she had seen, it was a profession that required a person to be a master at compartmentalisation. Given his rank, and how he had spoken earlier about his time working in the cities, Alex had likely had a fair bit of practice at it. Still, to be able to conduct yourself in so formal a manner when a family member had been murdered before you, well, it was something Maddie wasn't sure she could ever have done herself.

Slowly, Alex walked over to where James sat in the snug. Maddie watched him take in a deep breath and slowly let it out before pressing two fingers against the far side of James's neck. The side that had not been punctured by the corkscrew. Alex looked at his watch and held his fingers there for a good minute. The longest minute Maddie had ever known.

The surrealness of the scene was staggering. Tinsel sparkling gold, silver and red had been hung in a decorative flourish around the snug. The juxtaposition of this alone and James's motionless body made Maddie want to be sick. But the Christmas music had started again when the power had returned. The volume was low and yet the song felt so intrusive. Alex stood checking his stepbrother's pulse to the soundtrack of 'Silver Bells' by Dean Martin until he was certain there were no signs of life before turning back to the group.

'I'm afraid he is dead,' Alex said, confirming officially what anyone who had looked at James's body knew deep down was true. 'Which means I need everyone away from the fireplace, now,' he continued. His tone was commanding without being demanding; he didn't need to give an order. It was simply an acknowledged expectation that everyone would do as he said. He no doubt knew that everyone was likely to be in shock – well, everyone except the culprit – and thus didn't want to worsen the fear for the innocent bystanders in the room. But there was no mistaking the authority in his voice: he meant business and wasn't to be trifled with just now.

'This room is now officially a crime scene. Nobody is to approach this area of the pub for any reason. And I want you to stay clear of the path between the door and where the body is sitting. Understood?'

Everyone in the room murmured their agreement.

'Donny, over here, I want a word,' Alex said.

'Wait a minute!' said Zainab. 'I have to go and look for my parents. Anything could have happened to them. I need to make sure they're alright.'

'I understand,' Alex said, his tone firm but in no way confrontational. 'The thing is, Zainab, I need to keep everyone safe and I can't do that if we're all in different parts of the building looking for your parents. Finding them is my top priority, I promise you that. I'm just going to have a quick word with Donny, and then we'll start searching for them in a way that keeps everyone safe. Just, give me a couple of minutes, can you?'

'OK,' Zainab said, offering Alex a little nod.

'I know you're scared, I would be too in your place but I need to handle this strategically so nobody else gets hurt, understand?'

'I do. I'll wait here until you say so,' she said.

'Thank you,' Alex said, before turning to Don. 'DC Maynard, follow me to the kitchen, will you?'

A pale-faced Don strode straight over to his friend, and superior. The Christmas cheer that had previously flushed his freckled cheeks had completely disappeared. For all his talk of ghosts earlier that evening, he now had the pallor of a man who had seen one. And he wasn't alone. There wasn't a person in the room who didn't look shaken, weak even, from what they had seen. Mrs Fazakerley, the oldest member of the party by some margin, had collapsed into a chair and was fanning herself with one of the menus.

If the killer was in this room, Maddie certainly couldn't have picked them out based on the reactions she was witnessing. But then again, she couldn't presume that the murderer was in fact in the room. Not when there were two people as yet unaccounted for.

Alex and Don disappeared just behind the kitchen swing door so as not to be overheard but Alex didn't take his eye off the circular window for a second. Whether this precaution was to ensure people followed his directions and stayed away from the crime scene, to monitor the behaviour of the people left standing in case any of them gave anything away or even tried to make a run for it, or to make certain no further trouble broke out, Maddie couldn't say. The likelihood was it was a mixture of all of the above.

Curtis went back to the table they'd been sitting at earlier so he could rejoin his dog. Taking a deep breath, Maddie sat next to him and put a reassuring hand on the old man's arm. From local murder cases she'd covered on the paper, Maddie knew that he was likely the first person Alex would want to speak to. He was present in the room when the crime happened, after all. At the very least, he was an ear witness. There was another thought surfacing in Maddie's mind, that much as she tried to ignore it, would not be denied.

Could Curtis also be a potential suspect?

She looked down at her hand resting gently on his arm and had the strong urge to remove it. She managed to style out her sudden sense of disgust by patting Curtis's arm lightly, lifting her hand away and then picking up what was left of her Coke.

'Sorry, not sure why but my throat is so dry I think it's going to crack,' she said, before taking a sip.

Curtis offered a stiff nod, and nothing more.

Placing her drink down on the table, Maddie did her best to casually observe her companion. He seemed so kindly, the last thing she wanted to believe was that he had been involved in a murder. But Maddie had covered enough stories in her line of work to know that people were rarely what they seemed. As far as she knew, he had been the only person in the room when the crime happened. He had told them he had fainted, and that had seemed very plausible given the dramatic circumstances. But what if that had been a cover story for an ill deed? And then there was the hardness she'd seen in his eyes when they first met. Those eyes had looked like grey steel in the dark and quiet of the village. What if her first instinct about him when they had met at her car had been the right one?

Earlier, they had been laughing about the fact that Curtis had a reputation for appearing and disappearing as if from nowhere. That didn't seem so funny now. It seemed like more of a warning sign that this apparently harmless old widower who walked with a limp wasn't as frail as he'd have the world believe. Appearing as if from nowhere would certainly put a murderer at an advantage. The victim wouldn't know what was happening until it was too late.

Maddie shook her head and wished that she could shake these thoughts away at the same time. But there was no denying what had happened and the fact that somebody had done it deliberately. She couldn't quite see James from where she was sitting but the image of his wide eyes and slack jaw was burnt into her mind. In part, because those details reminded her of something she'd seen a long time ago. James's was not the first dead body she'd witnessed. She scrunched her eyes shut, trying to divert her thoughts in another direction. She didn't want to think about *that* right now. About Reelig Glen. About what she had found there when she had been holidaying with her parents as a child.

No. She didn't want to go back to that scene. Not now. Not ever.

When Maddie opened her eyes again, however, they inevitably wandered back over to the corner where James lay and, before she knew it, her journalistic curiosity had got the better of her. She didn't approach the snug. She was pretty sure Alex would have her hanged, drawn and quartered for going directly against his instructions like that. She simply sauntered over to the entrance so she had a clear view of James's body. Goodness knows what everyone else in the room would think of her for being so morbid as to stare at a corpse, but since she was already on her feet, it was too late to worry about that now.

After studying the body for a few moments, she noticed something she hadn't before. In particular, her stare fixed on the corkscrew protruding from his neck. He must have been stabbed with some force for the implement to break through the skin like that. Maddie felt sick at the very thought of dying that way. It was strange though. The weapon chosen by the killer was opportunistic: something that would have been lying around in the pub. But all other elements of the crime – the phone lines, the power cut – seemed very clearly planned. After going to all those other lengths, why wouldn't the killer have used a more efficient weapon to carry out their dreadful deed?

Maddie didn't have time to contemplate that any further

as Alex and Don pushed back through the kitchen door at this point. Casually as she could, Maddie returned to her seat next to Curtis.

'Right, folks, here's the situation,' said Alex. 'From what I heard of James's death, and given the cause of death, it was no accident. Let's be honest, it's very unlikely that he slipped, fell on a corkscrew and then managed to clamber onto a chair in the snug before he died. Whoever did this to him, placed him back in the chair for some reason. The fact that the phone lines have been severed, and the power to the pub cut out, only lends weight to the idea that we are dealing with a murder. And a premeditated one at that. I'm going to double-check my phone signal when I retrieve my mobile from the safe. But we all know signal is non-existent here so I would say we can't put any hope in that. The Dales Constabulary do have powerful 4x4 vehicles, but Maddie's predicament of not being able to get a breakdown service out here tells me that the roads are impassable. I've just checked outside the window and the snow is still falling. Even if I can get word to the Constabulary, I don't know when they'd be able to reach us given just how bad the drifts are out there. In short, we're stuck here.'

'Oh, this little speech of yours is doing nothing for my nerves, Alex,' said Mrs Fazakerley, fanning herself with the menu at an increased speed.

'I'm sorry, Mrs Fazakerley, I wish there was something I

could do about that, but right now there isn't,' said Alex. 'I know from my time on the job that the quicker officers act on a crime, the more likely it is to be solved. With that in mind, myself and DC Maynard will be starting some initial questioning, taking down certain records on paper and, once we get our phones back from Sofia, digitally recording the audio of any conversations on our phones. This will not be a substitute for formal questioning down at the station tomorrow but it may narrow the focus, i.e. it may mean that only a few of you have to come in for formal questioning.'

Alex took a breath to let all he had said sink in but not a soul in the place would have dared speak just then. Regardless of how much they might object to being questioned or any burning query they may themselves have had. Just like Maddie, the whole room seemed to sense that Alex had more to add.

He looked around each and every person in the room before opening his mouth again. 'Many of you are friends to me and I know you've had a shock this evening, as we all have. But murder isn't something you can treat with kid gloves. I'm going to ask you a lot of things you're not going to like and if you don't answer them here to my satisfaction, you will answer them under caution and on record at the station. Or, as is your right under caution, remain silent.'

Maddie glanced around at the other potential suspects. They were doing quite a good job of remaining silent already, and she understood why. Everyone else probably had the same feeling she did right now. That she'd better be very careful about what she said and how she said it until the true culprit was caught.

'There are very few sure things in a murder investigation, but the weather outside would very likely prevent any escape unless the killer wanted to die of frostbite by attempting a getaway on foot. So, I'm as certain as I can be that the murderer is on the premises. Perhaps hiding out somewhere or perhaps they are even in this room.'

Maddie, just like everyone else, involuntarily looked at the other people in attendance. Eyeing each in turn as if it were possible to spot a murderer just by looking at them. In doing so, she thought again about the fact that Mr and Mrs Kapoor were still missing. And what about Sofia? Jeannie said that she had run into Mickey but she didn't see his wife. No sooner had this thought crossed Maddie's mind, however, than the front door swung open, which in turn made everybody jump at once.

Mickey and Sofia bustled in a moment later, covered from top to toe in snow. A flurry followed them in, the white powder spilling all over the carpet and making it difficult for Sofia to get the door shut again. The sight of the snow falling in through the entrance like that at once made Maddie's body stiffen. Precisely how much snow had fallen out there? It must be banked up pretty high for that to happen and for Alex to say he didn't even think police vehicles could reach them.

'How many times did I tell you to buy extra batteries for the torch?' Sofia said to Mickey as she came in shaking her black winter coat and stamping her feet on the welcome mat to get rid of the snow that had settled on them.

'Alright, I've been just a bit busy on the run-up to Christmas, you know,' Mickey returned, swiping a grey woollen hat off his head and taking off his coat.

'Took us twice as bloody long as it needed to, that did. And in a bloody blizzard,' Sofia continued, uninterested in Mickey's excuses.

'Dad,' Alex said.

'Yeah, it's alright, son,' Mickey said. 'The mains switch 'as been sabotaged some'ow, don't ask me why. But the transfer switch for the generator were fine so we'll be alright for the night. It's unfortunate, but there's no need to worry.'

'No . . . Dad, please, just listen a minute,' Alex tried again.

At Alex's words the whole room fell silent, and Mickey with it. Maddie wasn't sure if it was the words themselves or the tone Alex used, but both Mickey and Sofia stopped what they were doing and looked over to where Alex was standing.

Slowly, Alex walked across the room towards them. James's dead body lay just to the right of where they were looking and Alex likely wanted to prepare them for what they were about to see before they clapped eyes on it accidentally. Gently, he shuffled them away from the door, in the direction of where all the other people were huddled.

'Something's happened,' he said.

''Appened?' Mickey said. 'What's 'appened?'

'It's James,' Alex said, his gaze shifting to Sofia.

Maddie felt a solid lump of anguish completely block her throat as Alex's eyes landed on the mother of the deceased. She hadn't been James's biggest fan but she certainly wouldn't have wished him dead. And the look on Alex's face; the mouth attempting neutrality but the eyes full to the brim with sorrow. How did anyone tell a person that their child was dead?

'What's 'e done this time?' Mickey asked.

Alex just shook his head in response and at once Mickey's expression changed. Every muscle in his face fell slack as he realised the kind of news Alex was about to deliver to them.

Alex took Sofia's hands in his.

'I'm sorry,' he said, looking into her soft, round face. 'James . . . he's dead.'

'Wh—' Sofia began, vigorously shaking her head. 'No, no, no,' she repeated over and over, breaking down into tears and beating weakly at Alex's chest with her fists. Alex merely stood there, stoic, allowing Sofia to pound her hands against his body until the tears overtook her and she collapsed on the floor in a heap.

Mickey was totally silent. His eyes wide. Neither of them knew yet that James's dead body sat in the corner, separate and alone from everyone else, who, as per Alex's instructions, were seated closer to the bar. Mickey's eyes were vacant. As though he was off, lost in some other universe. Far away. Where both of his sons were still alive.

'I'm sorry,' Alex said, looking between the two of them and extending both hands to help Sofia up off the floor.

''Ow – 'ow did 'e . . .?' Mickey seemed to force the words past his teeth.

'He was murdered,' Alex said. 'Please, don't look, not now. But his body is in the corner over by the fireplace.'

Almost involuntarily, both Mickey and Sofia's heads swivelled in the one direction they'd been cautioned not to look but Alex gently put a hand to each of their cheeks and turned their faces back to him. 'Please,' he said, a slight tremble in his voice. This was the first clue he had given that he had been affected by what had happened. Up until now, he'd been able to keep his composure. 'Don't look,' Alex repeated. 'It's not how you want to remember him.'

Slowly, both Sofia and Mickey nodded.

'What do we do now?' Mickey asked after a pause.

Alex took a deep breath and looked into his father's eyes. 'We find out who did this to James, and make sure they don't see the light of day for a very long time.'

CHAPTER ELEVEN

After the shock they'd had, it was understandable that Mickey and Sofia needed to sit down and collect themselves. Alex, with much tenderness, escorted them over to a table a few feet away from where Maddie and Curtis were sitting.

'Sir,' Don said. Maddie could not get over how serious his tone was. It was such a change from the guy who had been cracking everyone up with talk of sour cream Pringles and theories about Curtis being related to Houdini just less than an hour ago. 'Nobody should have to work their brother's murder. I can inspect the body.'

Alex looked over at his colleague and put a hand on his shoulder. 'Thanks, Don,' he said, for once calling him by the name he actually favoured rather than the pejorative *Donny*. 'But . . . I need to do it. I'm not going to feel like I'm doing enough to catch whoever did this unless I'm a part of every step. If at any point I think my judgement is compromised, I will step aside and let you take the lead.'

Don nodded. 'Yes, sir.'

'Keep an eye on everyone in here while I take a closer look at James, alright?' Alex said.

'Anything you need, sir,' Don replied.

'Zainab?' Alex said.

'Yes,' she replied.

'I haven't forgotten about your parents. I just need to take a quick look at James's body before we leave, make a couple of notes. Then, if they haven't come back to us by the time I'm done, I'll go in search of your parents.'

'OK,' Zainab said, her tone betraying the fact that she wasn't thrilled that Alex had other business to attend to first.

After casting a reassuring smile in Zainab's direction, Alex went behind the bar, picked up a waiter's pad and pen and strode over to the corner where his stepbrother lay dead.

'I should have done something,' Curtis said, drawing Maddie's attention away from Alex.

'Oh, Curtis,' said Jeannie, who had come to sit with them. Given that Jeannie had had the misfortune of being taken by surprise by James's cadaver, she too had needed somewhere to perch and collect herself. 'You don't get anywhere thinkin' along those lines. This isn't your fault.'

'Then why does it feel like it is?' said Curtis.

'There's really nothing you could have done,' Maddie chimed in. She still wasn't a hundred per cent certain Curtis hadn't played a part in James's demise, but in Great Britain you were innocent until proven guilty. And besides, from the aftermath of her discovery in Reelig Glen, she knew the burden of feeling like you should have done something all too well. Of course, in her case, it was true. She should have done something and had failed. But Maddie couldn't think of anything he could have done that wouldn't have resulted in his own death too.

'There must have been something,' Curtis said. 'The thing is, it all happened so quickly and then I felt the world slipping away. The next thing I knew, Barkley was yapping like a mad dog and you were calling through from the kitchen for me. If I'd just managed to stay awake, I might have something useful to tell Alex about who had done it. Or maybe if I were sharper, I could have found a way to stop the murderer in their tracks.'

'Trying to interfere might have got you hurt, or worse,' said Maddie. 'Whoever did this to James, they're not messing around and they don't strike me as the type who takes prisoners. They likely knew Alex and Don were here. That they are police officers. And despite the threat of being caught they committed the crime anyway. That's not the kind of person you want to go up against.'

'Oh crikey, I 'adn't thought of it like that,' said Jeannie, looking around the room again at the others, just as Maddie had earlier, knowing that someone standing close by could have taken a life in cold blood. 'Maddie's right, Curtis. It's no secret in the village that our Alex comes here on Christmas Eve. Everyone knows 'e wants to be around 'is family at this time of year. After, well, everything.'

Maddie wanted to know exactly what Jeannie meant by that. Especially since he had made some cryptic comment earlier about Christmas Eve being a weird time of year for him. Ultimately, however, Maddie decided it was too forward to ask since she didn't know Alex, or anyone here for that matter, very well at all.

'Whoever it was that did this knew our Alex would be here, and likely Don. And they didn't let it stop them. If you hadn't passed out you might not be here any more,' Jeannie added.

'And at any rate,' said Maddie. 'You didn't have a hope of helping James with the power cut out like that. Me and Alex couldn't see a thing in the kitchen. It took us all our time just to get out of there without being injured or falling. What could you have done when it was pitch black and you couldn't see a thing?'

'Listen to 'er, Curtis,' said Jeannie, 'she's talkin' sense.'

'First time for everything,' Maddie said, offering a weak smile. She knew it was a lame joke, but she couldn't help but at least try and lighten the mood. Yes, she'd been upset about not being able to get to her parents for Christmas Eve, but the cosy, festive cheer of The Merry Monarch had done a lot to soothe that, and it was just too much of an abrupt gear change to go from talking about Alex kissing Cindy Clawford under the mistletoe, to murder.

'I know, everything you're saying to me, well I would say the very same to someone else if this happened to them. But I can't help but feel responsible,' said Curtis. At this Barkley, seemingly sensing his owner's demeanour, nuzzled into his master's leg and rested his snout on Curtis's knee.

'The only person responsible is the person who killed James,' said Maddie, even though she was a hypocrite for saying it. She had felt that same sense of responsibility for years over the body she had found. Even though she'd been only five years old when she saw it.

'I agree with Maddie, you can't even think about blamin' yourself for this, it's . . . it's . . .' Jeannie frowned, sniffed the air and then shook her head.

'Are you alright?' Maddie asked.

'Aye . . .' Jeannie said, though she was still frowning. 'I'm alright. Never you mind. Just . . . I don't know, me mind is playin' tricks on me.'

At Jeannie's reassurance, Maddie's gaze once again drifted over to the snug where James lay. She couldn't see

James's body from this angle but she could just make out Alex scribbling notes on the waiter pad. He appeared and then disappeared as he strode back and forth, examining his stepbrother's body. It seemed like Alex was looking at every inch of space around the corpse. He studied the carpet. Stared rigorously at the table nearest to where James sat. Then he turned back to the body again and as he did so Alex's expression changed abruptly and he disappeared behind the wall of the snug. He reappeared a few moments later, his face creased with a mixture of disbelief and confusion as he looked down at something in his hand.

Alex's hand was obscuring the object, so Maddie couldn't see exactly what he'd found. Whatever it was, Alex stared at it for a good minute before grabbing a napkin from a nearby table, wrapping the object up and putting it in his pocket.

Maddie narrowed her eyes at this. Technically, Alex was a police officer collecting evidence from a crime scene. But should he be putting things in his own pocket?

In the time it had taken her to contemplate this question, his gaze shifted from James over to the table where Mickey and Sofia now sat. He seemed to be weighing something up.

Slowly, he made his way back to the group; specifically, he went over to Mickey and Sofia. He said a few words to them and then summoned the attention of the group as a whole.

'Right, everyone,' Alex said. 'The first thing I'm going to do is try and locate the missing members of the party, Mr and Mrs Kapoor. In light of everything that's happened, Zainab is understandably worried about her parents, so our priority is to locate them and make sure they are safe. With a bit of luck they took shelter when the power cut happened and just haven't found their way back to the group yet.'

As Alex said this, Maddie couldn't help but wonder whether this was truly Alex's top theory on the whereabouts of Mr and Mrs Kapoor. It was possible that one or both of them had fallen and injured themselves in the dark and that was why they had taken so long to rejoin the group. But other than that, Maddie was struggling to think of an innocent rationale for their increasingly long absence. Was Alex really so keen to locate them because he wanted to make sure they were safe? Or did he secretly suspect, as Maddie did, that one, or both, of them had had a hand in James's death? Out of everyone involved with the scavenger hunt, they were the only ones not to return after James's killing. Wasn't this more likely to be a sign of their guilt than anything else?

One thing was for sure, Maddie needed to tell Alex what she had seen and heard before the murder took place. Before now, the argument she'd overheard and the moment she'd witnessed between James and Mrs Kapoor had amounted to nothing more than idle gossip, which was why Maddie had kept these things to herself. But now, well, now this information could amount to motive.

'Once we've located Mr and Mrs Kapoor, we'll begin questioning you each in turn,' said Alex. 'Nobody is to leave this room under any circumstances. Toilet breaks can be taken but you must take at least two other people with you so your whereabouts can be verified at all times,' he added. 'I'm sorry it has to be this way but I'm sure you can all understand—'

Alex stopped in his tracks as Mickey reached out and grabbed his arm. A strange expression, somewhere between confusion and shock, was written across his face. 'Do you . . . do you . . . smell that, lad?' Mickey said, his voice almost quivering as he did.

Alex's eyes widened at his father's words, and he seemed to swallow back a response that he could not bring himself to vocalise.

Jeannie had also jumped at Mickey's words, and she turned around in her seat to face him and Alex. 'You – you can smell it too?' she said. 'I thought I were just imaginin' it.'

Mickey shook his head. 'You're not imaginin' it, Jeannie. I can smell it alright.'

'Smell what?' Maddie said. She had no idea what was going on here but the looks on Mickey, Alex and Jeannie's faces were just too unsettling to let their behaviour pass without comment.

Alex looked over at Maddie. He hesitated but eventually did speak. 'The smell . . . the one I mentioned before . . . it's my mother's perfume.'

Maddie sniffed the air. Now that she was concentrating, she could smell something she hadn't before. Something cutting through the scent of Sofia's turkey beginning to roast in the oven. A fresh, citrus fragrance. But it was faint, very faint.

A frown formed on Maddie's brow, as she tried to make sense of what this meant. Why this smell held so much gravity for Alex, Mickey and Jeannie. 'Your mother's perfume . . .'

'But,' Don said. 'Sir . . . your mother died . . . I mean, didn't she?'

Alex nodded. 'Ten years ago. On Christmas Eve.'

CHAPTER TWELVE

Maddie's eyes widened.

So that was the thing Jeannie had mentioned earlier and the weirdness Alex had alluded to before they went into the kitchen to look for the next clue. The reason Alex wanted to be around family at this time of year. He wanted to be with the family he had left after the loss of his mother. Her stomach sank as she thought of what Christmas Day ten years ago must have been like for Alex. Of all the stories Maddie covered at the paper, she always thought that the saddest were those in which a tragic event played out at what should be a happy occasion. Particularly, she ached for families who lost loved ones around the Christmas period. A time in which the world is obsessed with present-buying and Christmas trees and indulgent food, and happiness is expected. Looking over at Alex, Maddie didn't just see a police inspector, she saw the young boy Alex had been when Mickey had left to start a new family with Sofia and the twenty-two-year-old who lost his mum on Christmas Eve, a time when they should have been celebrating together.

And now this family had a new tragedy on the anniversary of an already grief-stricken occasion. But . . . could it be a coincidence? That James had died the same night as Alex's mother? And why on earth could Alex, Jeannie and Mickey smell her perfume? It wasn't like she'd been in the pub earlier and had left traces of it behind, the woman had been dead for a decade.

'Oh my God,' Don said, seemingly in response to Maddie's thoughts. 'I can't believe it. Why didn't I think of it before? It's so obvious. The ghost, who lives here. It's your mother.'

This comment was enough to shake Alex out of his surprise and shoot a sidelong look at his colleague. 'Don't be a daft sod.'

'It's possible,' said Sita from the seat she'd taken next to Mrs Fazakerley, nodding her head. 'Your family does spend a lot of time in this place, perhaps the spirit didn't want to leave you and this is the only way they can find to be close to you.'

'Or,' said Don.

'Oh God, here we go,' Alex half-said, half-sighed.

'She's got unfinished business in this world, right, and

is angry about somethin' that 'appened to 'er while she were 'ere. So, she's been trackin' you and yer family, choosing her moment, and is takin' the anniversary of 'er passin' as an opportunity to seek 'er unholy revenge for misdeeds done to 'er when she were alive.'

Mickey flinched at this. 'Misdeeds, what kind of misdeeds?'

'Could be anything. Could be being killed by your best friend because you were about to uncover 'is money-laundering operation, could be a parkin' ticket,' said Don. 'Ghosts are very mysterious and it's difficult to discern their motives.'

'That's true, they are,' Sita said with so earnest a head nod that, despite the seriousness of the situation, Maddie found herself suppressing a smile.

'They're also non-corporeal and therefore incapable of committing murder,' said Alex, a weary note in his voice. Maddie wagered this wasn't the first time he'd had to listen to a wild theory from Don.

'Of course ghosts can commit murder,' Don said, looking at Alex as though he was mad for suggesting otherwise.

'Really, how?' said Alex, his tone betraying the fact he was completely disinterested in Don's answer. At a guess, Alex simply wanted Don to exhaust his enthusiasm on this subject so he could debunk his arguments and resume the formal investigation.

'By movin' things with their mind, or by concentrating really 'ard on somethin' until it moves, like Patrick Swayze did,' Don explained in a manner that suggested he thought Alex an absolute amateur for not knowing this much already.

'Wait a minute . . .' Alex said. 'Being killed by your best friend because you're about to uncover a money-laundering operation . . . Please don't tell me you're basing your theories about this killing on the plot of *Ghost*. Because, even for you, that is beyond ridiculous.'

'Well . . . not entirely,' said Don. 'That one with Nicole Kidman is a good resource on the subject too.'

'I'm amazed you don't want to get Bruce Willis on the phone, see what he has to say about the subject,' said Alex.

Don paused. He clearly sensed Alex's mockery but couldn't help himself. 'Might not be the worst idea in the world,' he muttered, only just loud enough for Maddie to hear.

'Yes well, since my mother, to the best of my knowledge, wasn't about to uncover her best friend's money-laundering ring,' Alex said, his voice dripping with exasperation, 'and since I'm alive and well and she didn't smother me to death like Nicole Kidman did in that film you're on about, I think we'd better shift the focus of the investigation in a more sensible direction. Ghosts do not exist. A ghost did not stab James in the neck with a corkscrew.'

At this, Sofia let out a sob.

Alex's features softened. 'I'm sorry, Sofia, I didn't mean to – I didn't mean to say it like that. It's just, you know Donny drives me up the wall with this stuff. Please, forgive me.'

Sofia shook her head and reached for Alex's hand. ''S OK, love,' she whispered, before burying her face in a tissue.

Jeannie turned back around to face Curtis and Maddie, her expression utterly forlorn. 'I know 'e wasn't my nephew by blood like Alex is, and I know 'e was always in trouble but, 'e didn't deserve to go out like that. Poor lad, I still can't believe it.'

'Nobody deserves that kind of death,' said Alex. 'But it wasn't my mother's ghost that did it. Though, I'll admit, that is exactly how somebody wants it to look.'

'What do you mean, lad?' said Mickey. 'The perfume's a trick to try and make us think it were 'er? Oooh, if that's the case whoever's done this better 'ope you get your 'ands on them before I do.'

'The perfume's one thing,' Alex said with a nod, 'but there's something else. I found a ring belonging to my mother lodged in James's mouth.'

'What ring?' said Mickey.

'It . . . it was her engagement ring,' said Alex.

'But, Alex, I thought you said you never found her

engagement ring after yer mother passed?' Jeannie said. 'How the bloody hell has that turned up here?'

'You're right, Jeannie, I didn't find it when she died,' said Alex. 'I mean, sorry for saying this, Dad, but it wasn't worth anything.'

'No need to be sorry, lad,' said Mickey. 'I didn't 'ave two 'apennies to rub together when I bought it.'

'But it was worth something to me, sentimentally speaking. Which is why I looked for it. When I didn't find it amongst her belongings I wondered if she'd maybe sold it for whatever she could get for it.'

'If she did, that might explain how someone else got hold of it,' said Maddie.

'Yes,' Alex said. 'Either someone has come across it somehow in the last ten years, or someone took it and hid it away before she died. Regardless of *how* they got their hands on the ring, its mere presence suggests that whoever did this, they've been planning, if not a murder, then some act of cruelty for a very long time. Even if they hadn't been plotting murder from the very beginning, it's been in their head for a while. James was positioned in that chair so that the murderer could easily lodge this ring in his mouth. In a lying position, the ring might have fallen out or got lodged deeper in his throat than the killer wanted. It's much easier to arrange something like that in a sitting position. The details of this attack have been very carefully planned out.'

'But why, love?' said Jeannie. 'Why would someone do somethin' like this?'

'I don't know, Jeannie. I'm sorry. Why anyone would choose to try and frame my mother's ghost for killing James is quite beyond me. It's hard to believe anyone would think that would wash. But it's not washing with me. I am on the hunt for a flesh and blood killer. And before the night is out, I will find him.'

No sooner had Alex spoken these words, however, than three sharp knocks sounded out. The sudden and sharp nature of them made everyone in the room jump. Slowly, every head in the room turned in the direction of the disturbing thuds. The three knocks came a second time, and with each one Maddie flinched. It was the last sound anyone wanted to hear after the conversation had revolved around ghosts for the last twenty minutes.

'See,' Don whispered. 'I told you, it's the ghost.'

'It's not a ghost,' Alex hissed back.

Before Don could completely reignite their argument, the knocking came again and, was it Maddie's imagination or was each knock getting louder and louder?

She couldn't say who or what was making the sound, and part of her wasn't even sure she wanted to know, but it seemed to be coming from behind the fireplace, not far from where James's body still sat.

CHAPTER THIRTEEN

'I'm telling you,' said Don, 'it's yer mother's ghost. She's trying to communicate with us.'

'No it's not,' said Alex, walking towards the fireplace and pausing next to a wooden panel to the left of it. Using the end of his pen, he pushed the panel and, to Maddie's surprise, it wasn't just a panel but a door that opened.

Was this one of the secret passageways they had been talking about earlier? If so, it surely couldn't be a co-incidence that this one was located right next to James's body. A secret passageway would make it easy for a killer to surprise his victim, and to flee the scene.

Slowly, Alex nudged the very top of the door open, again with his pen, and within moments a somewhat dazed-looking Mr Kapoor collapsed out onto the floor.

'Oooh,' he said. 'Thank you, I didn't have the strength to

get the panel to open. Thought I was going to be trapped in there forever.'

Alex didn't speak. He simply studied Mr Kapoor, seemingly waiting to see what he would do or say next.

'Dad!' Zainab called from across the room. She rushed to her father's side and helped him to his knees. 'Wait a minute, he's hurt,' she said, looking up at Alex and then dabbing her finger to the back of her father's head to see if he was still bleeding. Given how red her fingers were when she pulled them away, it was clear that he was.

'I don't know exactly what happened, just that someone hit me on the back of the head while I was looking for scavenger hunt clues,' Mr Kapoor said. 'I didn't see who it was but they knocked me out clean. What's going on? Has someone resorted to violence to win the game? Has it really got that bad now?'

'No, I'm afraid it's a lot more serious than that,' said Alex.

'More serious?' said Mr Kapoor. 'How so?'

'It's James,' Alex said, holding out a hand to help Mr Kapoor to his feet. 'He's been murdered.'

'Murdered?' Mr Kapoor's eyes widened as he slowly looked around the room, his stare eventually landing on James's body, which from Mr Kapoor's perspective was partly obscured.

Mr Kapoor took a stumbling step around Alex to get

a better look. 'Murdered! But how did this happen?' he almost whispered.

'We don't know,' Alex said. His tone was flat, giving nothing away. He was still watching Mr Kapoor very closely. Still examining his every expression and gesture. From where Maddie was sitting, it didn't look like Alex was putting much stock in Mr Kapoor's story about being knocked out. But, then again, he did have the wound to prove it.

'You'd better come and take a seat, Mr Kapoor,' Alex added.

'Wait just a moment. Where is Javeria?' Mr Kapoor asked, and then when Alex didn't immediately respond he asked again. 'My wife, where is she?'

'We haven't located Mrs Kapoor yet,' Alex explained.

'Haven't lo . . .' Mr Kapoor trailed off and his eyes rested once more on James's body. 'We need to find her, now.'

'We were just about to search for you and her when you knocked on the panel. You stay here. I'm going to have a quick word with DC Maynard,' Alex said, waving a hand over in Don's direction, 'and then we'll start searching for Mrs Kapoor right away. And while we're on, Sofia?'

Sofia looked up from her seat at a nearby table.

'I'm sorry to bother you, but I'm going to need the mobile phones returning to me, in the kitchen. Take Dad to the office with you and Jeannie too, safety in numbers. And bring the phones to me. Can you do that?' said Alex.

'I'll sort it,' Sofia said with a gentle nod.

Once this was agreed, Alex turned on his heel and strode off back towards the kitchen, waving Don on to follow after him.

There was a period of eerie silence while Mickey, Jeannie and Sofia went to fetch the mobile phones from the safe. Maddie took a moment to glance out of the window, remembering all the snow that had fallen through the door when Mickey and Sofia came back from starting up the generator. It was still snowing now. Small, feather-light flakes zoomed past the window, their whiteness gleaming in the dark. Would this weather ever ease? Right now, it felt to Maddie as though she might be trapped in this place forever. A far from welcome thought when she had expected to spend the evening sitting in front of her parent's fireplace drinking sherry. Gazing fondly on the Christmas tree decorations she had made in her preteen years that were still dutifully hung regardless of how tatty they had become.

Once Sofia broke the silence by returning with the phones and dropping them off with Alex in the kitchen, a couple of people started talking and before long a murmur of conversation was rumbling on. From what Maddie could hear, some were wondering what had happened to Mrs Kapoor, others were suspiciously eyeing Mr Kapoor, and Sita was explaining how the ghost of Alex's mum could still be behind all this.

Looking at her own companions, Maddie caught Jeannie wearing a very curious expression. She was pressing her lips together and shaking her head as if wrestling with her own thoughts.

'Jeannie, are you alright?' Maddie found herself asking, not for the first time that evening.

Jeannie opened her mouth to speak. Then closed it. On opening it again, she asked, 'Was . . . were you with Alex when the murder took place?'

'Yeah,' Maddie said. There was something about Jeannie's tone that made goosebumps shoot right up Maddie's arms. It was getting a bit draughty in here with the fire out and the blizzard still raging outside, but no, it was definitely Jeannie's tone that was giving Maddie the chills. 'Why do you ask?'

'It's nothin',' Jeannie said with a weak smile that betrayed the fact it was a lot more than *nothing*. 'I'm just going to pour myself a drink. I doubt Mickey will mind under the circumstances.'

Jeannie stood and walked behind the bar. Maddie watched as she poured herself a glass of port and thought again about the answer she'd given.

Had she been with Alex when the murder took place?

Had she? Really?

She thought she had.

She thought they were in the kitchen together. He'd

come over to look at the phone wire. And then he made his way back over to the door because he was going to get Mickey and ask him about the phone lines being dead. But then everything went dark. Could he have sneaked out of the kitchen? In the dark? Without making a sound to betray what he was up to? Could he have picked up a corkscrew as he passed through the bar area and stabbed his stepbrother with it? That seemed unlikely.

How would he even know that James was in the vicinity?

And yet, the question still niggled at Maddie.

Was she with Alex at the time of the murder? Could she say for definite he was in the room with her?

She tried to get the order of events straight in her head.

After the scream, she had whispered his name. And he didn't respond. She had thought he just hadn't heard her. But what if he wasn't there? Mickey said that the electricity mains switch had been sabotaged but he didn't say how. Maddie didn't know enough about electrical supply to commercial buildings to come up with a theory about how Alex might have done this, but what if he had found a way? And then he'd taken his opportunity . . .

Maddie shook her head. Though suspicion still gnawed at her she couldn't bring herself to believe Alex was behind this. He must have been in the kitchen with her the whole time. Mustn't he?

'I think I'm going to fix myself a drink too,' Maddie said

to Curtis, who had barely said more than a few sentences since his ordeal – and who could blame him. 'Do you want anything bringing?'

'I'm quite alright without anything else to drink, thank you,' said Curtis.

Nodding in Curtis's direction, Maddie pulled herself up and approached Jeannie who was still standing behind the bar. Maddie looked over her shoulder and could see, through the circular window, Alex and Don deep in conversation a wee bit further down the kitchen.

'Jeannie,' Maddie said, keeping her voice low. 'Something's wrong, isn't it? Before, why did you ask me where Alex was during the murder?'

Jeannie took another sip of port. Her hands shook as she did so and her lips quivered as she drank. She set the glass down on the bar, straightened a festive beer mat that featured a herd of reindeer, sighed, and then looked up at Maddie. ''E never talks about it now. But Alex 'ad a really 'ard time when Mickey left. And then when Alice – 'is mum – died, well, I think 'e felt like the whole world 'ad abandoned 'im.'

'That's more than understandable,' said Maddie. 'I think almost anyone would feel the same under those circumstances, at least in their worst moments, but he said earlier that he'd had a lot of time to get used to it.'

'Mmmmm,' Jeannie said, with a nod.

'You . . . you don't think he's being honest with himself?' Maddie knew this was a sensitive subject and was using all the skills she usually implemented as a journalist when she had a source who was scared to talk. Offer calm, rational responses. Don't pile on the pressure, keep the questions as light as you can. Above all, listen more than you talk.

'I could be worryin' for nothin', I suppose. Maybe 'e 'as . . . put it all behind 'im, you know,' said Jeannie. 'After all, you were with 'im when it 'appened. When James was . . . you know.'

'Yes,' Maddie said, her tone not quite as convincing as it was before. ' . . . I was with him. In the kitchen.'

'So yes,' Jeannie said. 'There's no need for concern. Everything's fine. Everything will be alright.'

'I'm sure it will,' Maddie said.

Jeannie nodded but then frowned. 'It's just . . .'

Maddie gave Jeannie a moment to speak. When she didn't, Maddie prompted her. 'It's just . . .?'

'Well, when Mickey left and when Alex's mum died, in private, 'e . . . 'e . . .'

'What?'

''E did stuff.'

'What . . . kind of stuff?' Maddie said, gently, oh so gently. Jeannie didn't want to be talking about this, that much was more than clear. If Maddie pushed at all, there was no doubt the woman would clam up and Maddie would never know all she needed to about the seemingly virtuous inspector leading the investigation into his step-brother's murder.

''E got a bit violent, you know,' Jeannie said, her voice getting quieter the more she revealed. ''E would punch the wall, and 'imself. 'E even started a couple of brawls in 'ere that 'e were lucky not to 'ave got written up about. Probably would 'ave cost 'im 'is career in the police force.'

'Sounds like he was angry. And although starting fist fights isn't the best method of dealing with it all, again it's very understandable,' Maddie said.

'Yeah,' Jeannie said. 'But it used to scare me. The place 'e went to when 'e got like that. I used to look at 'im and think, all that anger, it's got to go somewhere. It doesn't just disappear, you know?'

'So, where do you think it went?'

Involuntarily, Jeannie's eyes flitted over to the snug in which James's corpse was sitting and then snapped straight back to Maddie. 'Alex . . . 'e was the one who found 'is mother when she died. We never found the engagement ring 'e's just pulled out of James's mouth. Since, when Alice died, it had been ten years since Mickey left her, I just assumed she'd long since thrown the damn thing in the Ribble or something. But . . . what if . . .'

'What if she didn't?' Maddie finished.

Jeannie offered a slow nod in response. 'Oh, God forgive me, I shouldn't be saying this. 'E's my nephew and I love 'im, as if 'e were me own kid. But what if Alex found that ring and 'as 'ad it all along? What does that mean about what's 'appened tonight?'

Maddie knew this was as close as Jeannie would ever come to insinuating that Alex had had some part in James's death. She hadn't outright said anything particularly incriminating. But there were threads in a tapestry, and the question Jeannie had posed hung heavy between them.

A moment later the swing door to the kitchen abruptly opened making both Jeannie and Maddie jump.

'Oh, sorry you two,' Alex said as Don slid past him back into the bar area. 'I didn't mean to startle you.'

'Then don't burst through a door right after a murder has been committed,' Maddie said, tacking a small smile to her lips. It seemed plausible, she thought, that she and Jeannie would be rattled by a sudden noise after what had happened to James. Hopefully, Alex would think so, too. Hopefully, he had no idea that just moments before Maddie and Jeannie had been placing their suspicions on him and had been startled by his sudden appearance.

'Duly noted,' Alex said. He didn't smile but his tone was light enough to convey that he understood the humour. 'Maddie, can you come into the kitchen for a moment? I need to talk to you. Alone.'

Alone . . . ?

'M-me?' Maddie stammered in a manner that was sure to rouse Alex's suspicions.

'Yes . . .' Alex replied, his eyes moving up and down as he studied Maddie's expression in much the same way he had Mr Kapoor's just ten minutes before.

'Sure,' Maddie managed to say, hoping her tone was casual enough to distract Alex from her obvious, earlier apprehension.

As Maddie circled the bar and walked towards the swing door, she could feel her heart beating harder and harder in her chest. Her mind raced. She tried again to get it straight in her head exactly what happened and in what order when the power had cut out, and she'd heard that awful scream. Was she about to be alone in a room with the man who was the real culprit behind James's murder?

As she pushed through the swing door into the kitchen she realised, one way or another, that she was probably about to find out.

CHAPTER FOURTEEN

'So, obviously this wasn't the Christmas Eve you were expecting when you walked into the pub tonight,' said Alex.

'You can say that again,' said Maddie, struggling to find a posture that looked relaxed, largely because she wasn't in any way relaxed. It wasn't just that the smell of the cooking turkey was getting stronger by the second, a smell that just twenty-four hours ago would have made her mouth water but now just left her with a queasy feeling in her stomach. It was her growing anxiety over all that Jeannie had just revealed and a growing sense of not knowing who on earth to trust in this situation. Alex came across as a firm but fair authority figure with a kind – at times even gentle – nature. But wasn't that sometimes the way with these things? That the person you least expected to do something heinous went ahead and did it? Wasn't that how they always thought they were going to get away with it? And it wasn't as though she'd need to be the one reporting the news to understand that police officers were capable of abusing their authority. If Alex had had a hand in James's death, he wouldn't be the first policeman to have committed murder, even in the last decade. She couldn't assume that he was innocent just because he had a badge. Many an ill deed could be hidden behind one of those.

Still trying to find a casual posture, despite the tsunami of unwanted thoughts, Maddie tried leaning next to one of the sinks and folding her arms. It may not have looked very relaxed, but it was a comfortable enough way to stand. That was better than nothing.

'I'm going to have to ask you some questions, about tonight and about the people in the pub,' Alex said. 'And I'm going to make notes on your answers.'

'OK . . .' Maddie said, a frown forming on her brow.

'You . . . have an issue with that?' Alex said. 'I did say I would need to question everyone.'

'No, no issue,' Maddie replied. 'Ask me anything you want, I'm just surprised that *I'm* the first person you want to talk to since I was with you when the murder happened. But I'm not a police inspector, so of course I'm just going to do as I'm told and bow to your wisdom.'

A strange smile that Maddie couldn't read the meaning

of crossed Alex's lips for a moment but just as quickly it disappeared. At the sight of it, Maddie wanted nothing more than to scan the room to see where the kitchen knives were kept. To at least know where a weapon might be waiting should she need one, but Alex's eyes were fixed on her, and they weren't budging. He'd notice if she started looking around and might even perceive her lack of eye contact as guilt. The last thing she needed after everything else was to be wrongly accused of murder. So, she'd just have to hope that Jeannie's theory and her own nagging doubts were wrong.

'Which of these phones is yours?' Alex asked, holding the tray Sofia had returned from the safe, in which lay all of the mobiles she'd collected earlier in the evening.

Maddie pointed to hers and Alex instructed her to pick it up and turn it on.

'Mind if I take a look at your contacts, messages and call history?' said Alex.

Maddie shook her head, inputted her PIN and handed the phone to Alex.

He took a good couple of minutes to scroll through several screens. Even though she knew he wasn't going to find anything incriminating, the process felt more than a wee bit intimidating. He could look at any of the messages she'd sent, not expecting them to be read by anyone but their recipient. She could only hope he didn't go far enough back through the threads to find the last messages between her and Lance. No death threats were issued, but they weren't polite either.

'I'm going to need to hang onto this for now,' Alex said at last. 'Though I don't see anything immediately incriminating, I've hardly had a chance to go through it with a fine-tooth comb.'

'I understand,' Maddie said with a nod while Alex returned her phone to the tray.

'Where did you start your journey tonight and where were you going when your car broke down?' Alex asked.

Maddie was about to protest that Alex already knew these details but then she noticed he was poised with the pen and pad, ready to jot down her answers. He wanted to record her response in her own words, officially. And may even be looking out for any differences in the story she'd told him earlier in the pub. Hoping to catch her in a lie.

'I set off from my offices in Trafford at about half four. I was going to just drive up the motorway to Edinburgh to see my parents,' said Maddie. 'But there was an accident on the M6. It caused a pile-up and the route was pretty much a no-go.'

'So, how did that change your journey?' Alex said, making notes on what Maddie was saying.

'The sat nav suggested a route through the Dales. It wasn't snowing at that point, at least not on the motorway, so it seemed like a good plan to basically get off on the next exit and bypass the traffic jam.' As Maddie said this, she considered just how much trouble that single decision had caused her. Yes, if she'd stayed where she was, she would be at this very moment still sitting on the M6. Probably broken down. But maybe the BAC would have been able to get to her there. One thing was for sure, she wouldn't be stuck in a pub in the middle of nowhere, being questioned by a police officer who might actually have had a hand in the murder of his own stepbrother.

'And why did you decide to stay at The Merry Monarch tonight?' Alex asked, his tone flat as though the two of them hadn't been laughing themselves silly over Don's addiction to sour cream Pringles just a couple of hours earlier.

'My car broke down in the village and Curtis directed me to come here in case the breakdown service couldn't reach me, which they couldn't,' said Maddie.

'Had you met Curtis before this evening?'

'No, never,' Maddie said.

'Had you met James before this evening?'

Maddie almost said that thankfully she hadn't, but since the poor guy was dead she realised just in time that this would be a rather insensitive comment. Especially when he was a member of Alex's family. 'The first time I met him was at the bar this evening.'

'What about anyone else in the pub?' said Alex. 'Anyone you were already acquainted with?'

Maddie shook her head, she could feel herself becoming exasperated by the pedestrian nature of the questions. 'No, I didn't know anybody here. I only wanted a bed for the night because my car had broken down. Trust me, if there had been a way to get home to my family tonight rather than be stuck here, I would have found it.'

Alex nodded, but it was a stiff nod. As though he hadn't even noticed Maddie's irritation growing by the second. He scribbled a few things in his notebook and then looked at her again. 'How much interaction did you have with James?'

Maddie sighed and then thought for a moment before answering. She knew she wasn't the murderer and that this was a waste of time. She just wanted Alex to move on to someone who might actually be responsible. To make that happen, however, she was going to have to tell him about all the events she'd witnessed that evening that revolved around James. 'I met him at the bar, he made some comment about a woman as hot as me not needing a hot drink to warm her up.'

At this, Alex winced, presumably at the poor calibre of the pickup line. It was the first glimpse Maddie had seen of the sensitive Alex she'd been chatting with before the power cut, before the murder had taken place.

'What else?' Alex said, returning his expression to the same neutrality as before.

'Mickey could see I didn't like him talking to me that way and told him off for it. I went to make a phone call and, when I looked over at the kitchen, Mickey and James were having a heated argument.'

'That's not so unusual,' Alex almost grunted.

'Yeah, well, maybe not, but it wasn't the only argument James was at the centre of this evening,' Maddie said.

'What do you mean?' said Alex.

'My room is next to the one the Kapoors are staying in,' Maddie clarified. 'You know I went upstairs for a shower. They were having an argument before I came down to have some supper. It was about James. Mr Kapoor was angry that he'd been making advances on Zainab. I mean, really angry. But then . . .'

'But then, what?' Alex pushed.

'I . . . there was also something going on between Mrs Kapoor and James. I mean, I don't know what exactly, this is really just speculation, but when I looked over at their table earlier, they gave each other this look when Mr Kapoor wasn't paying attention. There was something in it. They seemed almost mesmerised by each other.'

'You think they were having some kind of affair?' Alex said, a frown settling on his brow at the idea.

'I don't know, but they both flinched and looked

elsewhere when Mr Kapoor turned back around to face them and Mr Kapoor did not look happy that he'd caught them staring at each other,' said Maddie.

'But why would James be trying it on with Zainab if he was having an affair with her mother?' said Alex.

'I don't know,' Maddie said with a shrug. 'The only thing I can come up with is that maybe he was trying to make Mrs Kapoor jealous for some reason. But it doesn't make a lot of sense.'

'I'll make a note of it, see what shakes out in the rest of the interviews,' Alex said, his face assuming an even more serious expression than before. He looked hard at Maddie, straight in the eye.

'When I came back into the pub after having a word with Donny earlier, you were looking at James's body, why?' Alex asked.

'I'm afraid it was just morbid curiosity,' said Maddie. 'Something I'd seen when I first caught sight of him looked odd. I went back for a second look and realised it was the murder weapon. Everything else about the act had seemed so meticulously planned.'

'But the weapon was something the killer could have grabbed from anywhere in the bar?' said Alex.

Maddie nodded.

'That occurred to me too when I was examining the body for clues,' said Alex. But he didn't say any more than that. Didn't let Maddie know what he'd deduced or if he thought it might be important.

Again, Alex gave Maddie a long, hard look that, though she resisted the urge, made her want to shuffle on the spot.

'Did you have anything to do with James's death, Maddie? If you played any part in what happened to him, now is the time to tell me. It'll only be worse if something comes out later. Judges do not look kindly on people who try to deceive law enforcement.'

'I didn't have anything to do with James's death,' Maddie answered. 'But . . .'

'But?'

'Nothing, we haven't time, you need to go and find Mrs Kapoor. After all we've seen tonight, who knows what's happened to her?' Maddie said, at once regretting that she'd hinted she had anything else to say in the first place. Why on earth had she done that when she was almost free and clear?

'Let's make time,' said Alex, folding his arms across his chest.

Maddie pressed her lips together and thought for a moment. If Alex was the true killer then she really didn't want him knowing intimate things about her. Things she'd never told anyone before. But what was the real likelihood of him being behind this? She didn't have any concrete evidence. Just a few misgivings from his auntie, who didn't even want to think her nephew was capable of such a thing anyway. And the odds were that he had indeed been in the kitchen with her when the murder was committed. He couldn't have known James was outside and he would have had to work extremely quickly to kill James and get back into the kitchen without her noticing he was gone. For now at least, Maddie had to think of Alex as a police officer. Withholding anything about herself would only lead to her acting weirdly enough around him for his suspicions about her to deepen. Even more pressing than that, however, was the desperate feeling that was building inside Maddie. That had started to hatch the moment she saw James's dead body. She had to tell somebody. She had to get the secret out.

'Do you believe in karma?' Maddie asked.

'I might not go that far,' Alex said. 'But I've seen my fair share of what goes around comes around on the job. Why?'

'James's isn't the first dead body I've seen, Alex. It was a long time ago now. I was five, and my family were on holiday in the Highlands. We visited a forest up there called Reelig Glen. I'd run off on my own. You could, just about, still do that back then. Run around without parental supervision and not get kidnapped. It's a beautiful place, full of the tallest trees in Britain, and I loved being out there, being with nature.'

'What does this have to do with tonight?' asked Alex.

'Probably nothing,' said Maddie. 'It's just a . . . a feeling that I'm having. Because of what I found in the glen that day.'

'A dead body,' Alex said, putting two and two together.

Maddie nodded. 'There's a clear path that winds through the trees but I tripped while I was running around, fell down into this ditch. Got scratched to hell by thorns and stones. When I stood up and dusted myself off, I noticed it. Her.'

'A woman?' Alex said.

Again Maddie nodded. 'At first I just thought it was somebody sleeping or hiding. But then they didn't move, even when I'd made all that noise falling down into the ditch. And something about the way the body was lying there, I knew it was too still. And then, I knew the person was dead. Even though I didn't really understand what dead meant at that age.'

'Must have been scary. What did you do?' said Alex.

'Nothing. Before I knew what was happening my parents were calling me in the distance. And I jumped, clambered my way back up the path and ran back to Mum and Dad.'

'Did you tell them?'

'No,' Maddie said. 'I didn't tell them. I didn't tell anyone. Alex, I just left her there.'

'You were just a kid, you probably were scared, maybe even in shock, you didn't have the resources to deal with that kind of situation,' said Alex.

Maddie sighed. She'd tried to comfort herself with that kind of logic many times over the years but she knew the real reason she hadn't said anything about the body. 'But I *knew* it was wrong,' she explained. 'I knew I should have said something. I was just scared. Growing up, my parents were masters of making me feel like I might get into trouble for something even if I hadn't actually done anything wrong. I'm not explaining it very well but they would always shout at me first and ask questions later. I thought if I told them about the body I'd be in trouble for finding it. I thought they'd be mad at me. Like, somehow, I was responsible for the body lying there. Or that I shouldn't have found it, shouldn't have been off the path. I was only interested in staying in my parents' good graces. When that woman and that woman's family needed me to be brave, I failed them. I was a coward.'

'Again, let's remember you were five when this happened,' said Alex. 'Everything you're saying is totally understandable.'

'Understandable, maybe. But it's not exactly winning human behaviour, is it?' said Maddie. 'Years later, when I was training as a journalist, I looked into the newspaper archives to see if there was anything about the woman. Her body was found by somebody else. It had been classified as a murder. But the walker who discovered the body didn't find it for nearly a week after I did. There had been a lot of rain that had washed away any forensic evidence. They never caught the person who did it. Because of me.'

'There really isn't any guarantee that they'd have caught whoever did it even if you had told your parents straight away,' said Alex.

'I . . . suppose not. I'd never thought of it like that,' Maddie said. 'But what if – what if being here, caught up in this murder, is my comeuppance for failing that woman all those years ago? What if this is my punishment for leaving that woman's death unanswered?'

CHAPTER FIFTEEN

'You are as bad as Donny, you know that?' Alex said, some of the prior humour returning to his features. 'Look, yes it would have been preferable for you to report what you saw. But you were a kid. There's no changing what happened back then now anyway. And I don't think for a second that you're here to be punished. It's just an unfortunate coincidence . . . for you anyway.'

'What do you mean by that?' Maddie said, raising an eyebrow.

'I mean, it's going to be nigh on impossible for me and Donny to conduct a search for Mrs Kapoor, while keeping an eye on everyone in the pub. It's not safe for one of us to go off alone, we need to be a pair. But if we both go, then there's nobody to watch the people in the pub and the killer might make a break for it if they think they've got half a chance of surviving the snowstorm. In short, we haven't got the numbers we need to deal with this situation and keep everyone safe and in check at the same time.'

'So . . . I'm sorry, what are you saying exactly?' Maddie said, tucking her blonde hair behind her ears as she spoke.

'I'm saying you and me were in the same room as each other when the murder took place so we've got alibis and know it couldn't be either one of us,' Alex explained.

'Right . . .' Maddie said, though she still wasn't sure she could completely vouch for the fact that Alex hadn't got up to some terrible misdeed in the dark.

'So, I need you onside,' Alex said. 'To help out. I need you to come and look for Mrs Kapoor with me while Donny watches the group down here. Once I've got everyone re-united and in the same room, it'll be an easier situation to manage . . . At least that's the theory. But until then, well, I'm going to need you to pitch in.'

'I . . . suppose I could do that,' Maddie said, praying her uncertain tone wasn't betraying her thoughts just then. It was one thing for Alex to get her in a room on her own when said room was adjacent to one that held witnesses. There were plenty of people on the other side of the kitchen door, including Jeannie, waiting for her to emerge. They'd soon realise something was amiss with Alex if anything happened to her here.

But if she followed Alex off into another part of the

building, away from everyone else, well, he could say that anything had happened to her. And because he was a police officer, who was well respected in the village, everyone would probably believe whatever story he fed them. He knew she was an investigative journalist from their conversations earlier in the evening. If he had found a way of offing James, he probably wasn't counting on someone like her being in the room when he did it. If he even remotely suspected that she might uncover the truth of the situation, he might choose to get rid of her as soon as he got the chance. He may even get rid of her and try to pin James's murder on her.

Alex, seemingly sensing her hesitation, said: 'If you really do believe that you're here as punishment for not reporting that body all those years ago – not that I do, mind – then what better way to redeem yourself than help me find the person who did this to James?'

Maddie nodded, largely because she didn't really see that she had any other choice. 'Alright, of course I'll help.'

What else could she say? If she said she was scared because she didn't think it was safe, he would only say it was time to be brave now, braver than she was in Reelig Glen. And there was no other valid reason for hesitating, other than her currently secret suspicions about him.

'Thank you. It's hardly a conventional way of conducting an investigation but I'm in a tight spot. I've thought about trying to get to the nearest house on foot and asking for help there but it's a good half mile from here in the snow. It would mean leaving Donny on his own without back-up, which is never a good strategic move. And even if I did make it to a house to use the landline, with the snow falling the way it is I don't think even the constabulary 4x4 cars could get to us. And then there'd be the question of whether I could make it back to the pub without freezing to death. All in all, it's not worth the risk.'

'No, you're right,' said Maddie. 'Staying put and sticking it out seems pretty much the only sensible option.'

'It's probably going to be a long night. I'm grateful to have an ally. Not that I've completely stricken you from the suspect list, you understand?' Alex said, flashing her a grin as he walked towards the door.

'But, I thought you said we had alibis because we were together at the time of the murder?' Maddie said, following after him.

'Well, I'm ninety-eight per cent sure you weren't involved. But you are the only unknown quantity in the room. The mysterious outsider. For all I know, you and James dated two years ago and it ended badly. Or you could be some kind of accomplice.'

'You're going to have to come up with a more plausible theory than that,' Maddie said. 'Don's Patrick Swayze theory has a higher level of credibility to it than the idea that I would ever say yes to a date with your stepbrother.'

'Maybe,' Alex said, his grin widening. 'But that's just what a wronged woman would say under these circumstances. And you know that I can't check your phone and financial records from here. So, you could tell me anything. Let's face it, even if we do have an alibi in each other because we were in the same room when the lights went out, it doesn't mean you had nothing to do with what happened to James. You're a suspect. Everybody's a suspect. Even me.'

With that comment Alex pushed through the swing door back into the pub.

'That much we agree on,' Maddie said once she was sure he was out of earshot.

Alone in the kitchen, she could hear the wind howling outside. Beyond the windows, she could see white flakes shooting through the black of night. At any other time, she might have felt cosy and cocooned. The way a person does when the weather is abysmal outside and they are safely inside. But right now, the sturdy stone walls of The Merry Monarch and the snow beyond it felt like a prison. There was no escape, from the pub itself or from the feeling of being trapped here. Held hostage almost, against her will. The last thing Maddie wanted to do was follow Alex back into the pub. But, as he had just so clearly outlined, there was no way out of the pub that didn't end in hypothermia. Her chances of survival were likely, just about, better if she stayed indoors.

A particularly vicious gust of wind rattled the kitchen window just then. As if the weather were confirming to Maddie personally that there was no escape here. That only a cold and lonely death in the snow-laden dales of Yorkshire lay beyond the pub threshold.

Fully accepting that there was no other choice but to go along with the course of action Alex had suggested, Maddie sighed and slowly walked towards the kitchen door, pushing her way back out into the pub and wondering what on earth was going to happen to them all next.

CHAPTER SIXTEEN

By the time Maddie re-entered the pub, Alex was just starting to explain that the pair of them were going in search of Mrs Kapoor. Sita questioned why Alex was trusting the outsider, of all people, to help him and Alex duly explained that he had been with Maddie at the time of the murder and therefore knew she couldn't be responsible for James's death.

'Did anyone see Mrs Kapoor before the blackout?' Alex asked, once he had answered Sita's query. 'Anyone from her team know which room she was in at the time? Any direction to make this process quicker will be much appreciated.'

'Mum was supposed to be in the drying room, next to the library,' said Zainab. 'At least that's the room I think Dad assigned her.'

'That's what I remembered,' said Jeannie. 'I was fumblin'

around in the dark, but on my way downstairs I did open the door to what I think were the drying room – impossible to tell really – and called out for Javeria. I didn't get an answer but it could easily 'ave been another room considering I couldn't see a bleedin' thing, like. You'll probably 'ave a bit more luck findin' her with the lights on. What's funny – funny peculiar, not funny ha-ha – is that James weren't supposed to be anywhere near the fireplace. I think Mr Kapoor suggested 'e look for clues in the secret passageway near the pub toilets.'

'That's right, I did. I gave everyone somewhere to look. But he never did as he was told, did he?' said Mr Kapoor.

'That's my son you're talking about!' Sofia shouted across the room.

Mr Kapoor at least had the decency to look shame-faced about what he'd said. 'I am sorry, Mrs Beaumont,' he said to Sofia. 'I keep forgetting that this has really happened. I keep expecting it to all be somehow unreal.'

''S OK,' Sofia said, waving a hand at Mr Kapoor before burying her head in it.

Alex sighed. 'Thanks for the information. We'll go up and check the drying room for Mrs Kapoor and then expand our search if we don't find her there.'

'I still think I should come with you,' said Mr Kapoor. 'My wife could be dead and you're not letting me look for her.'

'Dad!' Zainab half-screamed. 'Don't say that. Mum isn't dead. You don't know what you're talking about.'

Mr Kapoor didn't apologise to his daughter, but the same look of shame crossed his face as it had just a few moments ago. He would no doubt think twice about assuming the worst in future when her delicate ears were close by.

'Look, I know it's difficult. I wish I didn't have to make this harder. But we've been over this, Mr Kapoor,' Alex said. 'You're injured and for all I know the killer is still somewhere else on the premises. I can't take someone who is a physical liability.'

Mr Kapoor muttered something, but he made sure it wasn't loud enough for Alex to hear the precise wording and so, perhaps wisely, Alex chose to ignore it and move on.

'In my absence, DC Maynard is in charge,' Alex said, making eye contact with each person around the room. 'What he says, goes. If anyone tries to go around that rule, they will immediately arouse my suspicions. Those of you who know me well know that would be a very, very bad idea. So, it's best if you all just sit tight and wait for us to come back.'

Alex made a move towards the staircase and gestured for Maddie to follow after him. Before doing so, she noticed Jeannie shooting her a concerned look. Maddie did her best to avoid maintaining eye contact with Jeannie. To pretend that she hadn't noticed her expression and that everything was going to be OK.

Despite her reservations, she had to hope for the best here. If Alex was who he seemed to be, there was no safer place in this predicament than at his side. If he wasn't, well there was no easy way of getting out of this situation now anyway.

'I didn't want to say anything in front of Zainab,' Maddie said, once she and Alex were halfway up the stairs and out of earshot, 'but, what exactly are we expecting to find here? I mean, do you think Mrs Kapoor is . . . OK?'

A large bowl of Christmas-scented potpourri sat atop a table on a landing halfway up the stairs. The refreshing zing of orange and cinnamon was a welcome change from the smell of the turkey in the kitchen and, as they passed, Maddie filled her lungs with it. Since it didn't look like she was going to be allowed back into the outside world anytime soon, it was as close to fresh air as she was likely to get.

'It's impossible to say,' said Alex. 'If that look you saw between James and Javeria was an indication that they were having an affair, and Mr Kapoor is behind James's death . . . well there's nothing to say he didn't take the opportunity to kill both of them. Jealousy can be a powerful driver for some.'

Of course, everything that Alex had just said had flitted through Maddie's mind, back in the kitchen, when she had explained all she had seen and heard that evening. But there was a piece of evidence that didn't fit that narrative. 'How could Mr Kapoor be the killer though, if he was knocked out by the person who committed the murder?'

'What, that? He could have done that to himself,' said Alex. 'Wouldn't be too difficult to injure yourself like that, and make it look like somebody knocked you out. Knocking the back of his head hard against the wall would do it.'

'I . . . hadn't even thought of that. It seems pretty extreme to me that someone would injure themselves that badly,' Maddie admitted. 'But I guess that's why you're the detective and I'm the reporter.'

They reached the top of the stairs and Alex offered a small smile at her comment. 'I'm glad you didn't think of it. It means you haven't seen the things I've seen. You'd be amazed at the lengths some people will go to in order to cover up a crime.'

Maddie swallowed hard as Alex said this and really wished he hadn't as it set her mind racing once again with the idea he might be the killer. Maybe after seeing the way people had covered their tracks over the years, he'd got a few ideas for himself and taken the opportunity to rid himself of his family rival.

Taking a deep breath, Maddie tried to push these thoughts from her mind. *Come on*, she told herself. *You're being ridiculous. Try and keep your cool.*

'We're going to have to end this conversation here now,' Alex said, reducing his voice almost to a whisper. 'Say the killer is somebody we haven't considered. Somebody who sneaked into the pub without us noticing. Or sneaked upstairs when Mickey ushered out everyone who wasn't taking part in the scavenger hunt. Or, say, Mrs Kapoor is somehow in on it. We don't know who is listening, or from what hiding place. It might seem paranoid but it's better to be that way than caught out by whoever's behind this, so keep any conversation casual.'

Maddie nodded, and followed on as Alex walked up the corridor.

On her first walk up the stairs, Maddie had not paid much attention to the common areas provided for guests at the hotel. She had been too busy trying to bustle into her own room and jump into a hot shower. But at the end of the hall on the same level as the guest rooms, she could see now that there were a few doors painted in different colours to the bedrooms, a simple way of differentiating them for guests with poor orienteering skills.

'The library is right at the end of the corridor there,' said Alex, gesturing to a wooden door painted purple. There was a small sign on it, too small for Maddie to read the text from this distance, but when they did get up close, it read GUEST LIBRARY, as she'd suspected.

Looking to her left, Maddie saw a blue door with a sign that read GUEST LAUNDRY. And to her right, a yellow door that was labelled as the drying room.

'This is the room Mrs Kapoor's team said she was sent to,' said Alex, his voice almost a whisper.

'Jeannie wasn't sure if she'd opened the right room when she left the library, but look, the rooms are right next to each other,' Maddie hissed back. 'Even in the dark, she probably did get the right one.'

'We still need to double-check,' said Alex, slowly turning the doorknob and pushing the door open a few inches. 'Mrs Kapoor?' he called.

No response.

'Mrs Kapoor?' he tried again.

Still no response.

Alex held a finger to his lips to signal Maddie to be quiet.

Slowly, Alex pushed the door so it swung wide open on its hinges, the creak so loud a band of pipers would have known they were coming. But still, Alex and Maddie kept their peace. The lights were on in the room and Maddie could see a row of metal racks designed for drying off wet socks, boots and raincoats belonging to walkers. But at first glance, Maddie couldn't see anybody. She did, however, notice Alex physically bracing himself as he entered the room. He clearly thought there was a possibility that somebody could jump out at them, which was an unsettling thought to say the least. Maddie had no idea what to do should such a thing actually happen but, hopefully, given his police training, Alex did.

With bated breath, Maddie watched him enter the room. Almost wincing at the shock she was sure was about to come. The moment Alex's head was around the door, however, he looked over to his left and at once his muscles seem to relax. His jaw, which had been clenched, slackened and he looked back at Maddie with sorrowful eyes.

'What, what is it?' she asked, more certain than she'd ever been about anything that she didn't really want the answer.

'It's Mrs Kapoor.'

'Is she . . .?'

'I don't know. She's on the floor. Looks like there was a struggle.' Alex started to move to where Maddie presumed Mrs Kapoor's body lay. Steeling herself, she stepped into the room after him. She didn't particularly want to see a second dead body this evening. But until she could be certain Alex wasn't involved, she needed to watch him. Especially around other potential victims. Maddie was pretty certain he wouldn't have been able to get all the way up here in the dark to bump someone else off, and what would have been his motive for killing Mrs Kapoor anyway? But then again, she was involved with James somehow and Alex had accused Maddie earlier of being a possible accomplice. What if he had an accomplice himself? Since she knew so little about these people, Maddie couldn't afford to take any chances. She had to keep an eye on him. If he did anything unusual, she'd notice right away and could regroup with Jeannie downstairs. Likewise, it would mean Alex couldn't cover anything up without her seeing it.

Mrs Kapoor was sprawled on the floor, face down in her turquoise trouser suit. It was impossible to see if she was breathing. Her once perfectly combed dark hair lay in thick, unruly clumps over her head and her arms were in such a position that suggested she had not managed to break her own fall when she went down.

Alex crouched next to her and pressed two fingers to her neck. 'She's got a pulse,' he said, 'and she's warm.'

Maddie breathed a sigh of relief. Thank goodness they weren't looking at another murder. Yes it was unsettling that someone else had been attacked, but the way in which James had left this world told Maddie that if the killer had wanted Mr and Mrs Kapoor dead, they would be so. Assuming they were both innocent of any wrongdoing, the likelihood was that the pair of them were just somehow in the killer's way of his real target. Which meant they would only be dealing with the one dead body this evening which, at any rate, was more than enough.

Gently, Alex turned Mrs Kapoor onto her side and swept her hair out of her face. 'Mrs Kapoor?' He shook her shoulder a few times in an attempt to rouse her. 'Mrs Kapoor?' he tried again.

A moment passed and it felt like a very long one. But then, a frown came to Mrs Kapoor's brow and she emitted a short moan. Another few moments and her eyes fluttered open.

'It's OK, Mrs Kapoor, it's me, Alex Beaumont. Your family are downstairs in the pub and they're safe too.'

Mrs Kapoor looked weak, drowsy, but then all of a sudden seemed to snap out of her stupor. She grabbed Alex.

'Ow!' he said, as Maddie watched her hand grip his arm tight.

Mrs Kapoor didn't even acknowledge Alex's response. Instead she started stammering.

'Y-you-you've got to h-help me. Y-you've got to believe me.'

'It's alright, Mrs Kapoor, like I said, you're safe now,' Alex explained, while patting her hand.

'N-n-no, not safe. Not safe here. Can't be. Can't be. It attacked me. It attacked me.'

'It?' Maddie said, her blood running cold. Mrs Kapoor

was almost ranting at this point, something had startled her. Some *thing*. 'What do you mean *it*?'

Because of her position, Mrs Kapoor clearly hadn't realised Maddie was in the room until this point, and sat bolt upright at the sound of her voice. On recognising Maddie's face, her eyes became a normal size for her head again.

'Oh, it's you, it's just you,' she said, almost sobbing at the realisation.

'What do you mean, *it*, Mrs Kapoor?' Alex asked, clearly no more enamoured with Mrs Kapoor's description of her attacker than Maddie was.

'You won't believe me. You won't believe me,' Mrs Kapoor said.

'Mrs Kapoor,' Alex said, taking one of her hands in his. 'You need to calm down and, if you can, tell me who attacked you.'

'It was a g-g-ghost,' came Mrs Kapoor's reply.

CHAPTER SEVENTEEN

'A ghost?' Alex said flatly. Maddie could tell he was only just managing to keep from rolling his eyes. After the back and forth he'd had with Don earlier, this was probably the last thing he wanted to hear. If Mrs Kapoor hadn't been so incredibly shaken by her experience, Maddie might have smirked at his obvious irritation.

'Yes,' Mrs Kapoor said. 'It was terrifying. I have never seen anything like it.'

'Can you describe this ghost in a bit more detail?' Alex said, his tone betraying the fact that he wasn't convinced at all by the idea that Mrs Kapoor had been attacked by a phantom.

'All the lights went out. I didn't know what had happened. I thought maybe there had been a loss of power like there was a few years ago. So I found my way to the door, feeling my way along the walls, and when I opened the door, it was there in the corridor. Glowing.'

'Glowing?' Maddie said, unable to stop herself.

Alex shot Maddie a look for interrupting his witness and, no doubt, for encouraging the bout of mild hysteria Mrs Kapoor was currently caught up in.

Sorry, she mouthed. Even as a reporter she knew better than to interrupt a person's testimony mid-flow. It was just, she hadn't expected the assailant to be glowing. This was hands down the weirdest detail she'd ever heard.

'Glowing,' Mrs Kapoor confirmed. 'It was not of this world, I am telling you. It was glowing.'

'What else do you remember?' Alex said. His tone was gentler now. Despite his exasperation at the ghost being named as the chief suspect, again. He had remembered himself, and that Mrs Kapoor, regardless of her wild accusation, was a woman seemingly very much disturbed by whatever had happened to her.

'It had a long black cloak, and hood. It looked like death had come to claim me. And its face . . . its face . . .' Mrs Kapoor whimpered.

'What about its face?' Alex nudged her when a moment or two had passed and she hadn't completed the sentence.

'It was . . . half shadow. Half light,' said Mrs Kapoor.

Alex frowned. 'I'm not sure I understand.'

But that description stirred something in Maddie's

subconscious. Something she had seen earlier in the evening. 'Was there anything else on the face?' she asked.

Mrs Kapoor nodded. 'I'll never forget it, not as long as I live. There was a single teardrop.'

Maddie rubbed a hand over her mouth as her suspicions were confirmed. 'It wasn't a ghost. I saw that face too this evening. Hanging on the wall downstairs. A hand-painted mask. It looked like some kind of memorabilia piece.'

'Oh, yes,' Alex said. 'That is one of the many hideous *vintage treasures* Dad hangs on the wall.'

'Earlier, I noticed it was missing,' Maddie said. 'Well, that's not strictly true. When all the teams left the pub and went off in different directions, I knew something wasn't the same as before but I couldn't work out what it was. It was when I noticed the fire was out. I thought that's all it was at the time. Or tried to convince myself that it was just the fire that was different. But, deep down, I knew there was something else. That mask had creeped me out when I saw it for the first time. I couldn't help but notice it when I first arrived. So, although I couldn't put my finger on it, I'll bet that's what was missing when I looked around the room. I bet when we go back downstairs that mask is gone and whoever did all this is using it to conceal their identity. And a ghost wouldn't need to use a mask.'

'No. No, you have to believe me,' said Mrs Kapoor. 'I

know the mask you mean, but what I saw . . . it wasn't human. It was a ghost. It was.'

'What did this ghost do to you?' Alex asked. 'What I mean is, did the ghost touch you? Make physical contact?'

'I – uh . . . no,' Mrs Kapoor said.

'No?' said Alex, his whole body deflating at the realisation that there wasn't going to be a simple way of proving to Mrs Kapoor that her attacker had been corporeal. 'Well, then how did it render you unconscious?'

Mrs Kapoor thought for a moment. 'When I saw it outside, I screamed and stumbled backwards into the room. It came after me. It came . . . towards me. I did everything I could to keep my distance from it. Edging backwards every time it inched closer. But then I tripped. I turned over onto my front and scrambled to get back up as quickly as I could. But then . . .'

'Then . . .?' Alex pushed, determined to have his answer.

'Then something hit my head. Not flesh. Not a hand or a fist. Something hard. Yes . . . see? Blood.' Mrs Kapoor touched the back of her head. Her fingers were spotted with red but it seemed the blow she had taken was nowhere near as hard as the one Mr Kapoor had received. Or, if Alex's theory was correct, that he claimed he had received.

'That thing,' said Mrs Kapoor, 'it knocked me out. But it . . . it didn't touch me with its hands. I don't know how it moved the object. But it was a thing. It was not a person.'

'Right, OK, bloody hell, Donny's going to have a field day with this,' Alex said.

'What?' said Mrs Kapoor.

'Nothing,' said Alex, possibly realising that they didn't have the time to stand here arguing over the existence or non-existence of ghosts. 'The main thing is, you're alive and we can sort that injury out,' he added, offering both his hands to help Mrs Kapoor to her feet.

Mrs Kapoor dusted off her suit but then something about Alex's words seemed to strike her.

'What did you mean by those words? Why would I not be alive?' Mrs Kapoor said, her voice suddenly taking on a note of suspicion.

'Well, um, though, as I mentioned your family is safe and, well, I'm afraid something terrible has happened, to James,' said Alex.

'James? What? What's happened?' said Mrs Kapoor, her voice on the brink of being frantic. That was much more emotion than Maddie would have expected to see if James was nothing more than a passing acquaintance that Mrs Kapoor saw off and on during visits to The Merry Monarch.

'I'm afraid there's no good way of breaking this news. He's been murdered,' Alex said, as softly as he could.

'Mur—' Mrs Kapoor began, but then her eyes narrowed. 'Where is my husband?'

'He's downstairs with everyone else, including Zainab,' said Alex. 'Why do you ask?'

'I want to see him, at once,' was the only response Mrs Kapoor was willing to offer.

Alex looked at Maddie in such a way that she knew he was reading something into this statement, and Maddie couldn't much blame him for that. On learning that James was dead, Mrs Kapoor hadn't asked any of the expected questions, such as how James died or if anyone else was hurt. Her thoughts had immediately turned to her husband and, from the tone in Mrs Kapoor's voice, it seemed obvious she suspected just what they did: that Mr Kapoor had taken action to make sure James didn't come near his daughter or his wife ever again.

CHAPTER EIGHTEEN

'I told you it were a ghost,' said Don, folding his arms across his chest with a certain degree of indignation as he listened to Mrs Kapoor's version of the events that had unfolded upstairs when all the lights went out.

'He's right,' said Sita, who was sitting at a table next to the newly reunited Kapoors. 'He did try to tell you. But no, you wouldn't listen. Your mind is closed, completely closed off to possibility. Just like the politicians when it comes to the climate crisis. The ignorance in this world never ceases to amaze me.'

'If I'd witnessed what Mrs Kapoor did, you would have had another dead body on your hands,' said Mrs Fazakerley. 'My heart wouldn't stand a shock like that.'

Alex, somewhat exasperated, rubbed his eyes and ran a hand through his sandy hair. It was clear to Maddie that he was going to have to waste yet more time debunking this ghost theory, so it was very likely clear to him too.

When they had made it back downstairs with Mrs Kapoor, Zainab had been overjoyed to see her mother was alive and, apart from a bump on the head, unharmed. Mr Kapoor had also tried to greet his wife with open arms, but received a cold reception with Mrs Kapoor refusing to embrace him in return.

It had not taken long for Mrs Kapoor to relay her story about the ghostly figure, and it seemed Don wasn't going to waste a minute in seizing his moment of glory.

'For God's sake, Don, come on,' said Alex, 'the mask is missing off the wall. Never mind how a ghost would take the mask off the wall, I'm assuming you think you've got that covered with your Patrick Swayze theory. But why, why would a ghost need to cover its face? You can't take a ghost to court. You can't lock a ghost up in prison. If a ghost committed these crimes, and I am definitely not saying one did, why would it need to conceal its identity? It makes no sense.'

This gave Don pause. He looked flailingly over at Sita for a moment. It seemed to Maddie that, given Don's crush on her, he wanted to find a way to hold onto this ghost theory. And find a way he did. 'Maybe, the ghost isn't yer mother,' said Don. 'Let's face it, from what everyone says, yer mother was a nice lady. Wouldn't 'urt a fly.'

'That much is true,' said Mrs Fazakerley. 'I knew Alice for years and she was never anything but lovely.'

'Right,' said Don. 'So then the question becomes, why would she be killin' people from beyond the grave?'

'Does it?' Alex said. There was no missing the fact that he was almost out of patience with this ghost business. As he said earlier, that was just what the killer wanted people to think. And wasting time indulging in the idea only gave the person who was really behind it opportunity to plan their escape.

'Yes, it does,' said Don, unwilling to be deterred by Alex's tone. 'And maybe she isn't. Maybe the spirit is someone else who is also dead, right? But yer mother and that ghost 'ave 'ad a falling-out in the afterlife so, this ghost is tryin' to frame your mother.'

'Really?' was all Alex could bring himself to say in response to that. 'At this point, I'm amazed you haven't started quoting from *The Muppet Christmas Carol.* How did you qualify for the same police force I did?'

'Well, they said I'd proven myself good at followin' orders, sir,' Don said, clearly wounded by Alex's question, though Maddie thought it a perfectly reasonable one under the circumstances.

'Yeah, I wasn't actually asking, Donny. You are very good at following orders,' Alex said.

'And I aced my physical, twenty-twenty vision, that's

what the doc said,' Don said, in a voice that was barely audible.

'Yes, yes, I know, I know,' Alex said.

'And during the siftin' questionnaire, I tested 'igh on bein' innovative and open-minded,' Don said, his voice, if it were possible, even quieter than before.

'Yes, alright, Don,' Alex said, putting a hand on his colleague's shoulder. 'I'm sorry. But despite what Mrs Kapoor said, we've got to move on to human suspects here.'

'I wouldn't be so quick to move on if I were you. Don's theory can't be ruled out as a possibility,' said Sita, 'The beyond is a very strange place, we can't pretend to know much about it at all. Anything could happen on that side of the veil.'

'Look, think what you want. But my name's not Peter Venkman. I'm not a bloody ghostbuster, I'm a copper. All I can deal with are the flesh and blood suspects. Spirits from the beyond are outside our jurisdiction, got it?' said Alex.

'Sir,' Don said, finally submitting to Alex's chain of command on this matter rather than Sita's baiting.

'OK, I'm going to interview people individually in the kitchen while—' Alex began, but he didn't get to finish his sentence.

'Inspector Beaumont, Inspector Beaumont!' Mrs Kapoor shouted before hurrying towards him.

Alex frowned. Looking for Mrs Kapoor had been a relatively swift job with a positive outcome but it had still got in the way of Alex actually finding out who was behind James's murder. Maddie imagined he was more than anxious to get on with the interviews without any further hindrance. It seemed, however, that his wish was about to be denied.

'Yes, Mrs Kapoor?' Alex said. It was obvious he was doing his best to be patient, but there was no missing the edge to his tone.

'I put my hands in my pockets to make sure nothing was stolen during the attack and—'

'I'm afraid we don't have time to deal with a theft just now, Mrs Kapoor,' Alex interrupted. 'If something important is missing, we might be able to recover it during the course of the murder investigation, but for now—'

'No, no, no, nothing is missing,' Mrs Kapoor interrupted in return. 'The opposite. I found this in my pocket. It wasn't there before.'

Mrs Kapoor handed a small black envelope to Alex, which had already been opened.

'Did you open the envelope?' Alex said, taking hold of it for himself.

'Yes, I wanted to see what it was. I didn't know if it was something I had forgotten about or, well, if it had been put there by somebody I knew.' Mrs Kapoor blushed as she said this and Maddie had an idea why. If their theory about James and Mrs Kapoor having some kind of secret tryst was true, she might have thought it some kind of message from him.

'But it is neither of those things,' Mrs Kapoor said. 'It is a message from the killer. When it attacked me, it must have placed the message in my pocket.'

Gasps flittered around the room at this revelation.

Alex opened the envelope and, making sure to only touch the very sides of the paper enclosed, read the contents with a grimace.

Taking a deep breath, Alex looked over at Mr Kapoor. 'You were also knocked unconscious. Anything unfamiliar in your pockets, Mr Kapoor?' he asked.

Mr Kapoor shoved his hands in his pockets but came out only with a set of keys and a wallet. He shook his head in response to the question he'd been asked and this made Alex's frown deepen. Did the fact that Mr Kapoor didn't have an envelope on his person make it more or less likely that he was telling the truth about being knocked out by a shadowy figure? Or did the fact that Mrs Kapoor's wound wasn't as serious and that the killer just so happened to plant a message on her, rather than her husband, make her the more likely assailant faking their injuries? Or were they somehow both in this together?

For the life of her, Maddie couldn't decide. How Alex did this for a living was utterly beyond her.

'Hang on just a minute,' Alex said, before disappearing into the snug that still housed James's body. A moment or two later he emerged with another black envelope. 'This was in James's pocket,' Alex explained, opening the envelope to read the contents.

'What is it, lad?' said Mickey. 'Does it give anything away about who the killer was?'

Alex shook his head. 'Not directly. But it is a note from someone asking James to meet them in the very snug he was murdered in.'

'I didn't see him enter the room and go into the snug,' said Curtis. 'And alright, I wasn't watching that part of the room but you'd think he would have said something if he saw me sitting there alone.'

'The note instructs him to be discreet,' said Alex, eyeing Mrs Kapoor. 'To make sure he isn't seen. So, whoever he thought he was meeting in here, it was possibly somebody he wasn't supposed to be meeting. He might have waited until you were looking the other way, Curtis, and then sneaked round into the snug. One thing is for sure. He was lured to this spot by whoever is behind the murder.'

Maddie felt her muscles tense at this revelation. Once again, she looked at Alex and thought about what Jeannie had said: *all of that anger has to go somewhere.* Previously, she had talked herself out of the idea that Alex was responsible for James's death because there would have been no way of him knowing that his stepbrother was just on the other side of the kitchen door, waiting in the dark to be picked off. But if James was lured, well, anyone could have put that note in his pocket at some earlier point in the evening. Including Alex.

'What about the note from Mrs Kapoor's pocket? What does that say?' said Sita.

'Yes! We're trapped here with this monster, if it's a message from the killer we've got a right to know what it says,' said Mrs Fazakerley.

Alex sighed. He clearly thought that sharing the contents of the envelope wasn't a good idea but, looking around the room at the faces of those he knew from the village, and Maddie's with them, he probably knew that he didn't stand much hope of keeping everyone's cooperation if he kept the information to himself.

'It's . . . it's written like one of the scavenger hunt clues,' said Alex.

'Scavenger 'unt?' said Mickey. 'Why the bloody 'ell would it be written like that?'

'I don't know, Dad. That's just what I'm seeing,' said Alex.

'Well, go on, what does it say?' said Sita. 'Like Mrs Fazakerley says, we've got a right to know.'

'Look,' said Alex. 'It's sensitive what's written in here. I have to show it to Dad and Sofia first. They can decide if I should share it with you. But if they say no, that's the end of the matter. No objections. Given the nature of the note, that's the right thing to do.'

With an apologetic look, Alex placed the piece of paper down on the table in front of Mickey and Sofia. 'Try not to touch the paper,' Alex said. 'There might be DNA evidence on it.'

The pair nodded and began reading. While Sofia only let out a stifled sob, Mickey's face turned red. The next thing Maddie noticed was a glower setting in and his teeth gritting. When he'd finished, he was quiet a moment but then he yelled out and stood up so quick he knocked his chair over backwards.

'Someone in 'ere is responsible for writing this. You want to know what it says, the rest of you,' Mickey practically roared out his words and grabbed the piece of paper off the table, completely ignoring Alex's prior instructions not to touch it. ''Ere it is, 'ere's what you want: *This mouse scuttled away from 'is family 'ome, from 'is little boy and 'is marital bed. Twenty years 'ave passed, and Vengeance 'as come. Now 'is bastard boy lies dead.*'

Despite the anger he'd displayed at the beginning of his speech, Mickey's voice broke as he read that last part out. And how could it not?

Maddie, for one, was shocked by what she had heard. It wasn't just the uncouth way in which the note spoke about James, who now sat dead in the corner. Though that was bad enough. It was the mocking tone to the wording. The killer, whoever they were, wanted Mickey and Sofia to feel shame over the fact that their partnership had had consequences for other people. As far as Maddie had understood, Mickey's departure hadn't been in any way related to the death of Alex's mum, Alice. There was a good ten years between Mickey leaving and Alice dying. But there was an insinuation behind the words that Alice never got over the betrayal of Mickey leaving her and wanted to unleash some kind of revenge on him and Sofia.

The note, and everything else about this evening, was unnerving to say the least, but Maddie wasn't about to let the human beings in the room off the hook that easy and put these events down to some kind of paranormal disturbance. That's what the killer wanted everyone to think; after listening to the wording of that note, there was no denying that. But it seemed to Maddie that the most likely scenario was that somebody who knew the family history was using it to manipulate them all in order to get away with murdering James for some other reason entirely. Some motive that had yet to be uncovered.

If that was the case, and it was certainly better than believing that the murder and the attacks on Mr and Mrs

Kapoor were committed by a ghost, then the killer, whoever they were, had overplayed their hand in this instance. The perfume and the engagement ring, those were relatively subtle touches that might play tricks on anybody's senses on a cold winter night once the power had gone out. But the note? This proved they were dealing with a human killer who was just trying to pull the wool over their eyes. Granted, Maddie hadn't had a close look at the paper Alex presented to Mickey, but she had seen enough to know it was a handwritten note, i.e. a note written by somebody with hands. Maddie was sure that Don would have some wild theory about how the ghost could move a pen using only the power of its mind but Maddie had yet to see any scientific evidence for such things. So, for now at least, she was on Team Suspect Is Corporeal.

'How much more evidence do we need before we understand that this is a ghost at work?' said Sita.

As Sita spoke, something struck Maddie that hadn't before. Largely because she had been so preoccupied with the poor relations between Mr Kapoor and James. Not to mention the seeds of suspicion that had grown from Alex's history and behaviour. But Sita was a specialist in ghostly matters. And just happened to be at The Merry Monarch on the night that a ghostly figure – or somebody dressed as a ghostly figure – was murdering and assaulting people. Moreover, she just happened, at this very moment, to be seated right next to the Kapoors. Could that be mere coincidence? From where she was sitting it would have been very easy for her to slip that envelope into Mrs Kapoor's pocket without anyone noticing.

But then, what motive could Sita have for killing James? Maddie certainly hadn't come across one so far. On the other hand, if there was one, given the way gossip worked in small villages, Maddie wagered it wouldn't be difficult to find out what it was.

CHAPTER NINETEEN

'Right, that's it. Everyone sit down and shut up, now!' Alex shouted, in a voice more booming than Maddie ever would have thought him capable of.

After Sita's comment, an argument had erupted between almost everyone in the room. Mickey and Sofia. Sita and Alex. Don and Mrs Fazakerley. Mr and Mrs Kapoor and Zainab. Curtis and Jeannie were the only two people sitting quietly like good children, shaking their heads at the rest of the rabble.

At the sound of Alex's command, however, the whole room did hush down and everyone found a seat. Perhaps because they knew this silly talk about ghosts was highly unlikely to stick and if they found themselves on the wrong side of the investigating officer, it might not end well for them. As the room quieted, the sound of the howling blizzard outside became noticeable once more.

Maddie couldn't remember the last time she'd heard the wind make a noise like that. She remembered too, from her walk to the pub earlier, just how cold it was out there. She shivered as her ears fixed on a tree branch that rapped against the window. Maddie was a logical person but between the remote location of the pub, the racket made by the storm and the murder that had taken place, nobody would have blamed her for getting caught up in this talk of ghosts.

'We are not going to point the finger at a ghost,' Alex said, 'until every human in this room has been interviewed first. If, after questioning, there are no obvious suspects then maybe we can start looking to the beyond for answers.'

A discontented mutter flittered around the room, but nobody dared challenge Alex directly on this. 'Don is going to keep an eye on everyone out here while the interviews continue to take place,' Alex said to the group. 'Mr Kapoor, I'd like you to come with me please.'

'Why me?' said Mr Kapoor.

Alex sighed. 'I could explain why you, if you'd like, Mr Kapoor. I could explain that in front of everyone, or you can come with me into the kitchen and I can tell you in private. Which is it going to be?'

Mr Kapoor looked around the room and then, with a scowl, rose to his feet and followed Alex into the kitchen.

Slowly, Maddie sidled over to the table where Jeannie and Curtis were still sitting.

'Stupid question, I know, but how are you two doing?' said Maddie. She couldn't dive right into asking about Sita. Somehow, she had to make the topic come up naturally in conversation.

'Relieved Mrs Kapoor's in one piece,' Jeannie said, making sure to keep her voice low. Like everyone else in the room, minus the killer, her heart was probably going out to Zainab right now. She was extremely young to be caught up in a business as grisly as this and everyone was being quite careful about what they said within her earshot. Particularly after Mr Kapoor's comments about the possible demise of her mother had shaken her so much earlier on.

'Agreed,' said Curtis. 'After all that has happened this evening. What you discovered in the drying room, well it could have been a lot worse.'

'She's convinced it was a ghost who attacked her,' said Maddie with a shake of her head.

'A ghost indeed,' Curtis said. 'It would be funny if it weren't so tragic that that's the best we can come up with when it comes to theories about the culprit. Granted the killer is doing their best to make it look as though a ghost is involved, but honestly, I've had to reassess my opinion of some of the people here tonight based on how adamant they are that a spectre is behind the crime.'

'Well, yes, Don for one is pretty sold on the idea,' Maddie said with a small smile. 'Though how much of that is an earnest belief in ghosts and how much is a bid to win Sita's affection, I'm not sure.'

'Knowin' our Donny, that ratio is probably twenty/eighty,' said Jeannie.

'He does seem to be rather keen for that to be the story behind all this,' said Curtis.

'Did Don and Sita know James very well?' Maddie asked, as casually as she could. This wasn't exactly a subtle way of breaking into the topic of Sita's relationship with James but Maddie had lost patience with the adroit route to getting information out of her companions quicker than she'd expected to.

'Donny knew 'im well enough from comin' in 'ere and kickin' about with Alex,' said Jeannie. 'But they weren't close. And as for Sita, well, should I even go there, Curtis?'

'Might not be good form with the chap sitting dead over there in the corner,' said Curtis. 'Maybe just the abridged version?'

Jeannie nodded. 'Sita went on a few dates with James.'

Clearly Maddie had accidentally pulled a face at this as Jeannie quickly added: 'You needn't look like that, love, it's alright for you city slickers, lots of men to choose from. When you live and work in small places it's slim pickin's, it is. One of the many reasons I've stayed single all these years.'

'What about meeting people online?' Maddie said.

'Well, say you do meet someone online. It don't ever go anywhere. You might 'ave a few dates but eventually if you like each other, sooner or later, the question of movin' in comes up. And will 'e want to move to the back of beyond for you? Probably not. And I'll do a lot of things when necessary but one thing I won't do is leave the Dales for a man.'

Maddie chuckled at this. She wished she'd been so headstrong about staying up in Edinburgh after she split with her fud of a boyfriend. Particularly when she found herself in such a dire situation, it would be easy to drift off into thoughts about the shapely peaks of the Cairngorms and the river spires of Inverness. But she couldn't be drawn into a bout of homesickness right now. There was a reason she'd started down this line of conversation, and she needed to stay on that track.

'Fair enough, I understand. So, I take it things didn't end well with James and Sita?' said Maddie. Not that this surprised her in the least. James might have had good looks on his side but he obviously wasn't the kind of person suited to monogamy.

Jeannie lowered her voice even further. 'Sita, bless her, is a bit of a romantic but she's never found the right person. She must not look at our Donny that way because, of course, 'e'd 'ave her in an 'eartbeat. So eventually, James must 'ave made a move and, thinkin' she had nothin' to lose, she agreed to go out with him.'

'Did he break her heart?' said Maddie, imagining the damage a person like James could do to someone with grand romantic notions.

'I'm not sure about that, exactly,' said Jeannie. 'But things got, well, you know, biblical between them and the mornin' after Sita wakes up, James is gone and she can't find a ring of sentimental value. Belonged to 'er great-grandmother, I think.'

Maddie winced. 'Oh God, don't tell me he stole from her?'

'James denied it flat out, even though everyone knows 'e were up to 'is ears in gamblin' debt and probably pawned the damn thing. Sita swore on all the weird and wonderful powers she prays to that the ring were gone and James were the only one with the opportunity to take it,' said Jeannie.

'So, what happened then?' said Maddie.

'Nothin',' Jeannie said.

'Nothing?' Maddie parroted.

'Sita reported the theft and Don looked into it for her,' said Curtis. 'But he didn't have any evidence that James had taken the ring. James even allowed the police to search his personal effects. I didn't practise criminal law myself back when I was a solicitor, but you don't have to be an expert to know that the police can't prosecute without evidence.'

'But, Sita still comes to The Merry Monarch and sees James here, or should I say saw James here, even after everything that had happened?' said Maddie.

'Not much choice,' said Jeannie. 'The last bus is four o'clock. Such is the government investment in infrastructure up 'ere. So, if you want to do something social on an evening and don't 'ave a car, The Merry Monarch's the only place in walkin' distance. And besides, like most people round 'ere, Sita understands that James is very much 'is own person and it's Mickey who owns this business. She wouldn't slight Mickey just because James 'ad done her wrong. Mickey would 'ave no bloody customers left if the village operated like that.'

'I see,' Maddie said, thinking over everything Jeannie had told her. Of course, Jeannie could be right, maybe Sita simply had no choice but to frequent The Merry Monarch, and maybe she didn't want to punish Mickey for James's sins. But it was also possible that she was keeping her friends close and her enemies closer. For there was yet another odd coincidence linking to Sita in Jeannie's story.

The ring.

Alex hadn't pulled a bracelet out of James's mouth. Or

an earring. Or a necklace. He'd found a ring in there. A ring of great sentimental value. Just like the one Sita had lost when James spent the night.

Maddie couldn't account for how Sita might have come across that particular engagement ring. But who better to pin a murder on a ghost than somebody who claimed to speak to them on a regular basis?

Sighing, Maddie shook her head. Would somebody really go to all this trouble, murder and all, over a piece of jewellery? Even one that had significance to them? Especially when they knew two police officers were going to be in the building when they did it. But then Maddie thought about the stories she'd covered at the paper over the last year or so and, had to admit, she'd seen people kill for a lot less and go to even greater lengths to cover it up.

'Yes, I don't envy Alex the task of finding out who did this,' said Curtis. 'I never had anything against the lad personally because we never really crossed paths except in here. But there are quite a few people out there who James has wronged over the years. A few of them in this room.'

''E was only a kid though,' said Jeannie, her eyes watery. 'I mean, I know 'e were old enough to know better and Lord knows Mickey and Sofia 'ave done their best to put 'im on a more righteous path, shall we say, more than once. But the scrapes 'e got into, well they were just that really. Scrapes. Nowt worth killin' over. And to think the person who's done it is trying to exploit our family history . . . I . . . I really don't know 'ow our Alex is holdin' it together when everyone's walkin' around blithely talkin' about 'is mother's ghost.'

'It's a terrible thing to do,' Curtis said, while Barkley also gave out a yap that sounded like agreement with his master.

'I feel for Alex, I really do,' Jeannie said. 'Not just because 'e's now got to find out who killed 'is stepbrother but also because 'e's been through enough without all this, 'asn't 'e? Dad left. Mum dying. James comin' along and taking 'is place to a certain extent.'

'Is that really how it is?' said Maddie.

'Oh, Mickey loves Alex, don't get me wrong. But 'e did leave, and that changes things. Even on just a financial nuts and bolts level. Sofia and Mickey are going to leave this place and the money they've made to their son when they go.'

'What do you know about that?' The question was almost spat at Jeannie and Maddie was shocked to turn and see that it was Sofia who had asked the question. The voice she had just heard was a far cry from the warm, welcoming tones the woman had used when talking to Maddie about her home cooking earlier in the evening.

'I-I-I, oh, I'm sorry, Sofia, I shouldn't be talkin' about

things like that. I don't know what possessed me,' said Jeannie.

'You're bloody right you shouldn't,' Sofia said, jabbing a finger into Jeannie's shoulder with such force that Jeannie cowered.

'Unless you're a solicitor and your name is Curtis Clarke,' Sofia continued, waving a hand in Curtis's direction, 'you've no idea who Mickey is leaving his worldly possessions to and it's none of your business anyhow. You're not in the will, I can tell you.'

'I-I-I wouldn't expect to be,' said Jeannie. 'Really, Sofia, I'm sorry. I was thinkin' about Alex, that's all. I shouldn't 'ave said anything. Not after what's just happened.'

Sofia grimaced at Jeannie and stalked back to the table she'd been sitting at with Mickey.

'Oh dear, oh dear,' Jeannie said, putting her head in her hands. 'What 'ave I done? When will I learn to keep my big mouth shut? Now I've upset a grieving mother. I don't think it gets much lower than this.'

'We all put our foot in it sometimes,' said Maddie. 'She's probably in part taking her anger out on you after what's happened to James.'

'Yeah, yeah, you're probably right,' said Jeannie, but she didn't sound convinced. And neither was Maddie.

She could understand that Sofia's emotions would be running high on a night like tonight. Her only son had suffered a violent death. Perhaps it was understandable that she would be angry at hearing somebody talking about financial matters, especially *their* financial matters, when the person who was likely the sole beneficiary was no longer around to receive their inheritance. But there was something about the ferocity of Sofia's reaction that didn't quite sit right with Maddie. She had practically bullied Jeannie into submission on the topic when all she needed to have done was tell her she didn't want to hear any talk about that.

Maddie looked again at Sofia, at those blue eyes that had seemed to sparkle when she first saw them. As the woman said something to Mickey and gestured over to Jeannie, there was an iciness to them that hadn't been there before.

Rubbing her hand over her face, Maddie decided that she must be tired and incredibly overanxious to be thinking along these lines. The likelihood was that Sofia just thought Jeannie's comments insensitive under the circumstances and wasn't able to control her response because of what had happened to James. Yes, Maddie told herself, it had to be that. There was no doubt from the way Sofia had reacted when Alex broke the awful news that, despite his many flaws, Sofia had loved her son dearly. And what possible motive could a loving mother have for killing her only child?

CHAPTER TWENTY

While Alex was interviewing Mr Kapoor, Maddie, Curtis and Jeannie had cleared it with Don to let Barkley out of the back door of the pub to relieve himself. The hound was not thrilled to be ushered out into the snow but seemed to understand their rationale for doing so and went about his business in a timely manner.

While standing there at the open door, Maddie took in deep breaths of the glacial air. Being trapped in a pub with a potential murderer wasn't anyone's idea of fun. But for a person who was claustrophobic, the ordeal was made all the more torturous.

Thus, Maddie stood for as long as she could on the pub doorstep while Jeannie and Curtis stood nearby, rubbing their arms and blowing hot air into their hands to stay warm. In the back yard, Mickey and Sofia had hung outdoor Christmas bulbs in an area that she assumed was used as a beer garden in the summer, and a space for smokers to stand in the winter. Gazing into the green and red bulbs, she began to wonder if Christmas would ever feel the same to her after all this. How would she get past the memory of seeing James's body sitting in that snug? Or the scream he had let out before he died?

Maddie shook her head. She had no answers. Not today. Maybe by next Christmas she would have some idea of any long-lasting effects this tragedy might have on her. Though she could have done with more time in the cool air, the weather only seemed to worsen in the few minutes they'd had the back door open and the ghastly howling of the wind and the groans of trees being bent and blown beyond their limits soon saw the trio usher the dog in from his constitutional, closing the heavy door behind them to ward off the elements.

About thirty minutes later, a somewhat deflated-looking Mr Kapoor emerged from the kitchen, closely followed by Alex. A certain hush fell over the group as the pair made their way back into the pub. As though they were expecting some kind of announcement. Instead, however, Mr Kapoor shuffled over to where his family were seated and Alex called Curtis next for interview.

Since Jeannie was in the toilets with Sita and Mrs Fazakerley, this would leave Maddie sitting on her own. Given her mild case of claustrophobia, however, and the fact she was cooped up at The Merry Monarch with these strangers for goodness knows how long, she would be thankful of a few moments to herself.

Moreover, if Curtis did have anything to do with James's demise, Maddie was fairly sure Alex would be able to recognise it when he questioned him. He seemed to know Curtis quite well, so any unusual behaviour would surely stand out.

Unfortunately, Maddie wasn't going to have that question settled anytime soon as there was yet more drama from the Kapoor family.

'Why are you interviewing anyone else?' Mrs Kapoor said to Alex, loud enough for everyone left in the room to hear. 'Why are you bothering with that? Don't you know my husband is the killer?'

Maddie's eyes widened. This was quite the U-turn in terms of what Mrs Kapoor had been telling them earlier on. Yes, she had seemed suspicious of her husband once they'd told her James was dead. But she had also been quite adamant that she was attacked by a ghost. Seemingly, she'd had time to think more carefully about matters and, between the mask being missing and the notes found in her pocket and in James's, decided that the ghost really was human after all. Not just human, but her husband. Maddie turned to see what Alex was going to make of this statement.

Unbelievably, Alex was completely unruffled by Mrs Kapoor's words. Unlike her daughter Zainab.

'Mother, what are you saying?' said Zainab. 'Why are you saying that about Dad?'

'Yes, Javeria, why would you say such a thing?' Mr Kapoor said, his brown eyes betraying just how wounded he was by her accusation. 'I wanted the boy to stay away from Zainab because he is – was – bad news. Everybody knew that. It was no secret and I didn't try to hide my feelings about it. But I would never kill a person over that. I would never kill anybody full stop.'

'I wish I could believe you,' Mrs Kapoor said. 'But the motive has nothing to do with Zainab. You thought you knew something, about James and me. That's why you killed him.'

Mr Kapoor threw his arms up in the air in exasperation. 'I have no idea what you are talking about. What did I know? You tell me, what did I know?'

'That he loved me,' Mrs Kapoor said, with a cool flatness to her voice.

'He loved you?' said Mr Kapoor.

'No, he loved me,' Zainab said.

Mrs Kapoor shook her head and put her hand on her daughter's arm. 'No, my darling. I am sorry, I did not welcome his affections, nor did I act on them. But he told me last Christmas that he loved me. Your father must have found out somehow. Thought that we were having some kind of affair, which we were not. And he took matters into his own hands.'

'I did no such thing, Javeria, I didn't even know the boy liked you. I thought he was trying to court Zainab, that's why I didn't want him on our team tonight. But, for the sake of saving face and avoiding arguments in public, I allowed him to sit with us. And now you air all of these accusations, in front of everyone. This is the first I am hearing of any of this. That's why he was looking at you so intensely earlier on? I thought he was just trying to manipulate you into siding against me when it came to Zainab,' said Mr Kapoor.

'He was not in love with you!' Zainab half-screamed at her mother. 'He told me I was beautiful!'

Maddie couldn't help but raise an eyebrow at this. How many women had heard James tell them they were beautiful? Granted, he'd called Maddie hot rather than beautiful but it was simply a variation on a theme. That old tactic some men used of making a woman feel good about themselves so they might be better disposed to sleep with them. Maddie was sorry for Zainab, that she was too young to spot a man like that. A man who had told her own mother the year before that he loved her. And who knew if that was even true? From all she'd heard, she wouldn't have put it past James to go after a married woman for the sport of it. Knowing that he'd never have to commit to her because she was already committed to somebody else.

'I am afraid James only doted on you because he was frightened that your father knew about his feelings for me. He worried that there would be consequences in my marriage and since he cared about me, well, it was a ruse to dispel any suspicions,' said Mrs Kapoor. 'I begged him to choose anyone else but he insisted that if he was flirtatious with you, there was no way your father would ever suspect he held affections for me.'

'This is the most humiliating thing that has ever happened to me. I hate you!' Zainab screamed in her mother's face. She was about to go running off upstairs but Alex caught her arm as she flew by him.

'I'm sorry, Zainab. I know you've been through so much tonight, but you can't go upstairs alone. We still don't know who the killer is or where they are. It's not safe.'

Zainab pulled her arm away from Alex's grip forcefully enough to make it clear that she didn't appreciate being told what to do at a time like this. She did, however, abide by Alex's instructions and sat herself back down in the pub, as far away from her mother and father as was humanly possible.

Maddie had never seen family drama aired so publicly. She had once listened to her parents argue all the way to a friend's party in the car, watched them dote on each other for several hours at the gathering and then resume their vicious argument the second they took her back to the vehicle. If Maddie's mum ever suspected her dad of murder, a policeman would only hear about it after she had torn several strips off him in private.

Alex approached the Kapoors and looked hard at Mrs Kapoor. 'Do you have any hard evidence to back up the accusation you're making against your husband? Because it's a serious one.'

Mrs Kapoor's eyes widened at this, as if she had only just realised the gravity of all she had just said. Slowly, she turned towards her husband and then looked back at Alex.

'No,' she said. 'I spoke out of turn. Hakim, my husband . . . he doesn't seem to know that James had any feelings for me. I just . . . his death is such a shock my mind ran away with me, and I thought the worst.'

'Given all that has come to light, you'll both be accompanying me and DC Maynard to the station tomorrow so we can get all of this on official record. I've witnessed all that has passed between you, as have Maddie and Curtis and your daughter, so I hope we won't see a change in your story come daylight.'

Mrs Kapoor shook her head. 'No, I will explain myself. I will explain why I said the things I said.'

Alex turned away from the pair, strode over to Zainab

and sat beside her. Considering everything she'd been through, and given how young she was, it seemed that Alex was doing what he could to spare her a hardline interrogation in the kitchen. Maddie smiled; even under the insanely difficult circumstances he was facing, Alex was still able to spare a thought for somebody as vulnerable as Zainab was right now.

Curtis grabbed Maddie's arm, startling her out of her thoughts.

'Oh God, Curtis, you scared the life out of me. What is it?' Maddie said.

Curtis waved his hands in a downward motion to indicate to Maddie that he needed her to speak a lot more quietly than that just now.

'What's wrong?' she hissed at him.

'Sorry. Didn't mean to startle you, my dear. But with Mr and Mrs Kapoor out of the running,' Curtis murmured, 'I think I know who the killer is.'

'What?' Maddie almost-whispered. 'Who?'

Curtis shook his head. 'I need to retrieve something first, from the cellar.'

'What? You can't just go on a ramble down to the cellar on your own. A) there's a killer on the loose, and B) Alex has insisted everyone has to stay in here,' said Maddie.

'I know all that. But a certain person visited my offices when I was in the process of making up Mickey's will.

They were trying to casually probe for information but of course I wasn't to be drawn. Mickey keeps all his papers in the cellar. If we're to confront the killer, I need something to back up what I'm saying. Supporting documental evidence, and if I'm right then the truth concerns Alex greatly,' said Curtis.

'What do you mean by that?' said Maddie.

'There's no time now. Listen, I'm going to go in for my interview with Alex. When I come out, I'm going to try and slip down to the cellar. I remember from last year's scavenger hunt, there's a secret passageway just near the lavatories that leads there. Come to think of it, I think it's the same one Mr Kapoor ordered James to search for scavenger hunt clues. At any rate, it should take me less than five minutes. I just need you to cover for me for that long. Alex will be in the kitchen interviewing his next suspect. I just need you to distract Don while I slip out. It'll take me no time at all, with a bit of luck he won't even notice that I'm missing, and then the horrible truth of this business will be out.'

'Why don't you just tell Alex about your suspicions when he interviews you?' said Maddie. She still wasn't sure about Curtis. He *had* been the only person in the room when James was unceremoniously offed. Why did he want to engage with all this cloak and dagger stuff?

'Because, if I'm right, Alex won't want to believe what

I've got to say. He's been through so much already, lost so much already. He will very likely dismiss the idea outright. And, Maddie, I have a strong suspicion that I'm right on the money with this. So I can't afford to be derailed. I hate to say it but, in the spirit of "trust no one", there's also a slim chance that if it is the person I think it is, then Alex may also be involved in all this somehow,' said Curtis.

Maddie took in a deep breath and let it out slowly.

Alex seemed such a straight arrow, one of the good people of the world. Yes, Jeannie had raised some red flags, but there wasn't really anything she'd said that couldn't be put down to the grief of losing his mother. The last thing Maddie wanted to think was that he might be in some way corrupt and had abused his position to get rid of an unwanted sibling. But, again, this wasn't the first time this evening that such a theory was being brought to Maddie's attention. And Jeannie had raised her concerns with Maddie separately, away from Curtis, so he had no idea that Jeannie had already raised the matter of Alex's complicated history with James and that it might have something to do with this.

Curtis made a move to get up, but Maddie stopped him.

'Wait a minute, wait a minute. This doesn't feel right. You're going to sneak down to Mickey's cellar. And retrieve, what? Mickey's will? Why on earth does he even keep the will in the wine cellar when he's got an office space? Shouldn't Mickey be involved in this given it's his property?'

'I understand your reservations,' said Curtis. 'But I drew up the will. It's not my property, but I have seen it before so no confidentiality is being broken. Mickey keeps it down there rather than in the office because in the holiday seasons he takes on extra occasional staff and they are always in and out of the office. I think he also didn't want James getting a look at it. So, he told me he was going to hide it. And yes, I could go over there and alert Mickey to what I'm doing. But then he'd probably alert Sofia.'

'And that would be . . . bad?' Maddie asked, trying to get to the bottom of whatever it was Curtis wouldn't say outright.

'The more people who know about it, the more likely it is that the suspected killer will either hear about the ploy directly or sense something is amiss. And we need the element of surprise on our side.'

Maddie thought about Curtis's words. She couldn't deny he was right about it being prudent to keep the number of people involved to a minimum. Regardless of a murder having been committed, this was still a small village pub and, as such, gossip and whispers would spread like wildfire round here. The last thing they wanted to do was give the killer a heads-up that they'd figured out their true identity.

'Alright,' Maddie said, though at this point she had no idea whether going along with Curtis's scheme was a good idea. Could she trust him any more than she could trust Alex? 'But, Curtis, you have to tell me who you think the killer is.'

'It's . . .' he began, but then stopped himself. 'Later,' he said.

'What's happenin' later?' said Jeannie, who had returned from the toilet and plonked herself back down in the seat she had been sitting in before.

'Well, um, the thing is,' Curtis said, stalling for time while he thought of something. 'Maddie was just asking about how Alice had died, and I didn't think you'd want to sit through that particular story just now.'

If it wouldn't have given away their clandestine plan, or at least strongly hinted at it, Maddie would have shot Curtis her most disgruntled look at this point. Couldn't he have come up with something more sensitive than that? Now Jeannie was going to think she'd been prying into their family history. Like that's what anyone needed right now!

Still, Maddie conceded that Curtis couldn't have told Jeannie what they'd really been talking about. It was downright cruel to draw any more people into this plot than necessary. Maddie's anxiety levels were already rising at the thought of having to cover for Curtis while he was down in the pub cellar. It would be just her luck for someone to notice he was missing about three seconds after his departure. She wasn't good at lying, never had been. Which should have been a virtue but, in this situation, would be a distinct disadvantage.

'Curtis,' said Alex, 'could you follow me through to the kitchen please?'

Maddie allowed herself to breathe again on hearing Alex's words. She had already agreed to help Curtis with his plan, there was no going back on that now. Not really. But at least she would get a few minutes to prepare herself for the grand deception while he was being questioned.

'Look after Barkley for me,' said Curtis. 'Hopefully, I shall not be gone too long.'

With that, Curtis and Alex made their way off to the kitchen. Barkley let out a couple of short, sharp whines as Curtis walked away. Maddie leant down, picked the dog up gently and placed him on her knee. 'It's OK, Barkley,' she said, stroking his ears. 'Curtis will be back soon.'

The dog settled into the rhythm of Maddie's strokes and stopped whining.

'Poor little thing,' said Jeannie. 'You know 'e was in the room when James died too. 'E's probably just as traumatised as Curtis but doesn't 'ave the luxury of vocalising it.'

'I'm sure you're right,' said Maddie. 'The wee pooch didn't ask for this any more than the rest of us.'

'About what Curtis was sayin' before, about Alice,' said Jeannie. 'It's only natural for you to ask, you know, considerin' all this crazy talk about 'er ghost and that.'

'Maybe,' said Maddie, less than thrilled at having to continue Curtis's lie for him. 'But it isn't really the time to be talking about that.'

'There's nothin' really to tell about it. Nowt as dramatic as what Donny would probably need to make 'is ghost story work,' said Jeannie with a small shrug. 'She were just very ill. All different kinds of ailments. 'Er immune system became so compromised 'er body it . . . it just couldn't go on. It were a particularly cold winter the year she died. She weren't old but she were weak.'

'That must have been very difficult, to watch someone you love decline like that,' said Maddie.

'Oh, it's the worst form of torture, make no mistake,' said Jeannie. 'Even now, I find it 'ard to focus on the woman she were before the illnesses took over. It's the kind of experience that 'as you wonderin' what kind of world we're livin' in. But there was nothin' violent about it. And definitely nothing supernatural.'

'And,' Maddie said, trying not to let any suspicion show in her tone, 'I suppose Alex must have found that difficult. Watching his mother decline like that.'

'Oh aye,' said Jeannie. 'And it didn't 'elp what the doctors told 'im after she died, either.'

'Why?' said Maddie. 'What did they say?'

'Oh, it were a load of nonsense,' Jeannie said, waving her hand in a dismissive gesture. 'It was the local doctor, Dr Everett, who'd treated Alice for many years. 'E decides to put it in Alex's 'ead that Mickey leavin' were the reason 'er illnesses started in the first place.'

Maddie swallowed hard. That wasn't the kind of thing a person wanted to hear. That an action from their father might have ultimately killed their mother. 'That's a dramatic statement to say the least. How on earth did he come to that conclusion?' she asked, doing her best to look confused by the insinuation. She tried to keep her tone casual as she spoke, but Maddie had that sense she sometimes got when an important piece of information for a story landed on her desk. She needed to know more.

'According to Dr Everett, Alice's first illness started not long after Mickey left because of the shock of it all, you know? I mean, I suppose I do understand to some extent that our emotions can have an impact on 'ow we feel physically in ourselves. But, with Alice, one illness led on to another. The doctor didn't outright say Mickey's leavin' 'ad caused it all but 'e said she wouldn't let go of the stress of the event and that 'ad prevented her from getting well again.'

'What did Alex say?' said Maddie. 'It's difficult to think of anything more upsetting to hear than that.'

'Oh, 'e were in a bad way about it at the time,' said Jeannie. 'We did a lot of talkin' about it. I think in the long run 'e accepted that there's good and bad 'ealth in the world and we can't control the 'ealth of other people. That the stress of Mickey leavin' might 'ave played a part in Alice's first illness – pneumonia – but the illness were really the problem because it weakened 'er immune system.'

'Alex has really been through the wringer, hasn't he?' said Maddie.

''E 'as love, 'e 'as,' said Jeannie. 'But it were all a long time ago until somebody decided to dredge it all up tonight.'

'Verdict rules I'm an innocent man, everybody!' Curtis shouted from the kitchen door. The sound of his master's voice made Barkley's ears prick up and Curtis made his way around the bar, back to the table, to greet his loyal hound.

'Innocent, for now,' Alex said, eyeing Curtis as he sat back down. 'Sita, can you come for the next interview, please?' he added.

Slowly rising from her seat, Sita trudged towards the kitchen. 'These interviews are a waste of time,' she said.

'It's not a—' Alex began, but then stopped himself. He

was unwilling to be drawn into that debate again. 'Let's talk about that more in here, shall we?' he corrected himself.

'It's alright, Barkley,' said Curtis when the dog leapt down from Maddie's lap to greet him as he returned to the table. 'I was only gone a little while. I always come back, you know that,' he added, bending to give the dog a rub around the ears. 'That said, I can't stop for long, I need to use the lavatory so I'll have to find some people to accompany me. Don't want to ruin my good name or invite another one of those interviews with Alex. He was . . . thorough, shall we say.'

'I'm sure you'll be able to find a couple of willing volunteers to help you out with that,' said Maddie, wondering how Curtis planned to use the secret passageway down to the cellar if he was going to take people with him on his excursion. But that was for him to figure out. She was far too concerned about how she was going to distract Don. There was the obvious Pringles angle but, given the severity of the current circumstances, such a conversation would definitely seem out of place and possibly rouse his suspicions. Then again, talking about the murder case directly might seem like she was suspiciously rooting around for information.

She'd just have to think of a way in with him. Even though she had no idea if it was the right thing to do.

Alex may have cleared Curtis of any wrongdoing, but he didn't know about his mysterious trip down to the cellar. He said he was planning to retrieve papers of relevance to the murder. But what if he intended to destroy them, getting rid of evidence that pointed at him?

Maddie sighed. It was too late to back out now. Curtis was already giving Barkley a farewell pat on the head. If she was going to distract Don, she needed to do it now.

'Jeannie, I need to go and ask Don something, will you be alright watching Barkley for a couple of minutes?' said Maddie.

'Aye, it's no bother,' said Jeannie. 'What do you need to talk to Donny about?'

'I will reveal all on my return,' Maddie said with a playful smile that she hoped would stave off Jeannie's curiosity long enough for her to actually think of something she would need to talk to Don about just then.

'Alright,' said Jeannie, 'I'll watch the little tyke. Don't worry, 'e'll be safe with me.'

Smiling, Maddie made her way over to where Don was standing. With every step, conscious of the fact that she had no idea if she was about to aid a friend or a foe.

CHAPTER TWENTY-ONE

Don was standing, almost to attention, with his hands clasped loosely behind his back. From his posture there was no mistaking that he was taking his orders from Alex very seriously, which only added to Maddie's sense of guilt as she drew near.

Just beyond him, however, she could see James's body. And this in turn made her think about the dead woman in Reelig Glen. About how all those years ago she'd been too scared to do the right thing. Maybe this was her chance to make amends. Maybe Curtis was to be trusted and would produce papers from the cellar that would serve to support his theory about who James's killer really was. After which, justice could be done. She couldn't change the way she had behaved as a child, but she had a chance, right now, to do something different, something better, something brave.

'Don,' said Maddie. 'Could . . . could I have a quick word?'

'What about?' said Don. His tone wasn't quite sharp but the words were definitely clipped. He wasn't about to easily forget he had a job to do. Perhaps he felt an even greater sense of duty after Alex had questioned his prowess as a police officer earlier.

Maddie walked around to the other side of him, so Don was forced to turn his head away from the part of the pub where Curtis had been sitting.

'I just wanted to say . . .' Maddie started, hoping something compelling was about to trip off her tongue. She paused for a moment, and then mercifully inspiration struck. 'I believe you. And Sita. About the ghost.'

'You do?' Don said, raising an eyebrow.

'Well, I wasn't convinced at first, I must admit. But I've been thinking it over and all the pieces fit. The engagement ring. The message in the black envelope. The fact that this thing, whatever it is, doesn't seem to have touched anyone with its hands.'

'Aye,' said Don. 'We've got to go through protocol and interview everyone 'ere, like Alex said, but if nothin' comes of that, we're going to 'ave to look elsewhere for an explanation. I've asked Sita if she'd be prepared to do a seance to get to the bottom of this and she says she would. That's what I've got my money on.'

'You're probably right,' said Maddie, while privately

hoping that she wouldn't end up taking part in a seance before the night was over. 'What I don't understand is, why Alice's ghost would wait ten years to take her revenge. It just seems a long time to wait.'

'That is a good question, like,' Don pondered, and then looking over in the direction of Mickey to make sure he couldn't be overheard, added: 'Maybe because that's 'ow long she suffered for after 'e left her, you know, before she died.'

'Surely not to the day though,' said Maddie. 'I mean, I know she died on Christmas Eve but Mickey didn't . . .'

Don's expression already gave Maddie her answer but he replied with words anyway. 'Aye.' Again Don glanced over at Mickey. ''E left her on Christmas Eve, twenty years ago.'

Maddie's mouth fell open at this. Really? He left her on Christmas Eve? With a small child? What a rotten time of year to end a relationship. Leaving someone on Christmas Eve was like leaving them on Valentine's Day or their birthday. Why on earth couldn't Mickey have waited, if not until the end of the bleak January days, at least until Christmas was over?

And what kind of Christmas had Alex had when his dad left? How had he even managed to celebrate this time of year since if it marked one of the most painful episodes in his life?

'Yeah, the look on your face pretty much sums up most people's feelings about that,' said Don.

'Sorry,' said Maddie. 'I don't really know anything about it. I shouldn't be judging. For all I know Alice was very difficult to live with, maybe even cruel. I didn't know her at all or their situation so I haven't got any right to be looking like that.'

Donny shook his head. 'You 'eard what I said earlier, didn't you? Alex's mum were a nice lady. From everything I've 'eard, she were very gentle. Alex has passed the odd remark over the years that Mickey took advantage of 'er gentle nature. Of the fact she weren't suspicious of people. 'E left on Christmas Eve because that's the date 'e closed the deal on buying this place. 'E already 'ad a plan to live here with Sofia. 'E's since admitted 'e was more selfish in those days but admittin' you were wrong doesn't turn back time, does it?'

'So, Christmas Eve isn't just the anniversary of Mickey leaving Alice, and her death. It's also the same day Mickey bought this place?' Maddie said, trying to digest the fact that this particular date in the calendar held yet another significance on top of what she had already gleaned.

'Aye,' said Don, 'so, knowin' all that, it makes sense, doesn't it?'

'Hm?' Maddie said, snapping out of her thoughts. 'Sorry, what does?'

'That the ghost would choose to 'aunt the pub. And choose to take revenge on Mickey's family on this particular day,' Don said slowly, sounding confused as to why this wasn't as obvious to Maddie as it was to him.

'Oh,' Maddie said, remembering her charade and adopting as earnest a face as she could. 'Yes, well of course, I had no idea about that. But after what you've told me, it makes perfect sense that the ghost would choose this place to visit. And direct its wrath at Mickey and Sofia on Christmas Eve specifically.'

'Aye, between you and me, I've been keepin' a keen eye on Mrs Fazakerley because I think the ghost might come after 'er, too,' said Don.

'Mrs Fazakerley?' Maddie said, looking over at the short but sturdy woman sitting with the Kapoors. 'Why would the ghost be after her?'

'Well, Mrs Fazakerley were good friends with Mickey's mother when she were alive, and she's notoriously not short of a bob or two,' said Don. 'So, she lent Mickey the deposit to buy this place.'

'Did she know Mickey was planning to leave Alice and Alex?' Maddie said.

'No,' said Don. 'Or at least she insists she didn't whenever the subject comes up. But there were a big showdown between Alice and Mrs Fazakerley at the time, apparently.'

'What kind of showdown?' said Maddie. 'Did it get physical?'

'Not quite,' said Don. 'Remember, it really weren't in Alice's nature to be aggressive. But after findin' out Mrs Fazakerley had lent Mickey the money to buy this place, well she couldn't keep 'er peace. Alex stopped them before it went too far but 'e told me they were shoutin' all sorts at each other. Alice accused Mrs Fazakerley of financin' Mickey's affair with Sofia. Which she sort of did, but she didn't know about that at the time.'

'But . . . earlier, Mrs Fazakerley said she'd never known Alice be anything other than lovely?' said Maddie, still trying to digest this new information about yet another complicated situation involving one of Alex's family members.

'I think Mrs Fazakerley is pretty ashamed of the whole event,' said Don. 'Felt really bad about the fact that something she did ended up leaving Alice without a father for 'er son. And then, of course, years later she died. I think Mrs Fazakerley just tries to pretend like that day never 'appened. Feels too ashamed about it all.'

'How come Mrs Fazakerley is still on good terms with Mickey then? Comes into his pub and plays his scavenger hunt?' said Maddie. 'If somebody redacted the truth like that with me, especially when the net result was leaving Alice with a young boy to provide for and raise on her own, I don't think I'd want to be in their company.'

'I don't know about that,' said Don, 'but 'e squared it away with 'er somehow because she lent James money too.'

'A lot of money?' Maddie said.

Don nodded. 'There isn't anyone in the whole village who 'asn't wound up slippin' James a tenner 'ere and there but word is 'e borrowed a good few thousand off Mrs Fazakerley. Unlike 'is dad, though, James weren't one for repaying 'is debt. I don't think she saw a penny of it back. Mickey were going to pay it off in instalments for his son but with the cost of livin' going up so much, Mickey and Sofia 'ave only just managed to keep the doors open 'ere, so 'e 'asn't been able to start repaying 'er yet. But 'e's given his word that 'e will.'

'I'm sure he will,' Maddie said, wondering just how many thousands James had owed to Mrs Fazakerley. Her head was starting to hurt keeping track of how many people James had done wrong in his short life. And by proxy, how many people would have had motive to bump him off.

Looking at Mrs Fazakerley, Maddie couldn't quite imagine her being able to overpower James in a struggle. That said, Maddie didn't know for sure that there had been a struggle. The lights had been out so he wouldn't have been able to see his assailant coming. And then something struck Maddie that hadn't struck her before: if the lights were out at the time of the murder, how did the attacker see enough to commit the act? James was stabbed in the neck with a corkscrew. Now, corkscrews were sharp, but to kill a person in one blow, you'd have to be able to see where you were aiming. You'd have to be able to make out the neck.

It was then that Maddie remembered something Mrs Kapoor had said about her attacker. That the figure in question had *glowed*. This detail had added to Mrs Kapoor's initial certainty that she had been attacked by a ghost rather than a person. But the more likely scenario was that the killer had found some way to gently illuminate themselves in the darkness. Giving them the aura of a ghost while also providing a light by which to commit their crime.

But how did a person make themselves glow? That wasn't really within Maddie's field of expertise. She suspected, however, that the answer to the question would dispel Don and Sita's ghost theory once and for all.

Maddie was about to ask Don if there had been rumours about precisely how much money James had owed Mrs Fazakerley when the moment was interrupted by Sita, followed by Alex, emerging from the kitchen.

'Well, everyone,' Sita said, 'I'm not a murderer either. Although I already knew that. Just a few more people to check and after that I vote we hold a seance to contact the ghost and release the negative energies once and for all. Don has already asked me if I am willing to do one if it comes to it. I always carry some seance essentials in my handbag so it won't take much setting up.'

Alex shot a glare at Don and then shook his head at Sita. 'When I want a supernatural consultant, I'll . . . Actually, you know what, strike that, I'll never want a supernatural consultant.'

'You are wasting your time,' was all that Sita said as she walked over to sit with Mrs Fazakerley.

Alex didn't dignify this with a response. Instead, he looked over at his aunt.

'I know it's weird, Jeannie, but I do have to interview everyone.'

'Of course you do, love,' said Jeannie. 'I'm sure Maddie can watch Barkley while I'm in there with you.'

Alex looked around the room until he caught Maddie's eye. He nodded, but that nod was swiftly followed by a frown.

'Wait a minute, where is Curtis?' said Alex. Had he been looking directly at Maddie when he posed this question, he would have seen her cringe and guessed immediately that she had something to do with the fact that Curtis was nowhere to be seen.

Luckily, Alex's stare was more meandering than that. He was surveying the room, perhaps hoping that Curtis would pull his world-famous trick of appearing out of nowhere. But Maddie knew better.

The same question that Alex had posed weighed heavy on Maddie's mind:

Where *was* Curtis?

The adrenaline had been pumping through her hard as she had talked to Don. At any moment he might have guessed that she was trying to distract him. Because of this, it was difficult for Maddie to gauge exactly how long she had been talking to him, but she had the distinct feeling that Curtis should have returned from his mission by now.

'He said he was going to the toilet,' said Jeannie.

'But, everyone else is here. After everything that's gone on tonight, nobody went with him?' said Alex.

'Um, Alex?' Maddie said, raising her hand as though in school. 'I, er, need to talk to you for a wee minute, in private. It's about Curtis.'

Alex's frown only deepened at this. He didn't say anything in response. He simply leant his head in the direction of the kitchen in such a way that Maddie knew even the worst tellings-off she'd had from her parents over the years weren't going to compare with what was to come on the other side of that swing door.

Scurrying behind the bar and through to the kitchen, Maddie did what she could to keep her breathing under control. She was really for it now, there was no doubt about it.

A moment later, Alex strode through the door, stopping only when he was standing directly opposite her.

'What's going on?' he said, in a tone of voice that made it clear he wanted sharp answers to his questions.

'Curtis had a plan,' said Maddie, 'to unmask the killer. He said he needed supporting documents from the cellar. A will . . . Mickey's will. He said it was in the basement and he wanted to retrieve it before he confronted the killer. I tried to stop him from going alone. I told him to bring you in on his plan, but he said . . .' Maddie hesitated, she absolutely couldn't reveal all that Curtis had said about Alex potentially being part of the murder plot in case it was true.

'What did he say?' Alex pushed.

'He said if it was who he thought it was then you wouldn't want to believe it,' said Maddie.

Alex frowned. 'Well, what the hell did he mean by that?'

'I don't know,' Maddie said. 'I didn't want to be a part of this but I couldn't talk him down.'

'You should have come to me right away,' said Alex. 'I thought we were supposed to be working together. And frankly, I thought better of you.'

'What's that supposed to mean?' said Maddie, her hackles rising.

'Oh, I'll tell you. I thought you had more sense! We were supposed to be working as a team,' said Alex. 'Trying to get to the bottom of this together. Doing what you do, reporting on all kinds of tragedies, I thought you'd understand the seriousness of a case like this. The importance of any information being passed on to me at once. Now, because you decided to keep this to yourself, Curtis is missing. After what happened to James, who knows what's happened to him? Don't you understand that I'm ultimately responsible for anything that befalls him? And you do this? Make it impossible for me to do what I'm meant to be doing. It's my job here to keep everyone safe. I could have talked to him, could have stopped him, if you'd just bloody told me.'

'Alright, I know,' Maddie said, a little louder than she meant to. 'I'm sorry. I made a mistake. Maybe I'm not in a place where I'm making the best judgments, but I didn't mean for this to happen.'

'Didn't mean . . .' Alex started, but trailed off as though he was too angry to say anymore. 'There's a lot more I could say to you, but what's the point? We can't waste any more time in here arguing about it anyway,' said Alex, running a hand through his hair. 'If Curtis is still alive, we need to find him before that changes. Which route to the cellar did he take, do you know?'

'He said he was going through the secret passageway,' said Maddie.

'I thought as much,' Alex said. 'Well, I'm going to have to go after him, and you're coming with me. If there's anything else you've conveniently forgotten to tell me, you can tell me on the way.

Given her claustrophobia, at the thought of having to navigate a secret passageway, Maddie felt as though her lungs were going to collapse in on themselves. But she didn't dare tell Alex that. He was livid about what she had done, and she couldn't much blame him. He said he was responsible for what happened to Curtis, but that wasn't strictly true. She was the one who had let Curtis go into the cellar alone. Deep down, Maddie knew what that meant. Anything that had befallen the man who had done nothing but try to help her was ultimately her fault, and no one else's.

CHAPTER TWENTY-TWO

'Any luck with the interviews so far?' Maddie said, trying to get Alex to talk more openly with her again after the dressing-down he'd given her in the kitchen, while, at the same time, taking her mind off where she was: a narrow stone passageway cut of rough stone. She had been hoping that she would avoid having to experience The Merry Monarch's secret passageways first-hand, but now that Curtis was missing it couldn't be avoided. Don had to stay with the group and watch them, so, despite her minor betrayal of withholding information, Alex had taken Maddie along to try and recover him.

It was as fitting a punishment as any for someone who was mildly claustrophobic. The rough walls scraped against her forearm with every step and the smell in here, Maddie couldn't describe it exactly but there was something old and deathly about it. Occasionally, the passageway widened, presumably to create a sort of passing place if people were coming in both directions. But those spaces didn't occur often enough for Maddie's liking and it was taking all of her might not to imagine those narrow stone walls closing in around her.

Alex was using the torch function on his mobile to navigate the passageway Curtis said he would be taking to the cellar. Maddie kept her eyes only on the next step ahead. In a place like this, she didn't want to be looking around too much. She imagined spiders and many other creepy-crawlies lived in dark crannies like this one and, though she may have loved running around the mud as a child, she could do without an impromptu minibeast hunt right now.

'And I'm sharing information with you because?' said Alex in response to Maddie's question about the interviews.

'Because you said you needed an ally in this?' Maddie returned, guessing in advance what Alex's retort might be.

'Yeah, well, when someone is an ally, the information sharing goes both ways,' Alex said, continuing at a steady pace despite the darkness and uneven surface of the stone floor.

'I told you,' said Maddie. 'Curtis was concerned you might stop him from getting the supporting documents from the cellar. He didn't think you'd want to hear about it, presumably because the person he had in mind is somebody you know well, and he was almost certain he knew who the killer was.' Once again, Maddie left out what Curtis had said about Alex's possible involvement. In any event, Curtis had just been speculating and, when they found him, wherever he was, if he had something to say to Alex, he could say it for himself.

'If he said that, then he clearly doesn't know me as well as I thought,' said Alex. 'This is a murder investigation, for Christ's sake. I'm not going to let personal loyalties get in the way of that.'

'Be that as it may, Alex, come on, let's not add another drama to this evening. You're not really mad at me, you're angry because you haven't got a strong suspect yet.' This was a long shot but Maddie thought it was at least worth trying to shift the anger onto something other than her collusion with Curtis.

'I *am* mad at you, make no mistake,' Alex said. 'And what makes you think I haven't got a strong suspect?'

'Mr and Mrs Kapoor were looking pretty shifty at the start of all this. But then they had that argument and the truth came out. Mrs Kapoor and James weren't having an affair—'

'So they say. We still don't know whether she actually did put that note in James's pocket. Or whether her husband did it to lure him there.'

'But Mr Kapoor had no idea James had feelings for his wife,' said Maddie.

'You're assuming that they were telling the truth,' said Alex. 'The argument could have been a charade. Either Mr Kapoor or Mrs Kapoor could have been lying about something. Or both of them could.'

'Looked real enough from where I was standing,' said Maddie. 'And everyone else you've interviewed so far has emerged from the kitchen declaring that they've been proven innocent.'

'And now you're assuming I'm telling them the truth,' said Alex. Though Maddie couldn't see his face because he was leading the way, she could almost hear the smirk in his voice.

'What do you mean?' said Maddie.

'Ask yourself this: what's the best way to get a criminal to relax and thereby somehow slip up?'

Maddie thought about this question for a moment but then realised the answer was obvious: 'Make them believe they've got away with it.'

'We have a winner,' said Alex. 'Give the lady a cuddly toy.'

'Wait. Is that what you were doing with me? When you took me on as your ally?' said Maddie.

'You'll never know for sure,' Alex said, before adding, 'But I'm fairly sure whoever is behind this is a lot more calculating than you are.'

'Not sure whether to take that as a compliment or not,' said Maddie.

'I don't think folk put the word *calculating* on their dating profiles in a bid to impress other people, so I'd say it just about makes it into the compliment column,' said Alex.

'Good to know,' Maddie said. 'Alex . . . are you, OK?'

The question was out of her mouth before she could stop it and the moment it was she knew this was the worst possible time to have this particular conversation.

Though almost everyone she'd spoken to had given her some reason to believe that Alex might have had something to do with James's death, Maddie's instincts told her he was working on the side of good here. But what if those instincts were wrong? Was a dark, enclosed space really the best place to start asking a potential murderer personal questions? Rousing their suspicions about how much she might already know, or be trying to find out about them?

And even if Maddie's instincts were right, even if Alex was the nicest guy on the planet and wanted to stop and talk about his problems, that was only going to delay them getting to the other end of the passageway. At that thought, Maddie was sure she felt her shirt getting tighter around her neck.

Alex manoeuvred himself into one of the passing places, turned to her and said: 'Why do you ask that?'

Grateful that at least they were having this conversation in one of the wider parts of the passage, Maddie took a deep breath of stale, damp air and tried to steady herself.

'Why? Well, let's start with the fact that you've lost your stepbrother this evening. And that someone is clearly exploiting your mother's passing as a way of escaping justice,' said Maddie.

'I know,' Alex said, 'But I can't think about all that right now. You saw Mickey and Sofia, they're in bits.'

'Despite your Dad leaving your mum for Sofia, you still really care about them both. Don't you?' Maddie said, with more than a little admiration showing in her voice. Not every person could do that. Care about the people who had basically been responsible for the breakdown of their family unit.

'I was young when Dad left. I didn't much like him then. Or Sofia. But after Mum died, I realised that besides Jeannie they were really the only family I had. And I could either stay bitter or find a way to get past it all. There'll be a time for me to be in bits but it's not right now. I can't afford that. We've got to find Curtis. Who knows what . . . we just, we need to focus. Obviously I'm not alright, deep down. But I've just got to push through.'

'OK,' Maddie said, more convinced than she had been all night that Alex was a person she could trust. 'Then,

I'm going to do my best to help you. No more side deals. I promise.'

Alex offered a nod and then continued on down the passageway.

'For the record, the agreement I made with Curtis. I was trying to help then. Trying to help you solve the case,' said Maddie.

'I know. But I've been on the job a long time. Why don't you leave the big decisions to me in future, eh?' said Alex, before adding, 'Here we are, this is the door that opens into the basement.'

Maddie looked at the heavy black door. Since James had been found dead, everything in this place had taken on a creepy, sinister aesthetic – at least in Maddie's eyes. This door was no exception. She watched as Alex turned a large metal ring to the left in order to lift the latch. It shuddered open with a deep creak. From the sound of it, you wouldn't have thought it had been opened in decades.

'I'll go first, you follow on,' Alex said, stepping into the next room.

Taking yet another deep breath, Maddie did as he instructed, her mind racing with some pretty sinister ideas about what they might find on the other side of the threshold.

CHAPTER TWENTY-THREE

The first thing that struck Maddie about the cellar was the smell. She'd never been behind the scenes at a pub before and the smell of hops down here was quite overwhelming. That, however, was not going to be the most startling part of her journey into the underground crevices of The Merry Monarch. About three paces into the room, Alex stopped in his tracks so abruptly that Maddie bumped into the back of him. It took her less than a second to understand why.

There, lying on the dusty floorboards of the cellar, was Curtis's dead body.

'Oh God, no,' Maddie said, burying her head in Alex's arm. She was past caring how overfamiliar a gesture this was. Poor Curtis had died at the hands of a murderer, and she was at least partly to blame.

Alex waited for her to lift her head before stepping

closer to the corpse. In a stupor, Maddie followed on, tears slipping down her cheeks as she did so. Just as he had with James, Alex held two fingers to Curtis's neck and looked at his watch as he did so. When a full minute had passed he took a deep breath and, looking at Maddie with glassy eyes, shook his head.

'I should never have let him come down here alone,' she said. 'This is all my fault.'

'No, it's not,' Alex said, and his eyes, which had remained on Curtis, flitted over to Maddie.

'I knew he was coming down here by himself. And I didn't tell anyone. And now he's dead. How can you say it's not my fault?' Maddie said.

'Because I know Curtis. If you hadn't helped him, he'd have found another way. Besides anything else, from the marks around his neck, I'd say he's been strangled. Unless you came down here and strangled him yourself, you're not to blame, got that?' Alex stared at Maddie hard enough to elicit a nod from her, though the guilt over what she had done was not going to dissipate any time soon.

Looking down at Curtis's pale face, Maddie choked back tears. 'He didn't deserve to die like this,' she said.

'This life is not about people getting what they deserve,' said Alex, his voice low, his tone dark. Slowly, Maddie looked from Curtis's body to Alex. He seemed almost caught in a trance as he spoke. 'Curtis didn't deserve to die like that. Mum didn't deserve to die like that. I didn't deserve to be left like that, just a kid.'

The more Alex spoke, the more Maddie began to wonder if this was the moment in which this previously calm and collected police inspector was going to snap. The moment in which she was going to realise that it had been a very bad idea to follow him down into a cellar alone.

'I've seen too much, doing what I do,' he continued. 'Nobody in this world gets what they deserve.'

At this point, Alex seemed to remember himself, slip out of his trance and notice the expression on Maddie's face. When he spoke again, it was obvious to Maddie that her trademark inability to mask her true feelings in a situation had struck again.

'Are you scared of me?' he said.

'Sh-should I be?' asked Maddie.

'God, no,' Alex said, as though the very idea was absurd. 'Why would you be . . . Wait a minute, you don't really think I've got a hand in this, do you?'

'No . . .' Maddie said, turning her head to look down at Curtis again in case her expression gave her away.

'You're a terrible liar.'

Maddie turned back to face Alex. 'Well, you were the one who said everybody was a suspect, even you.'

'I was being tart!' said Alex. 'Do you really think I'd throw my whole career away for James for Christ's sake?'

'Well, when you put it that way . . . maybe not,' said Maddie. 'It's just, he sort of took your place, didn't he? As number one son, I mean.'

'Maybe when he was very small,' said Alex. 'And we're talking like, when he was still in single digits. But James's ne'er-do-well schtick was wearing thin with Dad by the time he'd started secondary school. He often said he wished he was more like me.'

'Oh, well, I mean considering how James behaved towards me in the short time I knew him, I can understand that,' said Maddie. 'But what about the way you and Don were looking at me when I came into the pub earlier?'

'Well, what about it?' said Alex.

'It was unsettling. You were both staring at me. I don't know why, but something about it didn't seem right,' said Maddie.

'It's just standard police training kicking in. You notice when somebody new enters a room. You are trained to be observant. That's all. We were just wondering where you were going from and to.'

'That's it? Really?' said Maddie.

'Yes, really, so can we please agree that I am not the killer, or involved with my stepbrother's death in any way, and actually look for some clues as to who might be behind all this?'

'If you insist,' Maddie said, and when Alex shot her a disgruntled look, she added, 'You're not the only one who can be tart.'

Alex merely shook his head in response.

It was mid-quip that an idea had struck Maddie. 'Alex, his pockets. Is there an envelope in there? Like there was for Mrs Kapoor and James?'

Alex leant over to check both pockets on Curtis's trousers and on the waistcoat he was wearing.

'There's nothing in there,' he said.

'Worth a try,' Maddie said. 'Does it make any sense at all that we've found envelopes in the pockets of some people who have been attacked but not in others?'

'There's only one person it will make sense to right now,' said Alex, 'and that's the killer.' He began to look around the room on the hunt for other clues and Maddie did the same. Barrels of beer lined the walls, except for one wall which served as a wine rack. There were steps at the other end of the room that, Maddie guessed, offered an official route back up to the bar area. Her gaze circled back to the beer barrels and it was then that she noticed something lying on top of one of them.

'There,' Maddie said. 'There's a rope.'

Alex looked over to where Maddie had pointed. 'It's the blue stuff Mickey uses to hoist the barrels. Don't touch it. Or anything else. When we leave, I'm going to seal off this room. Prop something heavy against the door that leads out of the secret passageway and lock the other one. Forensics will be able to work with minimal contamination then.'

'Are you going to tell the others?' said Maddie. 'About Curtis?'

'I'm going to have to tell them something. But I don't know what, yet, I need to think about that,' he said. 'Did you notice anyone missing while I was interviewing Sita?'

Maddie took a moment to think about it. 'I'm sorry, I was too busy executing Curtis's plan of talking to Don in a bid to distract him.'

'Pringles?'

'Ghosts.'

'Oh,' said Alex. 'Yeah, that would do it. And you're sure you didn't notice anyone sloping off? Following Curtis?'

Maddie shook her head. 'I'm sorry. I wasn't looking at the rest of the room. The only person I really clapped eyes on was Mrs Fazakerley but I was only looking at her now and then. And because Don was looking at me, rather than keeping an eye on the room, anyone could have followed Curtis down here if they were subtle about it. Though, I'm a bit surprised nobody noticed.'

'People are getting tired. It's coming up to midnight now and the sheer amount of adrenaline people have been running on for most of the night will have left them exhausted and, crucially, not that observant.' Alex sighed. 'I need to go back up there and covertly ask each person if anyone left their table.'

'Wait, before we go back, shouldn't we try and find the will Curtis was looking for? If someone specific is mentioned in there, it might tell us who Curtis suspected and might even save you a lot of time in asking questions.'

'I suppose Curtis must have thought it shed light on this situation for a reason,' said Alex. 'Of course, there is a chance he already found it and the killer took it from him after strangling him.'

'I hadn't thought of that,' said Maddie. 'But let's check anyway. Better to try and uncover the will now if we can so we've got every advantage. Do you know where your dad keeps his papers?'

'He did mention something about them once. In a box behind one of the vintage bottles of wine, I think. Though why he was telling me, I don't know,' said Alex.

'You're his son,' said Maddie. 'I know he left but that's still true.'

'Yeah, but James was set to inherit all of Mickey's worldly goods,' said Alex.

Maddie remembered the spat between Jeannie and Sofia. How angry Sofia had got at Jeannie for assuming that James was a key beneficiary of the will. And she seemed to have been disputing the idea that James was going to inherit from Mickey. 'Who told you that James was going to inherit everything?'

'Mum, years ago,' said Alex, walking over to the wine rack. He looked along the row of vintage wines, found the one he wanted and pulled it out of the slot. Reaching behind it, he then produced a narrow wooden box. 'She said she wanted to prepare me for the fact so I wasn't shocked when it happened, or didn't bank on some big windfall if anything happened to Mickey.'

Mercifully, the box Alex had found wasn't locked so he was able to simply open it and pull out the documents that had been folded inside. 'There's the deeds to this place,' he said, flicking through the papers. 'And yes, here's the will Curtis drew up. It's . . .' Alex trailed off as he read.

'What, what is it?' Maddie said.

'James isn't listed as a beneficiary,' Alex replied.

'What? But I thought your mum said . . . Well, if he isn't then who is?' Maddie sidled up to Alex to get a better look at the papers.

'Sofia and me. I mean, the only real asset is this place. But it's an equal share, fifty-fifty.' Alex frowned. 'I don't understand. If James isn't even mentioned in these papers, then why did Curtis think they were important?'

As Alex said these words, Maddie thought back to Sofia's reaction when she found Jeannie and Maddie discussing the will. And something that had been said in this exchange suddenly took on new meaning.

'Why did your mum think James was going to inherit from Mickey?' Maddie asked.

'I . . . I'd always assumed Mickey had told her that,' said Alex. 'I mean, I wasn't bothered about it to be honest. I don't believe in waiting for people you care about to die so you can get rich off it. I make my own money. But maybe after Mum died, Dad had a change of heart and altered the will. Maybe he felt guilty, or sorry for me. Plus, James didn't exactly do anything in recent years to make Dad feel as though he was worthy of the inheritance.'

'That's all very possible,' said Maddie. 'But I think I know why your mum thought you were getting nothing. And if I'm right about that much, then I also know who the killer is, and why Curtis would have thought you'd hear none of it. Based on what's written here, I think I also know how we can draw the killer out.'

CHAPTER TWENTY-FOUR

'Right, everyone, listen up,' said Alex, about thirty minutes after he and Maddie had returned to the bar area. 'I know several have asked me, and I couldn't be drawn on it because I've had some things to sort out. But I have got some difficult news to share . . . about Curtis.'

'He's dead, isn't he?' said Sofia.

Alex and Maddie exchanged a quick glance with each other across the room, too swift and subtle for anyone else to notice.

'Yes, I . . . I'm afraid so,' Alex confirmed as a collective moan circled around everyone present. 'I know this will come as a shock to many of you who have known Curtis as long as I have – in some cases longer. There will be a time to mourn him properly. Right now, I have to manage the situation we find ourselves in. As such, the cellar is now a crime scene. It has been secured and is completely off limits. Anybody caught trying to access it, or the passageway leading to it, will be taken into the station for questioning tomorrow at the very least.'

At this, everyone looked around the room at each other. Perhaps trying to discern who, if anyone, would dare do such a thing.

'Obviously, I want to find out who's committing these crimes,' Alex continued. 'I had assumed, or shall we say hoped, that James's death was a one-off incident. But after what happened to Curtis, we can't be sure of anything. So, my top priority, even higher up the list than catching this killer, has to be preventing any further loss of life. With that in mind, it's clear that the system we've got going now isn't safe enough, otherwise we wouldn't have lost Curtis. So I've spoken to Mickey about alternative arrangements.'

'What kind of alternative arrangements?' said Mrs Fazakerley. 'Does it involve getting out of this place? I've had about as much of it as I can take. I won't be back for next year's scavenger hunt, that much I can tell you. This is a nightmare, a nightmare.'

'I really do understand, Mrs Fazakerley,' Alex said. 'But leaving here isn't an option. Due to the snow, the terrain is not passable outside on foot or by vehicle so we've had to come up with something else. Some of you already have rooms here tonight. There are a few going spare and then there's the communal rooms, all of which can be locked.

We're going to set up beds in those communal rooms so that everyone has their own place to bunk for the night. By the time we get everybody organised, it will be going on for two in the morning. It's been a dramatic evening, to say the least, so everyone will be assigned a room, and a key. You will lock your door, and you will not open it again until morning.'

A murmur ricocheted around the room at this. There was no hope of anyone leaving Alex's sight until the murders were solved, Maddie was pretty sure that would have been true even if there hadn't been a blizzard outside. But Alex's instructions only added to the oppressive atmosphere building in the room. Which was, of course, all part of their plan.

'If I haven't already conducted an interview with you, I will come to your room individually to complete those interviews and I will identify myself at the door with a knock signal. Everyone will be getting a knock signal, whether I've interviewed you or not, in case I need to enter your room for some other purpose. I will allocate a different signal for each person so it cannot be replicated by the killer. Only you and I will know the particular pattern you are listening for. Me and DC Maynard will take turns in sleeping and patrolling the corridor so there is no window of opportunity for the killer to strike again before more help can be summoned in the morning.'

'Why do we have to bother with a stupid knock system? Seems totally unnecessary to me,' said Sita. 'Why can't you just tell us it's you when you visit our room?'

'Because a voice through a door can be more difficult to identify,' said Alex. 'Someone might impersonate me to get to you. But if only me and the person I'm visiting know the knock code, that is far more secure. A person might guess at it, but their odds of getting it right are extremely, extremely low.'

'Is this really the only way?' said Sita. 'I think Don's right about the seance. Why don't we just do it and get it over with?'

'No, it is not the only way,' said Alex, his voice taking on a clipped, cold quality. 'but as the highest-ranking figure of public authority in here, it's the way I have decided to do it, and questioning a plan that I believe will keep everybody safe, Sita, only makes you look guilty.'

Sita's eyes widened at this and she looked visibly shaken by the idea that she might still be under suspicion, despite already having had an interview with Alex earlier. She didn't say another word.

Again, Maddie and Alex exchanged a barely perceptible look.

'I am going to come around each of you individually, tell you your personal knock signal, explain how any remaining interviews are going to be conducted and, crucially, give you the key to your assigned room. Dad, obviously I don't need to give you a key as you've already got one to your room but I'm going to start my conversations with you.'

''Ow come the Kapoors get to stay in the same room but I can't be in the same room as Sofia?' said Mickey, scowling at Alex.

'Because I've already interviewed the Kapoors about their experiences. Mrs Kapoor when we found her upstairs, Mr Kapoor later in the evening and Zainab individually. If anything happens between them now, it's going to be obvious the killer is amongst them as the windows are locked, the door is locked and any murderous happenings would completely debunk the story they've already told me. But I haven't questioned you or Sofia yet, and everyone has to be treated equally in that respect.'

'But we're James's parents, neither one of us is going to 'ave killed 'im, are we?' Mickey protested.

Alex waited for a long moment before answering him, looking between his dad and Sofia. 'I'm not your son right now, I'm a police officer. And I'm conducting an investigation. Everyone gets the same treatment until this matter is resolved.'

The scowl didn't leave Mickey's face but he didn't say any more. Alex waited for a low murmur of conversation to brew in the room before he began his own conversation with Mickey. He moved closer to his father and spoke to him in hushed tones.

As she and Alex had agreed in the cellar, Maddie began casually sauntering towards the table where Mickey and Sofia were sitting. They were seated at opposite sides of the table and Maddie sat on the one next to them in such a way that she could easily overhear Alex's conversation with Sofia. Alex had said he'd make certain Maddie could hear all that passed between them but she needed to do all she could to make sure she missed nothing.

Just as Alex finished his talk with his dad and began his discussion with Sofia, however, Jeannie walked over to Maddie with Barkley in tow.

'Oh, hi, Jeannie,' Maddie said, trying her best to train her ears on Sofia and Alex's conversation while desperately hoping that Jeannie wouldn't notice her divided attention.

'Hi, love,' Jeannie replied. 'Just terrible news about Curtis, are you alright? Must 'ave been a shock.'

Maddie felt terrible doing it, she really was upset about Curtis's death. He had done nothing but try and help her and then had died trying to bring the killer to justice. But she wasn't the kind of person for big shows of emotion in sad moments. She tended to do the opposite and go very quiet, very still.

That wasn't going to work for her just now, however. She needed to find a way of delaying a verbal response to Jeannie so she could clearly hear Alex's conversation. Since she only had a split second to choose a course of action, she went with dipping her head and putting a hand to her brow, feigning an outward show of the grief she felt deep inside.

'Aw, lovey,' Jeannie said, putting her arm around Maddie and pulling her close.

'But, Alex, love, I really don't think the killer will be after me,' Maddie overheard Sofia telling Alex. 'I can't think of a reason anyone would kill me and you can't really think it's Mickey? Why don't you let him stay with me? I'll feel more secure that way anyway.'

'Sofia, please don't fight me on this,' said Alex. 'I've already explained why you and Mickey need separate quarters. And for all we know, this person doesn't need a reason.'

'Everyone who kills has got a reason for it, haven't they?' Sofia replied. 'Even if it doesn't make sense to anyone else, they've always got a reason.'

'Whatever is going on in the killer's mind, we're not taking any chances,' said Alex. 'Now listen, the knock I'll give you is one knock, pause, three quick knocks, pause, one knock. Got that? Don't open the door for any other signal.'

'I understand,' said Sofia. 'I've got the key to my room safely in my pocket and I won't open the door unless I hear that signal.'

'Not until morning?' Alex checked.

'Not until morning,' Sofia agreed.

Satisfied that Sofia had understood his instructions, Alex moved on to talk to the Kapoors.

'Are you going to be OK?' Jeannie asked, rubbing Maddie's back.

'Yes, yes I think so,' Maddie said with a nod. The plan she and Alex had cooked up together was well in motion now and she'd played her part in the trap they had set, so she could focus on talking to Jeannie. 'I just got a bit overcome there, I'll be alright.'

'I don't mean to add more problems into the mix, but what are we going to do about Barkley?' said Jeannie.

On hearing his name spoken, Barkley looked up at Maddie with his soulful, dark eyes. When all this was over, as Maddie hoped it would be soon, she would talk to Alex about allowing Barkley to see Curtis's body. Animals may not have intellect enough to earn themselves PhDs or diplomas, but they understood things. Primal things. As cruel as it might seem to let Barkley see Curtis's lifeless form, considering the bond Maddie had witnessed between the pair, it would be much crueller to leave Barkley thinking his master had voluntarily disappeared on him.

But that particular level of canine closure must be kept for another time. Right now, the more pressing question was what to do with the wee mutt in the interim.

'What do you think we should do? Who would he be best placed with in Curtis's absence?' Maddie asked.

'Hard to say,' said Jeannie. 'Alex loves dogs but 'e's a bit preoccupied at the minute so I don't think 'e's got the 'eadspace for a furry companion. I'd take 'im but I've not got any experience with dogs. Never 'ad one and, to be honest,' Jeannie lowered her voice to a whisper at this juncture so that the hound wouldn't overhear her next words, 'not that keen on them.'

'Well, if there's nobody obvious to look after him, I can take him in for now,' said Maddie. 'We've had dogs in the family and he doesn't seem much bother.'

'That's very kind of you, love,' said Jeannie, handing Barkley's lead over to Maddie.

'It will actually be quite nice to have a bit of company in the room for the night,' said Maddie. 'If anyone does try to get at me, Barkley will probably live up to his name and yap his head off.'

'Eee, that's a good point,' said Jeannie. 'If I 'adn't been bit as a child, I might feel safer with a dog in my room.'

'Sorry to interrupt, you two,' Alex said, approaching them. 'But I need to talk to Jeannie about her knock signal and make sure she's secure for the night. Whoever did this is trying to pin the murders on Mum's ghost. With you being her sister, Jeannie, well, we need to make sure we keep you especially secure, so I've organised for you to have the guest library room. Now, there is one of those bloody secret passageways in there, I've already been in to secure the door to it and make sure it can't be opened from either side, so you should be safe. But the particular reason I want you in there is that the main door has an added security measure. It locks but it's also got a bolt you can lock from the inside.'

'Oh, thank you, love,' said Jeannie. 'I don't know what the killer 'as got against our Alice, but whoever they are, they've got a nerve makin' it seem like she – dead or alive – would ever 'urt a fly.'

'I know,' said Alex. 'And I do want to find out who it is. But I can't focus on that tonight. I need back-up and resources I just don't have. So, for now, let's concentrate on keeping everyone safe until the sun comes up. We can find out who is dragging Mum's memory through the mud tomorrow.'

'Alex has already given me my knock signal and my key when we were talking to Mickey earlier. So, I'll leave you two alone so Alex can give you your knock signal,' said Maddie.

'Oh, you don't 'ave to leave, love. You wouldn't kill anybody,' said Jeannie.

'Jeannie!' Maddie said. 'You mustn't trust anyone! Not even me. We don't know who the killer is. It could be anyone, that's the way you've got to think.'

'She's right,' said Alex. 'Now is not the time to be trusting.'

Jeannie nodded, but did not look at all convinced by their collective show of paranoia. Turning away from them and gently tugging on Barkley's lead so he followed after her, Maddie started towards the staircase.

As she did, Sofia, who was already on her own way upstairs, turned around to take a long look at the room below her. A strange, unreadable expression crossed her face and, eventually, her ice-blue eyes locked with Maddie's. Almost as quickly as they did, however, Maddie averted her stare elsewhere, hoping the gesture didn't look in any way suspicious or out of place. She might be a terrible liar, and her face might always, somewhat against her will, betray her true feelings, but right now she had to fight those instincts. The last thing she and Alex needed was for the wrong person, the very person they were trying to draw out, to suspect a trap had been laid.

CHAPTER TWENTY-FIVE

Sofia sat at the dressing table in what was usually her and Mickey's bedroom, combing her hair before bedtime. She wasn't going to get any sleep, of course. Though she felt strangely exhausted, she was sure of that much. The loss of her son was unreal. Probably always would be. And the surrealness of it would keep her awake. She had heard Alex's words of course. Understood them and what they meant in physical terms. She had seen the body, also. Despite Alex's protests that she shouldn't, she had sneaked a look into the vacant eyes of her lifeless child as if that would somehow help her to understand the incomprehensible. But still James's death seemed like it had happened in a parallel universe. Or maybe even on a TV show. As though it was all pretend and Sofia would go into his room on Christmas morning and he would be there, half hanging out of his bed in some strange sleeping position, and snarl at her as he always did if she tried to rouse him before noon.

But no, she knew in her heart that, although it didn't feel it, although she may never really and truly believe this had happened, this was real. And even if she was overwhelmed by the emptiness that had slowly quarried out all that had once lain inside her over the past few hours, even if she wanted nothing more than to close her eyes and lose herself to oblivion, she couldn't. The gnawing, rat-like thoughts wouldn't let her. And she took a moment to wonder if they would ever let her sleep again.

In a bid to quiet her mind after all that had happened that evening and all that might possibly transpire before dawn, she had turned out all of the big lights in the room and looked at her reflection in the mirror solely by the light of the lamp sitting on her bedside table.

She sighed at the old woman looking back at her, and tears formed as she did so. What was she supposed to do now? How would she face tomorrow? And the day after that? Knowing that her son was no longer in this world with her. He may not have been perfect, far from it, but good mothers loved their children regardless of their shortcomings, and Sofia was a very good mother.

Unable to look herself in the eye any longer, she stood from her stool, walked towards her bed and began pulling back the covers. Not a moment later, a knock came to her bedroom door.

One knock. A pause. Three quick knocks. A pause. One more knock.

Yes, that was definitely the signal Alex had given her.

Checking her terry towelling dressing gown was covering all it should be, Sofia walked slowly towards the door. Taking a deep breath, she turned the key in the lock and opened it.

But Alex was not there to greet her.

With wide eyes, Sofia let out a yelp of shock and stumbled backwards into her room, trying to take in the figure in front of her. Sofia had thought Mrs Kapoor had been exaggerating before when she'd relayed her story of being attacked. But it was just as she had described it. The ominous shape emerged from the darkness of the hallway without a word. The only sound was the rustling of its long black cloak along the carpet as it strode into the room. Sofia could barely stand to look at the thing. She recognised the mask on its face as the one that usually hung on the wall downstairs. Painted half white and half black, with a teardrop on one side, she had thought the vintage mask quaint when they bought it at a flea market in Skipton. But now, seeing it actually fitted to a face, and the face of the person who killed her son no less, she found it nothing short of terrifying. Adding to the fearsomeness was its luminosity. Sofia didn't know how it was possible, but this thing, this ghostly presence, was glowing.

Suddenly, perhaps just as Sofia's survival instincts kicked in, she noticed the one detail she should have been fixated on all along: what was in the figure's hands. She inspected the weapon as closely as she could from the few paces she'd managed to keep between her and the killer. She surmised that the killer was brandishing the carving fork from the kitchen, the same one she used to serve up the Sunday carvery to customers at The Merry Monarch.

The gleaming form continued its advance towards Sofia. She could barely breathe as the fork was raised high in the air, preparing to make its deadly blow. Before the killer could strike, however, the door to Sofia's bedroom slammed shut with a loud bang.

Startled by the sound, the ghostly shape swung around to see what had caused it. A moment later, the big bedroom light blinked on.

'Put the fork down,' said Alex, who was standing with Maddie between the wardrobe and the door, and had been since everyone had locked themselves in their rooms an hour ago. 'It's over. It's all over. Don't make things any worse than they already are.'

At these words, the figure's shoulders slumped. They lowered their head and it looked as though a sigh rippled through them. For that moment, everyone in the room would have been forgiven for thinking the assailant was going to do as they were told. That they understood there was no fighting this now. They had been caught, red-handed no less, trying to end another person's life. Their third attempt on a life that evening. The jig was up.

As Alex walked towards the figure, however, something unexpected happened. The figure began to shake, quite violently, and a moment later a strange, primal scream emanated from it. There was barely a breath between this unforgettable shriek and the attacker lunging at Sofia once again, the fork raised high in the air in one last desperate attempt to make sure the next victim didn't see morning.

through the door. For that moment, everyone in the room would have been [illegible] of the [illegible] was [illegible] that they [illegible] there was no fighting [illegible] [illegible] [illegible]

As Alex walked towards the gate, however, something [illegible] happened. [illegible] began to [illegible] quite [illegible] and a moment [illegible] through [illegible] There was barely a breath between [illegible] Sofia [illegible] the [illegible] raised high [illegible] one last desperate attempt to make sure [illegible] didn't see [illegible]

CHAPTER TWENTY-SIX

'Noooooooooooo!' Alex shouted.

Maddie's mouth dropped open as she watched Alex leap after the figure in black and knock them to the ground before the fork reached its target. That fork was sharp. Such a manoeuvre had all the makings of a terrible accident. And sure enough blood was soon drawn.

Alex fell on top of the assailant and they both crashed down to the lime-green carpet. As this happened another scream rang out, again from the killer, this time a yelp of pain. As Alex turned the killer over, Maddie saw they had fallen on the fork and punctured their lower arm, quite badly. Deciding that Alex was perhaps best placed to deal with that particular emergency, Maddie dashed over to Sofia and did what Alex had instructed her to do when they formulated this plan: make sure the intended victim remained safe. As such, Maddie grabbed Sofia and pulled her back over towards the door. If, even in their injured state, the cloaked intruder somehow got the best of Alex and tried to take another swipe at her, the pair of them would be able to escape easily and quickly through the door and lock themselves in Maddie's room.

Before Alex had a chance to do anything else, the killer grabbed hold of the fork, pulled it out of their arm and threw it away. Blood gushed from the wound and with a contusion like that, Maddie would have expected immediate surrender. But, it seemed, adrenaline had somewhat overtaken them, likely caused by the fear of their true identity being revealed. Consequently, Maddie and Sofia watched on for a terrible minute as Alex wrestled with the killer. First defending himself from the various and frantic hits and kicks coming from his opponent. Then pinning the attacker's arms to the floor, waiting for them to give up the fight.

'You are going to bleed to death if you don't stop, is that what you want?' Alex said, breathless from the struggle, but still the killer flailed and twisted. 'If it is who I think it is under there,' he said, trying a different tack, 'you won't want to hurt me. Not really. And you know, I won't go anywhere until you are brought to justice. Until this is finished. So, give up, now.'

At these words, the figure in black stopped their thrashing. In fact, it was more severe than that, the body went completely limp. When it was clear the killer would resist no more, Alex dragged both himself, and them to their feet. Then, without wasting another minute, Alex pulled down the hood on the cloak, yanked at the ribbon on the mask and watched as it fell to the floor.

There, before them stood the killer, unmasked.

There, before them stood Jeannie.

Sofia had been appraised of who the suspected killer was when Alex and Maddie recruited her as bait but she still let out a gasp of surprise when the mask fell to the floor. And Maddie could well understand why. Of all the people Maddie had suspected that evening, Jeannie hadn't made the list. Above all, it was difficult to believe that someone, especially someone as seemingly kind as Jeannie, would use the memory of their dead sister to try and get away with murder. But that was just what Jeannie had done.

'When Alex told me he thought you were the one who'd stabbed my James to death, I told him right away that I thought he was mad,' said Sofia. 'She wouldn't do that, I told him. She's known James since he was a little lad. Watched him run around in the grass. Splash around in the Ribble. Play in the shadow of the grand old viaduct. She's seen him grow into a young man. All those years, she's watched him. She couldn't have done it, I said. She couldn't have been the one to rob the world of my little boy.'

For a moment, Jeannie didn't speak. She simply stood there holding her wounded arm. Her face was red. Her teeth, gritted. Her eyes full with tears that refused to fall. When at last she did speak, her voice was that of a broken, defeated woman. 'What are you doing in this room?' she said to Alex. 'Sofia were supposed to be alone.'

'We tricked you,' Sofia said, her voice full of spite. 'We got you.'

'Jeannie Lewis,' said Alex. He spoke in an almost robotic tenor, and Maddie couldn't much blame him for that. In the space of one evening, he'd had to work the case of his stepbrother's murder. And then arrest his aunt for the crime. Emotional detachment from all he was going through was likely the only strategy he had for making it through from one moment to the next. 'You are under arrest for the murder of James Beaumont and of Curtis Clarke and for the attempted murder of Sofia Beaumont. You do not have to say anything. But it may harm your defence if you do not mention when questioned something which you later rely on in court. Anything you say may be given in evidence.'

''Ow did you know it were me?' Jeannie said, at last, her voice that of a woman who is broken, defeated.

'All will be explained,' Maddie said. 'Once we get everyone downstairs again.'

'What?' said Jeannie. 'You're going to make me stand out there, in front of that lot?'

'That's the least you deserve,' said Sofia. 'What you've done to me can never be undone. And I want everyone to know what you did. And how you did it. I want them to know how twisted you are. It was the only condition I had when I agreed to being the bait in the plan to capture you. My suffering will never end. Yours can last for at least tonight.'

'Alex,' Jeannie said. 'You're not going to make me do this. You're not going to make me sit in a room and watch you tell everyone what I've done. I did it for you.'

'I didn't ask you to,' Alex bit off. 'I never would have asked you to. As if chins don't wag enough about our family history in this village. And you go and do something like this. Bring yet more shame on us all. And rub out James's prospects like that.' Alex snapped his fingers. 'If you think you were so justified in what you did, then you won't mind having the whole thing explained to the people who have been held captive here all night, fearing for their lives, because of you.'

'And just so you know, Jeannie,' Sofia spat out, 'you killed our James for nothing. Alex said it was something about the will. You wanted to make sure he was the heir to Mickey's possessions. That he wasn't cut out of his wealth because of James or me. Well, Mickey made sure he already had fifty-fifty share with me. James wasn't in the picture, we knew he couldn't be trusted with anything financial. So Alex had his stake. You took two lives and the thing you wanted all along, you already had it.'

At this, the tears that had so far merely filled Jeannie's eyes, now fell.

'Everything alright in 'ere?' Don said, as his figure filled the bedroom door frame.

'Woken up after bein' asleep on duty in the corridor, 'ave you?' Jeannie said through her teeth.

'Oh, did you really think I were asleep?' said Don. 'Maybe I should 'ave gone into acting, instead of police work. I would've quite fancied that. More limousines, less larceny.'

Alex didn't have it in him to smirk as he marched Jeannie towards the bedroom door but the glint in his eye told Maddie he appreciated his colleague managing to find some humour in the situation. Even though said situation was, at least personally for him, nothing short of dire.

'Yep,' Don continued as they walked down the hallway, 'I could buy a lot of sour cream Pringles on Leonardo DiCaprio's salary.'

CHAPTER TWENTY-SEVEN

'Alright, everyone, settle down,' said Alex, once everyone had been reassembled in the drinking area of The Merry Monarch. Using bedsheets and clothes pegs, Maddie, Alex and Don had managed to construct a makeshift screen to shield the corner of the room where James's body still sat. There had been no time to do this before, all of Alex and Don's attention had had to be focused on watching people in the room who were still alive in case the killer did something that gave them away. Now, however, they were about to recount to the others all they knew about his murder and Curtis's, and it didn't seem fitting for anyone, but particularly Sofia, to have James's corpse staring at them while they did so.

At Alex's words, the room hushed down. Eager to hear what he had to say. It had been decided that Maddie would do most of the talking, since she had hatched the plan to catch Jeannie and been witness to her capture. Don would provide support with the explanation when he could. Alex had privately admitted he didn't really want to have to go over the whole affair again right now. Especially when he would have to do so more times than he could count when he got back to the Yorkshire Dales Constabulary later on Christmas Day. Besides anything else, hearing the theory spoken aloud by someone else would give him distance enough to get everything clear in his head for the case file he was going to have to prepare before this case went to trial. Since Jeannie had already confessed the crime after being cautioned by Alex, and had been caught attacking Sofia in the costume donned by the person believed to be the killer, there was no hope of her escaping justice.

'As you might have gathered by now,' Alex continued, his head tilting towards Jeannie who was sitting off to the side of him, 'we have caught the killer.'

Jeannie sat silently with narrowed eyes. Maddie and Alex had used The Merry Monarch's first-aid kit to bandage the two slashes to her arm where the fork had pierced it. Mercifully the bleeding had stopped so they were confident she would be OK until they could reach official medical services later in the day.

After the resistance Jeannie had put up in Sofia's bedroom, however, Alex wasn't about to give her the opportunity to slope off and try her chances of survival in the surrounding snow. He had tied her to the chair with the same kind of blue rope she had used to strangle Curtis. There was no escaping judgement. Not in the courtroom. Not in this room right now.

'Jeannie?' said Mrs Fazakerley, shaking her head in disbelief. 'There must be some mistake or somebody must have put her up to it . . . threatened her or something.'

'There is no mistake,' Sofia shouted. 'She attacked me. Alex and Maddie caught her trying to stab me with a carving fork.'

A silence fell across the room, interrupted only by an occasional gasp. Eyes widened. Heads shook.

Maddie watched Jeannie close her eyes, as though that would somehow make her invisible.

'How do we know you're not in on it?' Sita said to Alex with her trademark lack of tact. 'She's your auntie and this was all somehow tied up with your mum, wasn't it?'

Alex sighed, but managed to take a deep breath and keep his cool. After all he'd been through, and given that Sita had been getting at him all night, Maddie didn't know how he stayed so calm. 'Maddie is going to take you through all the details. Hopefully, Sita, by the end of the explanation you'll be satisfied that I'm not involved.'

Sita folded her arms and simply said, 'We'll see about that.'

'When we asked Sofia to essentially act as bait to draw

out the killer,' Alex continued, choosing for now to ignore Sita's interjections, 'she insisted that the person in question would have to face you all after the fact. And we knew that after being kept here all night, fearing for your lives, you would expect, if not demand an explanation.'

'You're right about that,' said Mrs Fazakerley, 'worst night of my life so far. And I'm no spring chicken.'

'Yes,' Alex said, 'it's certainly up there for me too, Mrs Fazakerley. Maddie was actually the one who devised the plan to capture the killer, and followed up on what Curtis was trying to do when he died – trying to retrieve a document that would indicate a motive for the original murder. So, it's over to her for now.'

'The credit for catching the killer should be given to Curtis,' Maddie began; she still couldn't quite bring herself to say Jeannie's name and equate it with the killer. She never would have guessed the unassuming woman she'd met at the beginning of the evening was capable of double, almost triple murder. 'Before he died, he came up with this scheme to go down to the cellar and retrieve something, a document of Mickey's. A will. He mentioned that somebody had been to see him around the time Mickey was drawing up his will and that they were trying to dig for information on it. He was going to tell me who he suspected before he went down to the cellar, but we were interrupted before he had the chance.'

'But it was Jeannie?' said Sita.

'Given everything we know now, we assume so, yes. Curtis was stopped from getting at that document and didn't return from the cellar alive.'

'How did she kill Curtis without anyone noticing she was missing?' said Mr Kapoor.

'I am going to tell you that,' said Maddie. 'But I can't start the story half way through. As most of you know, I'm a journalist and the best way to understand a story is to start at the beginning.'

'I suppose I'd better find a more comfortable seat,' said Sita, moving over to sit in an armchair. 'Sounds like this is going to take some time.'

'I'll be as brief as possible,' said Maddie. 'But it is a complicated and intricate crime so all the different strands are going to take some explaining. Some strands of the story go back as far as Alice's death.'

'She took her sister's ring when she died, didn't she?' said Mr Kapoor.

'We assume so,' said Maddie. 'We assume that Jeannie found the ring before Alex did. Perhaps at the time, she wasn't planning on using it in a murder. Perhaps she took it for sentimental reasons. Or as an enduring symbol of the grudge she held against Mickey for leaving Alice and, from her point of view, slowly killing her.'

'It weren't just me!' Jeannie half-shrieked as she glared

over at Mickey and Sofia. 'The doctor thought Mickey killed Alice too.'

Maddie was surprised by the remarkably cold, calm voice Alex used to reply to his aunt. 'We're going to speak to Dr Everett to ascertain exactly how that conversation really went,' he said. 'But whatever was said, I can assure you it won't justify double murder.'

At this Jeannie quieted and when she was sure she wasn't going to be interrupted again, Maddie continued.

'Considering Jeannie went to visit Curtis when Mickey was putting together his will, it's obvious she has always been fixated on what her nephew has lost, or might lose, because of Mickey's other relationship and his other child – James. At some point over the years, a plan started to hatch to get rid of the other heirs to Mickey's wealth and, in Jeannie's mind, taking something back from the man who had taken so much from the people she loved. Then, last year, she saw an opportunity thanks to Mrs Kapoor.'

'Me?' said Mrs Kapoor, startled at hearing her name suddenly mentioned in this story. 'But I have nothing to do with the murders.'

'I'm not suggesting you're involved, Mrs Kapoor,' said Maddie. 'I'm saying a personal situation gave Jeannie an opportunity to place the blame elsewhere. Who was on your scavenger hunt team last year?'

'It was my husband and daughter, DI Beaumont, Jeannie and James,' Mrs Kapoor answered.

'Alex mentioned to me earlier that he was on your team last year, but he didn't say who else was. It was only when we discussed it later when we were down in the cellar that I realised that somehow, last year, Jeannie worked out that James had feelings for you. And from this piece of information, a plan hatched. The next year, which happened to be ten years to the day since her sister died, and twenty years to the day since Mickey left said sister, she would kill any heirs to Mickey's fortune. In her mind, she was delivering justice on those who robbed her sister of her life and happiness.'

'She used my situation with James to divert attention from herself as a suspect,' said Mrs Kapoor.

Maddie nodded. 'It's no wonder James suggested that your team split up after he found that note in his pocket, thinking it was from you. If he hadn't suggested it, Jeannie probably had a plan to suggest it herself in order to get a chance to make her move.'

'It is so sad,' said Mrs Kapoor. 'He thought he was going to meet someone he had feelings for, and instead met with his end.'

Though Maddie wasn't sure just how deep James's feelings ran for Mrs Kapoor, she agreed with the fact that it was a very sad way to go out.

'I know,' Maddie said. 'He wouldn't have suspected a thing. But to get away with it, Jeannie needed to confuse the situation as much as possible. She already knew she could find a way of implicating the Kapoors in the murder, but that wouldn't be enough. So, she devised other distractions. Using her knowledge of fabric as a seamstress, she made herself a cloak in just the right kind of sheer material to create a ghostly costume. She knew that Sita would be in the pub when she struck, a person who has more than a passing interest in the paranormal. She also knew that Sita had a personal history with James involving a ring of sentimental value.'

'Alright, move it on. The less said about that episode, the better,' Sita said.

Duly, Maddie moved swiftly on. 'She knew that Don also believed the place to be haunted. Told me herself that she'd heard him go on about it numerous times. With all these variables, she hoped to convince people that Alice's ghost had returned to exact revenge on Mickey, or that Mr Kapoor was using this as a ruse to cover his own crime of killing James to protect his marriage. Or that Sita had decided to kill him for the humiliation she suffered at his hands. And, with the exception of there actually being a ghost in the pub, these are all theories that the police would entertain in their investigation.'

'So dismissive,' said Sita. 'If there really was no

supernatural presence, how did she make herself glow like a ghost? And what about the perfume?'

Maddie sighed but had to admit she somewhat admired Sita's commitment to her beliefs. Even after all she had just explained, Sita was clearly still not quite ready to accept the fact that a human being was behind the killings after all.

'I can answer the question about 'ow she made herself glow,' said Don. 'When we removed 'er cloak we found one of those body torches runners use for visibility underneath the garment. It straps on across the chest and the black fabric sort of dims it to make it look like more of a glow.'

'We don't know about the perfume,' said Maddie. 'We're assuming some kind of diffuser. We just haven't had time to search for it yet. But given everything else was a trick, it's safe to say that was too. Even moments where she was being seemingly helpful, it was all part of the plot to kill James and then Sofia. Earlier in the evening, Jeannie took some glasses through to the kitchen to help out. I checked with Mickey, she had also done this before when I was on the phone with my mother. She had interrupted the argument he was having with James by bringing the glasses through. When they both dispersed, she used that opportunity to cut the phone line at the junction box in the kitchen. On her way back, she probably grabbed the mask off the wall and hid it in whatever crevice she had stashed the cloak and gloves she wore while masquerading as the ghost.'

'What about the lights going out? How did she manage to go outside to cut the power off?' asked Mr Kapoor.

'Through a secret passageway,' said Maddie. 'Jeannie was in the guest library and there's a secret passageway that leads down to the back door. She'll have slipped down there in her ghost costume without any concern of being seen. Sabotaged the electrics and then returned back to the guest library to set her plan in motion.'

'Starting with attacking me,' said Mrs Kapoor.

'That's right,' Maddie said. 'Jeannie deliberately joined your team so she would know where you, Mr Kapoor and James were at all times. She knew you were in the drying room so she attacked you and then planted the note in your pocket. Then she went downstairs through the secret passageway that comes out at the fireplace, knowing Mr Kapoor would be in there looking for clues. She attacked him, without leaving a note, probably thinking that would make him more of a suspect. She then pushed her way out into the snug next to the fireplace where she knew James would be waiting.'

'And then she killed him!' Sofia shouted with a sob.

Maddie took a moment before speaking and then gently said, 'Yes, I'm afraid so. Afterwards, she made her escape back through the secret passageway, stashed her costume and then went in search of the others to feign her surprise at the discovery of James's body.'

'How come Curtis didn't see any of this if he was in the room at the time?' said Mrs Fazakerley.

'He fainted,' Maddie explained. 'The shock of the lights going out closely followed by James's scream knocked him out. Until we pieced everything together, I wasn't sure exactly when he'd fallen unconscious but it must have been fairly quick. It was pitch black and the sight lines between where he was sitting and the chair where James's body was left are not good, so it prevented him from being an eyewitness. Also, remember, he wouldn't have been expecting a murder to take place. To begin with, he'll have just thought it was a power cut. It wouldn't be the first time there'd been one at The Merry Monarch, that's the whole reason Mickey has the generator out back.'

'This all explains 'ow she killed our James,' said Mickey. 'But what about Curtis? 'E's been a good friend for many years and thanks to 'er 'e's gone. Like my son.'

Maddie gave Mickey's words a moment to settle and then answered his questions. 'When it comes to Curtis, she took a risk,' she said. 'A terrible risk. All of the people at her table – me, Alex and Curtis – left her alone with only Barkley as witness. We assume she simply tied him to a chair when she left to commit the crime. Alex was in the kitchen, interviewing suspects. I was over on the other side of the room, completely engrossed in distracting Don so Curtis could make his way down to the cellar unnoticed. She followed him down there using the secret passageway, killed him and returned without anyone noticing. That's why there was no envelope in Curtis's pocket. The murder wasn't planned. She used a murder weapon that was on hand – although she did this in all instances. Probably knowing that procuring a specialised weapon would put her at greater risk of being caught. There's no doubt given the premeditation of the killings – Curtis aside – that she will have decided far in advance which weapons of convenience she was going to use. Stabbing weapons when it comes to James and Sophia. But she couldn't find anything sharp in the cellar, and so improvised with the rope.'

'Could it really be done that quickly?' asked Mrs Kapoor. 'Strangle a person, I mean?'

Alex nodded and chipped in with his knowledge. 'A person can lose consciousness within seconds, and can be dead in a matter of minutes. Curtis, despite his strange ability to disappear and reappear without warning, was not particularly strong and not young. I doubt it will have taken long at all.'

'I saw her,' Zainab said. 'Coming back from that corner of the room, near where the passageway is. She was carrying a bowl of water that she put down for the dog.'

'That was possibly going to be her alibi then,' said Maddie. 'That she'd just popped to get some water for the dog from the nearest tap. But I don't think she came here tonight expecting to kill Curtis. She thought that conning you into the idea that the deaths were paranormal, Alice's ghost seeking revenge, or that this was all to do with some marital dispute with Mr and Mrs Kapoor, would throw anyone off the real motive behind the killings. But when Jeannie returned from a trip to the bathroom, she and Sofia had an altercation about the will. Which probably set Curtis's cogs turning about the visit Jeannie paid him when he was drawing up the document in the first place. And Jeannie will have guessed this. She'll have realised that Curtis was a solicitor, a man of intellect and reason. That her spat with Sofia about Mickey's estate will have registered with him.'

'Stupid old fool,' Jeannie muttered, 'he should 'ave kept out of it.'

'I'll not 'ear you saying that about Curtis in my pub,' Mickey shouted over at Jeannie.

'Dad,' Alex said. 'Just keep your cool. We've got her. She's going to do her time.'

When Maddie was sure that the peace Alex had ordered would be respected, she continued with her explanation. 'Curtis may also have noticed something Jeannie said just after her altercation with Sofia. "What have I done?" she asked herself. She made out at the time that she was referring to talking about the will and making Sofia angry. But with all the information he was armed with, Curtis read into those words and began to suspect a motive. And I think Jeannie suspected Curtis had guessed it was her.'

'What was so important about the will?' said Mrs Fazakerley.

'Nothing,' said Maddie. 'Nothing at all. What is important is what Jeannie thought was in the will. She thought all of Mickey's possessions would go to James and Sofia. That Alex would be cut out completely. She was so convinced of it, she told Alice that's what would happen when she was still alive, which, ironically given the motive here, might have actually contributed to Alice's stress and worry over her child and hastened her death.'

'That's not true!' said Jeannie. 'You don't know what you're talking about!'

'I know that feeding a single mother poisonous lies about her child's father and what he may or may not be left for inheritance is a far from admirable thing to do,' Maddie snapped at Jeannie, the anger over what this woman had put everyone through suddenly hitting her. Yes, it seemed that Mickey had been pretty callous and self-serving in the way he had left Alice. And yes, it must have been nothing short of torturous watching your sister slowly decline into illness and death. But that didn't justify what had happened here tonight. People all over the world suffer these things and worse every day and don't use it as an excuse for manipulation and murder.

From Jeannie's perspective, having assumed Alex would be cut out of the will, Mickey was leaving Alice's child in the lurch for a second time. He would be left with nothing. Again. But Alex hadn't thanked Jeannie for what she had done in his name and, from what Maddie knew of Alex's mother, Alice wouldn't have either.

'It was only when I read the will,' Maddie continued after Jeannie's previous interruption, 'and realised that James wasn't listed as a beneficiary but Alex was, that I began to piece together who the killer was. There were only three people who had mentioned a will to me this evening. Curtis, who was dead. Sofia and Jeannie. The odds of Sofia killing her own son seemed very small, if not non-existent. Plus, she had an alibi in Mickey. So, we were left with Jeannie. Who had no alibi. Who had been overly interested in talking about the will. I had hoped I was wrong but, sadly, my suspicions proved correct.'

'How did you know she would go for Sofia?' said Mr Kapoor. 'How did you know Sofia would make good bait?'

'Using the will as a motive,' said Maddie, 'we logically concluded that Jeannie would expect Mickey's wealth to go to two beneficiaries. James, who was already dead, and Mickey's spouse. If the killer wanted to make sure

Alice's child received a full inheritance, rather than see it go to the family he left Alice for, it was obvious that Sofia was likely to be the next target. So we went to her and Mickey, explained that we wanted to lay a trap. It was important that the killer knew Sofia would be alone, so we asked Mickey to argue with Alex about that in front of everyone. We then predicted that Jeannie would either try and take Sofia's door by force, perhaps using some kind of tool to ram the door open, or that she would try and find a way to learn what Sofia's knock signal was. We still weren't one hundred per cent sure that Jeannie was the killer until I deliberately positioned myself right next to Sofia and Alex as they were discussing the knock signal. When she came over on the pretence of asking how I was, however, that was a big sign that we had the right suspect. So we allowed her to overhear the knock signal, knowing we would be lying in wait in Sofia's room when she came to call.'

'Hey, what about the patrol in the hallway though?' said Sita. 'Wouldn't she think it strange that there wasn't someone on guard?'

'I'm glad you asked that, Sita,' said Don, more than happy to demonstrate to the object of his affection how he had played a heroic role in the downfall of the killer. 'Alex asked me to pretend I'd fallen asleep in the corridor. I fooled her good, I did. Played the part to perfection.'

'Yes, we were ninety per cent sure Jeannie wasn't going to hurt Don, because he wasn't her intended target.'

'Yeah that's ri—' Don started but then cut himself off. 'Wait, what? You mean you thought there were a ten per cent chance she might murder me? Oh, thanks a bunch. You didn't mention that at orientation.'

Maddie shot a little smirk at Don and shook her head before continuing. 'We didn't know for sure that Jeannie would go after Sofia the way she had gone after James but their altercation over the will earlier in the evening seemed to make it more likely. And catching her in the act of trying to kill somebody else was the best chance we had of making sure the murder charges stuck.'

'And that was it?' said Sita. 'It was all about a will?'

'Not completely,' said Maddie. 'Which was actually what enabled us to be sure that Jeannie was the killer. She told me that Alex had blamed Mickey for Alice's death because of something the doctor said. That his leaving had triggered her run of terrible health. But when I was talking to Alex in the cellar, I learnt this wasn't true. In fact, I learnt that almost everything Jeannie had told me was false. Alex never blamed Mickey for his mother's death. But Jeannie did. And from what Alex told me, it took years for her to stop insisting this was true. She's told a lot of lies this evening. As well as feeding me information that might implicate Sita, she also tried to insinuate Alex might have had a hand in it. She was probably hoping to confuse the police so much that they'd never figure out who had done it. Hoping nobody would suspect the sister of the woman whose memory the killer was exploiting.'

'So, killing James was revenge then?' said Mrs Fazakerley. 'Revenge for Mickey leaving and making a new life with Sofia?'

'It were revenge for killin' my sister!' Jeannie shrieked. ''E runs off and starts a new fairy tale with a woman he's been seein' behind my sister's back for the best part of a decade, and she dies. You're all talking about justice bein' served. Alice got no justice, and none of you care about that one bit.'

'That's enough,' Alex said to Jeannie, and the firmness in his tone was enough to keep her quiet.

'What will happen to Jeannie now? After all that she's done?' said Mrs Kapoor.

Alex looked over at Jeannie and she looked right back at him, her eyes full of fear. 'She'll be tried and sentenced,' said Alex. 'With two murders and an attempted third, it's unlikely she'll live to see freedom again.'

Maddie wasn't sure if Alex meant for those words to seem so cruel. She supposed she couldn't blame him if he did. He already had so much in his past that was an emotional burden to him. Now he was a police officer with a murderer in the family. She wasn't sure how he was going to get through the coming weeks and months but she knew, without a doubt, that she would do all that she could to help him.

CHAPTER TWENTY-EIGHT

Though it was still freezing cold on Christmas Day, Maddie smiled at the welcome sunshine as she pulled her car up outside The Merry Monarch. The snow of the night before had begun to melt, making it possible for Alex to walk to Mrs Fazakerley's house, the nearest of those who had spent the night in the pub, and call the Dales Constabulary. By mid-morning, Alex and Don's colleagues had managed to navigate the roads to The Merry Monarch in order to collect the bodies, formally arrest Jeannie and begin cataloguing evidence.

Once Alex had assured Maddie that she was free to go about her business, she had managed to get the British Automobile Club to come out to her and get her car started again. She had already given full witness statements to Alex and Don and used the landline at Mrs Fazakerley's house to call her parents and let them know that she was OK and on her way home, but with a story to tell.

All that remained was to say her goodbyes, drive the remaining distance up to the outskirts of Edinburgh, and enjoy some of her mum's home-cooked food slightly later than originally scheduled. The very thought of the glazed ham sitting on the table was enough to make her want to cry with homesickness. She was relieved to have survived the night, of course, but she wouldn't truly feel like she'd escaped the horrors of last night until she was pulling crackers with her parents while scooping up spoonfuls of Christmas pudding and brandy sauce.

After all that had happened, however, Maddie couldn't leave before making sure Alex knew he could give her a call if he ever needed to talk. He had been through so much, not just in the past fourteen hours, but in the past twenty-odd years that, especially given it was Christmas, it felt only right to remind him that he wasn't alone.

Getting out of the car and walking up to the path to the pub entrance, she asked a young, uniformed PC where Alex and Don were. She didn't want to interrupt what was bound to be a very busy Christmas morning for them, but she had promised she would stick her head through the door before leaving the village of Quernby.

'They're just over there, madam.' The young PC pointed over to the bar area.

Sure enough Alex, Don, Mickey and Sofia were all standing together with their backs to Maddie. They seemed to be looking down at something. Walking towards them, she suddenly got the sense that something very serious was happening, though with the killer now safely in custody, she couldn't quite grasp what that might be.

'Everything OK?' Maddie said.

The group turned at Maddie's words.

'Aye,' said Alex. 'Barkley's just having a few moments with Curtis before the paramedics take him.'

'Oh,' Maddie said, looking down to where the others had been staring before. Curtis's body lay on a stretcher. His eyes were closed now, which made him seem more peaceful. Barkley lay with his front paws across his owner's chest. His usually pricked ears were flat to his head and he whined slowly, sadly for his master.

'Poor wee doggy,' said Maddie, tears rising in her eyes at the tragic sound of the hound's lament. 'What's going to happen with him?'

'We're going to keep him at the station for now,' said Alex. 'He'll come home with me when I've finished my shift. I know he's a well-behaved dog and will just sit at the side of my desk quietly. We'll probably have to find another system in the long-term but, much as I love dogs, we've got more pressing issues to deal with right now than rehoming the little pooch.'

'Of course you have,' said Maddie. 'Has . . . has Jeannie already written a full confession?'

'She's at the station doing it now,' said Alex. 'I counselled her on the fact that judges look more kindly on a situation if a guilty plea is entered as soon as possible, and if remorse is shown. But I think she's going to have to work hard to convince them about that second part.'

'No, she didn't exactly seem full of remorse when we were talking everyone through what had happened last night,' said Maddie.

'That's putting it lightly,' said Sofia. 'You'd think when confronted by me, the mother of . . .' her voice broke but she managed to regain her composure, 'the mother of the man she killed, that she'd at least look shame-faced about what she's done. But she didn't, and I don't think she will. She still thinks she did what was necessary.'

Alex rubbed a hand over his face, clearly still trying to fully digest what had taken place. 'Even after everything I've seen on this job, I still can't believe she's gone and done this. I clearly missed some worrying signs from her. I always tried to check in. Make sure she was OK. But working for the police, doing what I do, well it doesn't leave much time or head space for recreation.'

'I don't think there's any way you could have seen this coming,' said Maddie. 'I was a complete stranger here last night. Was meeting Jeannie for the first time and didn't suspect her at all until I put all the pieces together. I think part of the reason she did it is that she thought nobody would suspect her. She thought that was how she'd get away with it.'

'I've known Jeannie a long time, obviously,' said Mickey. 'Even after the falling-outs we've 'ad over the years, I would never 'ave thought I'd see the day when she did somethin' like this. To our . . . to our James.'

Alex rubbed his dad's shoulder and gave it a squeeze.

'You can't blame yourselves,' said Maddie, wondering if it was even her place to make the speech she was about to make. But looking at the expressions on the faces of Alex, Mickey and Sofia, she simply couldn't keep her peace. 'I can't pretend to know how you move forward from this but, whatever it looks like, I want you to know it's not your fault. You'll no doubt all go through times when you think it is. When you wonder if James and Curtis would still be here if this or if that. But I want to tell you that it's Jeannie who did this terrible thing. Who took something from you that can never be given back. And although we're all human beings and make mistakes, we don't deserve to die for them, or have those we love taken from us prematurely.'

'We'll try and remember yer wise words, lass,' Mickey said while Sofia merely nodded and offered an apprecia-tive smile.

'I'll do my best to remember your words too,' Alex said. 'But it's going to be a tough week ahead.'

'Yeah, sir, on that note,' Don started. 'I were talking to Maddie earlier and she's invited us up to Edinburgh for New Year. I've never been to Edinburgh and I know you won't feel like celebratin', but we can't stay 'ere now that the only pub is a crime scene and that, so why don't we just get away for a few days?'

'Are you asking me to go on a minibreak to Edinburgh with you, Donny?' said Alex. Maddie could hardly believe Alex had it in him to make a joke just then, but it seemed to her that it was a very good sign. That though there were undoubtedly dark times ahead, he would make it through them.

Don, however, wasn't looking too impressed by Alex's little jest. 'Why've you always got to make things weird?' he said, shaking his head.

'You're one to talk,' Alex replied. 'In all seriousness, Edinburgh's a nice idea but I really don't know if I'll be able to get all the paperwork tied up from this mess between now and then.'

'I thought you might say that,' said Don. 'So I've 'ad a word with the other officers at the station and they've all said they're going to chip in to make sure it is done by December thirtieth. We 'ad New Year booked off anyway. So me and you can take a road trip all the way up to

Edinburgh, well, Queensferry, actually, and get out of Quernby for a couple of nights.'

'So, four hours with you in New Year traffic, in a car filled with the smell of sour cream Pringles, that's supposed to be a holiday, is it?' said Alex. Maddie couldn't remember the last time she'd seen him smile, but she could see the glimmer of one trying to surface on his lips just now.

'Come on, sir, it'll be good for you,' said Don.

'Alright, if the paperwork is done, then we'll go and put upon Maddie for a couple of nights.'

'You won't be putting on me,' said Maddie. 'But you'll come back a lot heavier. Mum will be feeding you up with all sorts from the moment you arrive.'

'Now that does sound worth four hours in a car with him for,' said Alex.

Maddie smiled. 'Well, you've got my number. Just keep me posted . . . Oh, and sorry for finishing on a note of business but, it's been nagging at me. Did you find out how Jeannie made the room smell of your mother's perfume?'

Alex nodded. 'One of the team found a couple of oil burners hidden behind some of the vintage junk—'

'Oi! Watch it, lad,' Mickey said.

'Er, I mean vintage memorabilia, on the shelves around the room. They were vintage-looking items in and of themselves so even if they had been spotted, they wouldn't have looked out of place.'

Maddie sighed. 'I thought it would be something like that. I'm going to be in awe of how much trouble she went to for a very long time, I think.'

'You and me both,' said Alex.

Maddie nodded but then sensed Alex and Don really had to get on with the job at hand. 'Well, if there's nothing else you need me for, I'm going to get on the road and pray my journey to Edinburgh is less eventful than my journey from Manchester.'

'If there's any other questions we can call you for the answers,' said Alex. 'You get home and be with your family.'

A lump rose in Maddie's throat as Alex said this. With his mum long dead, his stepbrother murdered and Jeannie now headed to prison, his family had been severely culled. She could only hope that he, Sofia and Mickey would bond over their loss rather than be driven apart by it. Though they had all lost so much, they still had each other and there was something to be said for that.

'Thank you for helping Alex get to the bottom of what happened,' Sofia said to Maddie, giving her a big hug. 'We might have had to wait a lot longer for the truth to come out if you hadn't been here.'

'Thanks for the confidence in my investigative skills there, Sofia,' said Alex.

Sofia, in spite of all she was going through, reached out

to give Alex a playful tap on the arm. Maddie took this as a positive sign that what love remained between these three would only grow in the months to come.

After shaking hands with Mickey and Don and looking respectfully one last time upon the now-deceased Curtis while giving Barkley a rub between the ears, Maddie made her way back to her car and started it up. She had never heard a better sound in her life than the engine revving. It was a sound that was going to carry her all the way home into the arms of those she loved. Back to the place where, in her heart, she knew she belonged. And if she ran into Lance while she was back home, well, so what? After all, once you've faced down a murderer, facing down a good-for-nothing ex-boyfriend was small fry.

EPILOGUE

Maddie, Alex and Don sat on a wall overlooking the Firth of Forth, not far from the world's smallest working light tower, each with a bottle of beer in hand. They were all wrapped up in their winter coats and hats, their noses glowing red with the cold, almost the same hue as the Forth Bridge itself, which lit a crimson pathway across the water.

Barkley lay across Alex's knee sporting a rather snazzy tartan coat. Maddie could hear singing and cheering emanating from the nearby pubs of Queensferry as midnight on New Year's Eve approached. But, she privately admitted, this New Year's Eve was different to any other. After all that had happened at The Merry Monarch some seven days ago, Maddie realised, perhaps for the first time, just how lucky she was to see another year in. Many weren't so fortunate, and like almost every other person she knew, she had never given that much thought, until now.

'I'm glad we did this,' Alex said, looking out over the water and taking a sip of his beer.

'Well, we could 'ave stayed local and got wrapped up in a murder perpetrated by a rogue family member, but we did that on Christmas Eve,' said Don, flashing a cheeky grin.

For a moment, Maddie didn't dare move. She wasn't sure how Alex was going to react to Don's quip. He seemed to take a minute to weigh up his options, but, to his credit, he did ultimately laugh.

Maddie and Don joined in, relieved that even after the darkness of the past week, Alex could find his way back to good humour.

'Just don't crack jokes like that in front of Sofia and Mickey,' Alex said.

'Come on, Alex, I know it's not always obvious but I do understand there are lines in the sand to be drawn,' said Don.

'You're right,' Alex said, 'it's not always obvious.'

Maddie chuckled at Alex's retort but Don didn't look particularly amused by it.

'It's probably a very stupid question, but how are they doing with all that?' Maddie said. She had done her best to talk about anything except James's death since Alex and Don had arrived at her parents' house late the night before. But since, thanks to Don, the conversation had at last drifted in that direction, she may as well find out how everyone was in the aftermath of Jeannie's actions.

'They're as you'd expect,' said Alex. 'In hibernation for the foreseeable future. The pub hasn't reopened. They're talking about selling the place and moving out. But after what happened there, they may not have buyers biting their hands off. I've told them it's best not to make any big decisions just now.'

'They need time to grieve, properly,' said Maddie.

'They'll be grieving for the rest of their lives,' said Alex.

A sentence which stopped Maddie in her tracks. She'd never heard of grief really being spoken about in those terms before. Most of the time, people talked about it as a thing you did for a fixed period. But then, Maddie had only ever grieved for someone who had died at about the time you'd expect them to: when they had reached a very ripe old age and enjoyed a good life. It was still sad, yes. But easier to accept as part of the natural order. James's death wasn't like that. His parents would never have expected to outlive him. To live without him for who knew how long and all the while mourn the son they'd lost.

A fresh stab of sadness for all that Sofia and Mickey had to face pierced right through Maddie's heart.

'I'm not saying you're wrong,' said Don. 'And obviously, I am here for you and Mickey and Sofia, but I also can't 'elp but notice it's going to be midnight in less than a minute, so let's get down to the serious question: who's kissin' who?'

'Wha-a-a-at?' Maddie said through a chuckle. 'There were no kisses promised when I invited you up to Edinburgh, Don.'

'And you're not kissing me,' Alex said, eyeing his friend closely.

'I'm a step up from kissin' Cindy Clawford,' Don grumbled.

'Not necessarily,' Alex replied. 'And anyway, Cindy Clawford is a sore point and you know it.'

'Why's that?' Maddie asked.

'In her confession, Jeannie wrote that she hid the cloak and hood in Cindy Clawford's mouth a few days before she committed the murders, rolled up, like, really small so that it would be there waiting for her.'

'Ugh, yeah,' said Maddie. 'That would be enough to put you off another kiss under the mistletoe with that particular feline.'

'Yeah,' said Don. 'But since we're back on the subject of kissin' again, what're we doin' at midnight?'

'I'll tell you,' Maddie said, opening her handbag and pulling out three shot glasses and a wee flask of whisky.

'We are not going to kiss. We're going to toast. Beers down, whisky glasses up.'

'That sounds much better than Don's proposal,' said Alex. 'Oh, not that I think kissing you would be – I mean, I was talking about kissing him. I mean, what I meant to say was . . . I like toasts.'

'Good, because you're in Scotland,' Maddie said, trying to hide her amusement at Alex's tongue-tied little moment. 'And in Scotland we raise a glass in times of festive cheer.'

While taking in the view across the firth, Maddie thought again about that woman she found in Reelig Glen. About James. About Curtis. Should old acquaintance be forgot . . .

Never, she decided there and then. She would never forget them. Those lost along the way were a reminder that tomorrow is never promised. That there will not be a new year for everyone. That those lucky enough to see one have a duty to make the most of it. With that in mind, Maddie made a secret resolution to cherish each coming day much more than she had of late. Not just for her own benefit, but in honour of those who could no longer cherish each sunrise for themselves.

'Listen, the pubs are startin' the countdown,' Don said, as crowds of people hanging out of pub doorways and on heated pub patios began to chant: *ten, nine, eight.*

'Well, here you go then, quick,' Maddie said, handing them a glass apiece and pouring them a dram. 'To Curtis.'

'To Curtis,' Alex and Don said as the crowds continued to count down: *five, four*.

'To old friends, and to new,' Maddie said, knocking her glass against Alex and Don's and downing it in one just as the crowds burst into cheers of *Happy New Year* and the tune of 'Auld Lang Syne' began to play on the bagpipes.

Maddie, Alex and Don wished each other well for the new year, embraced and then turned back to the water to watch the fireworks. Streams of silver, gold and crimson light danced over the Forth as the singing and cheering continued.

ACKNOWLEDGEMENTS

I would like to thank my publisher, Quercus, for the opportunity to write this book and to have it published. Quercus have been ceaseless champions of my prose and I am very grateful to them for all their positivity about my work.

Many thanks also to my agent, Joanna, and the team at Hardman & Swainson who have been nothing short of a gift to me on my journey through the world of publishing.

Much appreciation is also extended to Hazel Nicholson for all the time she puts into offering such valuable feedback and guidance on police procedure.

A huge debt of gratitude is owed to Ann Leander and Dean Cummings who remain the best writing partners a writer gal could hope for.

Thank you also to my loved ones and dearest friends. My writing no doubt shines brighter for all the warmth and support I receive from those who know me well.

ACKNOWLEDGEMENTS